# *Sam's Song*

## Brenda Lambert

PublishAmerica
Baltimore

ISBN: 978-1-60749-436-2 (softcover)
ISBN: 978-1-4489-1168-4 (hardcover)
PUBLISHED BY PUBLISHAMERICA, LLLP
www.publishamerica.com
Baltimore

Printed in the United States of America

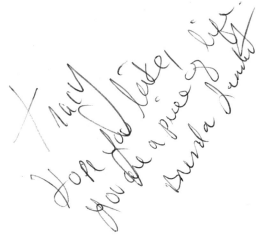

Tracy

Hope that later in life you are a piece of [illegible]

Brenda [surname]

I'm sure it has been said before, and I surely can't imagine that I would be the first, after all; life is long and words are many, but in the end, we all leave a legacy behind, some are hard to define, for they come in a cry or a whisper that is not yet heard or noticed. So comfort that cry, and listen for the whisper. And then leave your own legacy…

This book is dedicated to Babette…My sister.

# *House of Pain*

Marshall Perry sat on the top step with the cool October breeze ruffling his dark hair. The grey clouds rolling over in the sky fitted his mood. His quilted jean jacket didn't seem warm enough. A tear rolled down his cheek as his mind focused on something other than the grief that his grandmother was in, for the loss of her beloved husband.

Across the brown brushy field was the old boarded up house that stood as a monument to this northern Wisconsin community as the house of pain.

Marshall has heard all the stories behind the house from Grandpa, Grandma and his

Uncle Tony. He used to share them with his friends.

He heard the door creak and open behind him; his Uncle Tony stepped outside still dressed in the suit he had worn for the funeral. Tony sat beside him then let out a heavy burdened sigh.

"How's Gram?"

"You're mom gave her something so she can rest. She was going on and on, saying; she can't stay in this house anymore. We are going to have to figure something out soon and get her out before snowfall."

"Yeah, she didn't hold up very well when Grandpa was put into the ground."

Tony nodded with tears filling his already bloodshot eyes. "Yeah, well maybe it wouldn't have been so bad if we had some kind of notice…we could have been prepared."

"No offense Uncle Tony, but it sounds kind of selfish, Grandpa did have a bad heart."

"Yeah, he did, but he dropped right in front of her. I can't imagine." Tony replied with his tearful eyes fixed ahead where the house of pain sat.

Marshall took notice. "Uncle Tony, where's this David Pane today?"

"I didn't know where he was fifteen, twenty years ago and I sure don't know where he is today…Maybe your mother knows, you should ask her."

"I have, she don't like talking about him…He can't be normal…would you think?"

"Don't suppose he is, can't say that he was normal to begin with. But doing what he did. Nobody can get over that."

"He did what he had to do; right…? He had to shoot his ole man."

"He was too late to save his mother,"

"So did he, like get prosecuted for it?"

"No…he didn't even get manslaughter…It was the law that didn't keep that man behind bars. And that foolish woman who kept taking him back in…I missed it, you know…that night."

"Yeah, you were at camp that week…Grandma too, right?"

"She was the cook, we didn't know about it until we got home a couple of days latter."

"Have you ever been in there…? You know, like after it happened?"

"Course, haven't you?"

"No, it just doesn't seem right."

"Good kid…your mom is very proud of you…How's school going? This year,"

"It's going," Marshall replied with a shrug.

"Still want to be a writer?"

"Yeah, but it's a pipe dream."

"Who say's?"

"I say, it just is."

"Are you still taking that creative writing class?"

"Yeah, it's, the advanced class."

"Advanced? How's that going for you?"

"I just turned in my first essay of the year."

"You still have that same teacher, Mister Ross?"

"Yep, he's the only one. He teaches drama too. He defines drama by quoting Alfred Hitchcock; Drama is life with the dull bits cut out. End quote. He's real cool, everybody likes him,"

"Hey, I would like to read some of you're work sometime when you're ready."

"Okay, I'd like that…but I don't know if I have what it takes to be a real novelist. I can tell a story, show affections, and paint a brief picture here and there, but I can't find it in me to come up with all that, jibber jabber that a novel is supposed to contain."

"Oh, you mean all that, dull stuff in between." Tony chuckled then added "Well that's something you're going to have to work on kid."

"I guess so." Marshall replied as the door opened once again.

Marshall's mother, Gwen, stepped out.

"You ready to go Marshall?"

"Yeah mom I am. How's Gram?"

7

"She's resting, she's okay hon." Gwen replied folding her arms across her small waist line fighting off the cold chill of the fall air.

Tony stood up, bearing the cold air. "So what are we going to do?"

"Well, she could come live with us. I have plenty of room. And we will just, you know, she will have to sell the house. I just want to make sure this is what she wants to do first…She needs time to think."

Tony nodded. "Right, we have to be sure."

"In the meantime she's all right, for tonight anyway. You go on Tony, I'll check on her in the morning."

"Yeah…Pam and the girls are probably about done cleaning up at the church."

"Give them my thanks again for their help."

"I'll do that…see you soon, and give me a call…if you need me."

"Tony…call mom…you got to call her often…every day if you can, and it doesn't take but a minute to pick up the phone."

"Yeah…yeah I know sis…I will"

Marshall stood by feeling his uncle's guilt inside of him. Gram was Gram. Grandpa's side kick, the one that put up with his silly puns day in and day out, though she has heard them a thousand times she always laughed, just that act in itself sent every body around Gram and Grandpa laughing, she was his hero, and now she was alone, how could she cope?

"This is going to get harder on her Tony, in this empty house."

"I know Gwen but you have to remember that I live two hours away."

"A phone call Tony…I'll take care of her here, but she has to hear from you more than before."

8

"I said I'll keep in touch!" Tony protested clasping onto the small deck's railing. Gwen was always the pestering big sister of two years. Somehow Tony thought that once they became adults with families of their own, this pestering would stop. He hasn't been sure if it has even eased. It just seemed that he could never do right by her.

"I'm sorry Ton—" Gwen cried taking her hand from out of her pocket and patting her bothers back.

Tony stood his ground with his back to his sister. "I got to go," he cried and then sprinted off the porch.

"I Love you." Gwen cried.

Tony turned for a second and waved. "I love you too."

# Conner

The twelve year old boy woke, he had been restless, and sleeping hasn't been easy lately. The living room light shinned in from his opened door, His dad didn't know when to call it a night anymore. Conner sat up in bed, the moonlight from the window above him beamed onto his bald head.

Conner Bear has accepted the fact that he would probably die from this cancer. The problem was that his father has not. Conner's heart ached for his father. His dad's world was crumbling before his eyes. He knows his dad tries so hard most of the time, as far as he could tell anyway. His dad used to have so many plans for him, but he say's little about the future now, in fact he says very little at all these days.

Conner got himself out of bed, and then used the bathroom. He walked out to the living room not surprised at what he saw.

His father was asleep, sitting up in his lounge chair. A half a bottle of whiskey on top of the T V tray beside him, the television was still on. Conner nudged him on the shoulder.

"Dad, wake up." Conner replied, his father did not wake, nor did he stir.

Conner was disappointed. He took the bottle from the tray then walked away with it into the kitchen. He raised it over the supper dishes that were still inside the sink and empted it, nearly gagging from the smell of the alcohol; he ran the faucet for a moment, and then carried the empty whiskey bottle back to the TV tray. He began to walk away and then he turned back picking up the bottle once more and placing it into his fathers open hand.

Conner nodded, pleased at what he had done, for when his father wakes in the morning, he may have to believe that he had drank the whole bottle, and how can he do so at a time like this? It would be something he would have to ask himself, having a living son to take care of and all.

"Good night Dad," Conner whispered, then walked back into his room leaving the lights and television on, he crawled into bed knowing that he had to talk to Sam about this. Sam would take care of his father; Conner had no doubt about it. And

When the time comes, Sam will help his dad get over his death. Though he has never asked Sam but he knew; Conner knew. Conner drifted back to sleep

# *Sam*

Marshall was disappointed with the grade he had gotten on his essay in his creative writing class. He angrily tossed his books into his locker with his friend, Luke standing beside him, Luke took his eyes off of Marshall as Cindy walked by. He gave her a smile, looked back at Marshall.

"So he gave you a C…hey I get the average grade all the time, your grandpa died. Doesn't that count for something dude?"

"It has nothing to do with my grandpa's death. I finished it before he even died."

"He doesn't have to know that, ask him for a redo. I'd do it"

"I don't know…it seems like cheating to me."

"You are to soft man. You're not going to get anywhere in this world if you keep going by the book. Come on you have time, go give it a shot, it's not like you're teachers pet or anything."

"You think I'm a teachers pet?" Marshall asked slamming his locker door shut.

"No, I know you are, it blows my mind that he gave you a C. you, of all people."

"What's that supposed to mean?"

"Hey dude, just go talk to him. He's probably still hanging out in his class room."

"Yeah, maybe I will, see you tomorrow." Marshall replied then took off into a fast walk leaving his friend Luke behind grinning.

The halls of the third floor were now empty. 309 was Mister Ross's class room. The door was open. Sam Ross was in front of the blackboard whipping it clean, Marshall walked in quietly behind him. He remembered his freshman year. The basics of creative writing, Mister Ross did nothing but write on the blackboard all year long. Marshall had received his average grade three periods ago and he was still upset.

Sam Ross heard the footsteps behind him. He paused, briefly in the frozen moment of time. Why now, he thought to himself, he was displeased for allowing himself to let his emotions out, before he left the building. Sam took in a deep breath, as he heard the words behind him.

"Excuse me, Mister Ross?" Marshall called out.

Sam ran his thumb and his index finger under his eyes quickly, and then turned around acknowledging one of his students standing before him. He hoped his demeanor would go unnoticed, but he thought not. Marshall was too, taken by surprise. He saw before him, a different man than Mister Ross. The calm and collected, witty, charming man Marshall knew as his teacher, was not in his facial features now, instead Marshall saw a drained and tired man copping with tears of sorrow.

"I'm..., I'm sorry..., if this is a bad time...I'll come back tomorrow"

Sam Ross set the damp cloth down that he was using to wipe the board onto his desk, at the same time he quickly set his troubles to the back of his mind.

"You're not happy with the grade I gave you Mister Perry?"

Marshall shook his head. "No...I just would like to know what was so bad about it."

Mister Ross turned his attention to his desk drawer; it seemed to be stuck for a moment, it then opened with a tug. He pulled out his large wire bonded folder and opened it, flipping the pages, he protested. "That's strange; I could have sworn I gave you a C."

He nodded landing his finger onto Marshall's name. "That's what I have here. Didn't I write that on you're essay Mister Perry?"

Marshall nodded, cracking a subtle smile at his teachers sarcasm, in fact, he felt welcomed by it. "What did I do wrong Mister Ross?"

"I'm glad you asked. Marshall this is an advanced class you signed up for. Do you know why I have only one advanced class.?"

"I don't know, because it's a harder class?"

Sam Ross cracked a smile shaking his head. "Come on, you can come up with a better explanation than that."

"Well...I guess, one has to be more dedicated...I am Mister Ross."

"Do you still have the desire and determination?" his teacher asked putting his folder back into his drawer.

"Yes I do...you don't think so?"

"I didn't see it in the essay I received from you."

Marshall sighed. "My grandfather died and I wasn't yet finished with it. Can I have a redo, please?"

"Oh, I'm sorry, I wasn't aware of that. You have missed a couple of classes and that went unnoticed. Yes by all means you may have a redo; you have a week to do so...does that sound fair?"

"Yes, it sounds good, thank you." Marshall replied with a shrug. "Well I'll see you tomorrow"

"Yes, see you then" Mister Ross nodded taking the damp towel back into his hand. Marshall turned away and began to walk out only to stop in his tracks.

Sam was back washing the board down at the same time aware that Marshall hadn't left the room yet. He turned around to see his student, again before him.

"Mister Ross, I sort of lied, my grandpa did die, but I was finished with my essay before he died suddenly. I'm sorry I'll just do better next time."

Sam sighed, putting his hands into his black denim jeans.

"I appreciate your honesty. Marshall, you as a writer; can play god with your characters, you are their master. Can you feel the power in that?"

Marshall nodded. "Yes I can, I guess, I'm afraid to just let it out"

"At least you are aware of it, you know, I felt overwhelmed with the facts you gave in you're essay, I didn't feel you as the narrator were in it at all. I need opinions you were to afraid to voice. What's your take on life on other planets? It was an interesting concept, but you were lost in the shuffle. You need to expose yourself, every true writer has got to take off their mask, and that is why I have only one advanced class."

"I get it now, I really do. I'll do better on my next paper. Thanks and, I'm sorry."

"If you really want a redo, you got it. You provide me; A; material, I will give you a; B; the choice is yours."

"I'd like that chance, thank you."

Sam took his hands from his pockets. "You got it, you best be getting busy."

Marshall smiled. "See you tomorrow."

Sam nodded as if to excuse him from the room. Marshall left with a smile on his face.

He walked outside; the trees were already dropping the colored leaves all around him. The student parking lot was empting fast, He didn't care to see that Todd Martin's car was parked next to his truck; he was inside with his stereo blasting loud with one of his friends sitting inside. Marshall looked away; he didn't want to know what kind of drug deal was going on inside if any.

He got into his truck thinking of what Mister Ross had said to him. He felt bad for lying to him, but content that he came clean with it quickly.

He wondered why he was crying, starting the engine he realized his teacher hadn't been quite the same since the beginning of this school year. He pulled out onto the street, a song played on his stereo…Somewhere only we know; it was he, and Becky's song or it used to be.

Marshall wanted to believe that he would not tell any of his friends about it, he just couldn't, not after today. He remembered his freshman year when he tried out for Mister Ross's Drama class, he didn't make the cut. Mister Ross suggested he try his creative writing class instead. Marshall took his advice, and realized it's where he was supposed to be. He had no harsh feelings what-so-ever, and was happy to support the drama team, and encouraged his friends to do the same, they got together to help set up stage when ever help was needed, and there was always a thank you from Mister Ross.

He was excited to get started on his essay, he had a lot of work ahead of him, and he was backed up. Now he had two assignments from Mister Ross, and his science report hanging over him, maybe he should have just taken the c from Ross and try to get a fresh start next time around.

His mind was racing with different ideas on both of his writing assignments, at the same time he kept his attention on the busy street, not quite rush hour, yet congested enough for this small town just thirty miles outside of the twin cities where his mother owned a tailor shop and commuted back and forth almost every day. He was happy here, it's only been five years since he and his mother moved back here to Hudser Wisconsin. He wasn't born in this town, but born and raised in Dallas Texas until he was twelve. Marshall's father left him and his mother long before that. He hasn't seen him since. The big shot lawyer can kiss his butt for all he cared.

He was proud of his mother; she did well for the two of them. A dedicated woman who worked hard to get what she wanted, Marshall wanted the same for himself, and now, at this moment, he was glad he told his teacher the truth, and he was ready to take on the extra assignment to do so.

He was not too surprised to see his mothers van parked in their short driveway so early in the day; at times she would come home to do her work. He parked beside her van, grabbed his back pack and went inside.

He noticed the door to his mother's sewing room was shut, more than likely she was inside working on those bride maids dresses. He never bothered her unless he absolutely had to, perhaps Mister Ross should have had his door shut, he thought to himself as he walked into the kitchen sniffing the aroma. He opened the oven pleased to see his mother's famous meatloaf and baked potatoes inside. He opened the refrigerator and retrieved a soda, popped it open flinging his back pack off his shoulder he carried it to his room, eager to start on his work, he sat behind his computer.

Gwen's silky brown hair was falling out of the large barrette she had loosely fastened on the top of her head as she jogged herself into the kitchen.

"Oh please don't be burnt," she huffed opening the oven. "Oh thank god." She replied taking supper out of the oven." Marshall, dinner is in five!" She bellowed.

Marshall heard his mothers call, and because he knew better, he pulled himself away from his computer. Quickly he washed his hands then entered the dinning room.

"Supper is early tonight mom."

"Yes, Nancy is having one of those, Holiday décor parties, and I just have to go to it, yawknow. So anyway I called your grandma and asked her if she would like to come along, well, but she said no. I wish she would want to get out."

Marshall nodded sitting himself down at the table while his mother did the same.

"Has she decided whether or not she wants to move out of the house?"

"Well hon I think she is going to stay for the winter, she's all right with that, and I know you are busy, but whenever you can find the time, I encourage you to pay her a visit here and there."

"I will, we can have her over for supper anytime, right?"

"Right, but we also have to go to her, Marshall she's in a depressed state right now."

"Well, do you want me to bring her a plate of this meatloaf? I can, but I have to get back, I'm swamped with homework right now mom."

"That's all right; I was planning on it myself."

"I was thinking I should be there on Saturday, and maybe stay late,"

"Oh; why is that?'

"Saturday is Halloween Mom. You know, grandpa always kept an eye on the house of pain, called the cops when ever kids would want to break in and party."

Gwen shook her head with a sigh." You never did that, did you?"

"No, course not, that house gives me the creeps."

"I just wish they would send a bulldozer through it, and be done with it for everyone's sake." Gwen huffed, and then took a bite of the meatloaf.

"So what's your next assignment with Mister Ross?"

"Well, it's a twilight zone episode. I have to write one. Class has been a hoot, this past week we've been watching some of those old episodes. So I can be as bizarre as I want and get away with it."

"One of you're own?"

"Oh of course, no one is going to get away with plagiarizing, apparently Ross has the whole library of the twilight zone, and I guess that makes him a, zone head."

Gwen smiled. "I guess it would. So, what do you have planned for it?"

"I'm still stuck on a couple of ideas; right now." Marshall replied chasing his food down with a gulp of his milk.

"Mom, when, well, I went to see Ross after school today to ask him about the grade I had gotten on my essay, I guess I caught him off guard."

"Why, what was he doing?" His mother asked curiously.

"Well, he was crying."

Gwen was a bit relieved, and she questioned herself to as why, for she has heard nothing but good things concerning Marshall's teacher. Now she was concerned.

"I'm sorry to hear that, what was he doing? Maybe he was reading one of his student's stories?"

"No, it wasn't that, he was washing the board down, apparently thinking he was alone for a while.'

"Sounds like he's going through a crisis of his own, maybe he has a loved one that is sick or dieing, he's married, right?"

"Yes, he is. I meet his wife last spring at the play the drama class had put on. I guess he could be having problems with his marriage."

"Hon, if you're concerned, ask him how he is, he deserves your respect. If he doesn't want to talk about it, at least he knows you care; after all, you are his best student."

Marshall smiled with a shrug.

"Not this year mom."

"Its early, so you had a setback, you will get back on track."

# *David*

David Bear walked out of his bathroom with a towel around him, and then he knocked loudly on his son's bedroom door.

"Conner, it's almost seven thirty, time to get up!"

"Yeah dad, I'm getting dressed." Conner replied already dressed, he was sitting on the edge of his bed. If he could just sit a while longer, his light headiness may subside. This wasn't going to be one of his better days, only if he could just stay home today, instead of sitting at his mothers, and all day he would be waiting for his dad to return. He is old enough to be home alone.

Conner believed that by age twelve he could be left alone for hours at a time. He believed that it was a legitimate request, perhaps one that he will never be granted.

Wouldn't it be nice though, to go to school with his house key in his pocket, walk home, bundled up from the approaching winter, and fix him self a bowel of Tricks cereal, and just to sit in front of the TV to veg-out?

His father didn't want him going to school at this time because his immune system is too susceptible to colds and flues that go around in public schools as they tend to do. He still hangs on to the hope that a marrow donor match will be found suitable for his sons needs.

David knows the odds are slim to none, but he can't, he just can't take that chance.

Conner lifted himself from off his bed, and reached for his cap that read: Bears Auto Repair, he put in on and felt better, so he assured himself, it worked some of the time, and he left no room in his mind for doubt. He carried his back pack out to the kitchen with him, and then set it down near the outside door. His father was stirring his chocolate milk. Scrambled eggs and sausage was cooking on the stove.

Toast popped up from the toaster, Conner grabbed the toast, took it to the table and began to butter it. David continued with the morning ritual, placing three different pills in front of his son. Conner popped them into his mouth, and then drank a healthy portion of his milk. Most mornings David would eat breakfast with his son. Conner was quick to notice that his dad didn't have a plate of eggs and sausage in front of him, instead he only held a cup of coffee in his hand.

"Aren't you going to eat something dad?"

His father rubbed his own forehead, and then ran his fingers through his coarse dark hair. "I'm not hungry today…"

"Are you sick?" Conner asked seemingly knowing the answer.

"Did you sleep all night?"

Conner nodded turning his eyes away from his father. "Yeah," he said taking a bite of his toast.

"You didn't get up at all?"

"I went to the bathroom once,"

"You must know by now that I'm having a drink or two at night."

"I guess so…you sure look like it"

"Have you been empting my whiskey down the sink?"

"No, why?"

"Don't lie to me Conner; I didn't drink the whole bottle last night, or the night before."

"You must have."

"I'd be puking my guts out right now if I had."

Conner lifted his eyes to his dad's bloodshot eyes, "Well, you don't look so good right now."

"You think that just because you're sick you have the right to lie to me. It's not happening Conner,"

"And you think that just because I'm sick you can get drunk every night…You drank half a bottle last night, two nights in a row." Conner replied with a cry in his voice.

"I am an adult; I have a right to unwind at the end of the day," his dad bellowed.

"I don't want you to be a…alcoholic when I die!" Conner cried.

David shook his head. "You're not going to die Conner! You hear me, you're not!"

"Then why are you drinking so much?! I can't wake you up…what if I needed you? Don't you care!?"

"I care, you know I do, you are supposed to be in bed at night and I don't appreciate these tricks you have been playing on me!"

Conner dropped his toast down onto his plate sneering at his father.

"You were passed out drunk! You are in, what do you call that, denial! Denial about, me dying…You are drunk every night now, because I'm dieing and you don't want to believe it!"

"You are going to get another bone marrow transplant…!"

"No I'm not…" He cried with anger. "I'm telling, I'm telling Sam on you!"

"Do you want to die Conner?" David now cried.

Conner shook his head folding his arms across his chest." No, I want to stay here with you."

"Then let's work together on this. I'll make you a deal and cut back on my drinking if you stop believing that you are going to die."

Conner jumped up from his chair and rushed over to his fathers arms. He cried out loud. "I don't want to die dad!"

"Lets fight it pal, we can do this together. " David cried as he embraced Conner.

"Okay dad." Conner cried.

David didn't mind that he was late for work. He listened to Conner's view; He wanted to go to school. He promised Conner he would consider it. though, he was hesitant, He wanted Conner to be happy for the rest of his life, and, yes, it was time for him to secretly realized that if his son was to recover somewhat, it wouldn't be from a bone marrow transplant for It's highly unlikely that a perfect, or nearly perfect match was out there. This remission that Conner was in just has to stay.

Sam says to have faith. David believed that faith was for the weak and meek, just like Sam. It was all false hopes in David's eyes.

David wanted a break from Sam, but he believed Conner didn't, it was time for Conner to feel these small hints of false hope; it just seemed to be the only way. It was time to slowly prepare for the unthinkable.

This has been a long time coming. If such a God existed, David believed he had paid his dues. A life for a life, he has already paid that. He's paid it, what more did God want?

Why do some people give and give, until there is just nothing left, David had no answers and no solutions, but only the comfort he embraced at the end of the day, that very comfort, Conner wanted to take away from him. Tonight he would have to take his bottle of comfort into his bedroom; turn the light off, Conner would be less the wise.


Marshall sat behind his desk, joined by his classmates, with all their attention on their teacher, Mister Sam Ross who was pacing the floor with his energy and enthusiasm in tact, spoke to them.

"So how are your characters going about introducing them selves to the reader, I ask you…Do you want your first character to look in the mirror and reveal what is seen? I hope not, to fast, much to fast…I've spent hours—days with some people and still don't know what color their eyes are, heck, sometimes I forget what color my eyes are." {The class laughed,} "Do they part their hair on the right, or the left…? It's not important people…Who cares about personal preference! What I do know though, is whether they have bad breath…{Again, the class laughed.} I know the color of their hair, their general physique and how they dress…"

Marshall then took notice of his teacher's attire. Last year, and the year before his teacher wore mostly dress shirts that buttoned up and down, sometimes with a tie, when he wore his ironed kakis, this school year, Ross has been wearing a lot of jeans and knit shirts, and sweaters. It could indicate a marriage separation or divorce. If he were sitting closer to the front of the class and if his teacher were not speaking with his hands as he paced it would be much easier to tell if, Mister Ross was wearing a wedding band or not, Marshall couldn't be sure.

"…If I were going to introduce you to one of them in a story, then I'd begin with something like this:

BRENDA LAMBERT

Light sparked off his gold platted tooth; he was much too huge to be afraid of being mugged because of it. I shook his hand in a greeting. He said

"Hi Sam, great meetin ya," My fingers slid off his damp sweaty hand, as we took the booth together, he bowed, somewhat before me and I almost gagged as his breath entered my air space, quickly, I reached for my coffee cup, and brought it closer to myself…Did I paint you a picture?"

The class continued to laugh; in agreement Marshall's smile faded as the bell rang.

"Dismissed!" Sam called out. His classmates still wore their smiles while they gathered their books and slowly exited the room. Marshall moved much slower, he fiddled with his backpack.

Sam was gathering his papers on his desk, and he lifted his eyes to see Marshall standing before him. Marshall saw no ring on his teachers' finger; instead, he saw the whitish line where it used to be. They both locked eyes. Marshall sighed.

"A divorce?" He asked.

Sam nodded, saying nothing, only looking solemn.

"I'm sorry…I just want you to know that Mister Ross."

Again Sam nodded. "Thank you Marshall."

"And thank you for the…I don't know how to say it, the shove in the right direction…I won't let you down again…Is there, anything that I can do for you Mister Ross?"

Sam cracked a smile. "I don't believe so, but thank you for asking. You best be getting a move on, or you'll be late for your next class."

Marshall took the hint with a grain of salt. He did what he felt he had

26

to do, even if he had gotten booted out the door. He sprinted up the stair well nearly running right into his old girlfriend Becky. She smiled.

"Hi." She said, flinging her long blond hair over her shoulder. Marshall nodded without returning her smile with his, and then continued walking up the stairs.

When he first started dating Becky last spring, a few of his friends had warned him that she; had issues. What kind of issues could they be referring to? Such a relative statement, that they didn't know how to answer. Just; Issues, they said. At the time Marshall just wanted to date a pretty face.

It was no where near a perfect world, for some, Issues; don't wipe off one's sleeve as well as they do for others, instead, those issues, soak through their skin and builds a wall, letting nothing else in.

It didn't take Marshall long before he had seen the scars that issues had left behind, under the long sleeved blouses and sweatshirts that she wore to keep them hidden. She explained to him that it made her feel better when she was down or mad to cut herself now and then, and he ought to try it sometime for the high.

"Lots of people do it."

"It's crazy…how can it make you feel good?"

"It just does…try it and you will see."

"Not happening…" Marshall replied with sarcasm.

Latter on that evening he had called her on the phone and broke up with her. He wondered how many cuts his action was going to call for that night. He worried about her, but she was in school the next day, and even though it was a warm spring day Becky wore a sweatshirt. She was right, she wasn't alone, and some of her friends also wore long sleeves. Word had got out, with a little help from him, they were all called the Cutters...Why does one beat them self up? Marshall wondered. Have they forgotten, they were inside?

Conner put on his ski jacket, then reached for his cap from the coat rack. Surely, his mother would take her eyes off of Wheel of fortune and take notice, and put out her cigarette knowing that his father was coming soon. She did, butting out her cigarette, with a smokers cough.

"Honey bear isn't it about time you trade that baseball cap in for something a little warmer?"

"Yeah, I will' Conner replied picking up his shoes and walking over to the couch, he sat down slowly not feeling very well at all, it could be that it was just a bit to warm here in his mothers house. Her house used to be cooler for she was a penny pincher when it came to the heating bill. Conner slipped off his coat for now. His dads timing wasn't always prompt on Fridays.

Wendy puffed out her oversized tee shirt, for it was getting bunched between her breast line and her stomach roll. She picked up her empty beer can and potato chip bag and walked into the kitchen. Conner sighed, he knew what was coming next, and he had to prepare himself, it wasn't even the good kind, Conner wondered what cheap imitation fragrance would engulf his lungs this time.

Conner cupped his hand over his nostrils while his mother walked through the living room spaying heavily. Who was she fooling, but herself; surely she could get a little more creative. A little less lazy would do her no harm either, now that the days were getting colder, Wendy choose not to step out side to smoke her cigarettes.

From the small picture window, above the couch Conner had seen his dad's truck pull onto the curb.

"He's here!" Conner said loudly.

"Okay." Wendy huffed, quickly; she reached for the doily from the coffee table and vigorously, fanned the air around her. She only stopped when the sound of David's foot steps walked up the porch. She sat herself down not a second to soon.

After a brief tap on the door, David let himself in as he always had. He stood tall and rugged, his finely groomed beard agreed with him.

"Hi dad." Conner called out putting his jacket back on he knew, this arousal thing wasn't working.

"You got your books together?" his dad asked in his deep voice.

"Yeah, I got them in my backpack." Conner replied standing and picking up his pack.

"You want to wait in the truck a minute."

"Okay." He agreed walking his way to the door; David reached for his sons pack, leaving Conner's hands empty.

"Bye honey bear, I love you."

"I love you too mom." Conner replied before he stepped out side.

"What did I tell you, about smoking in front of him!?" David shouted.

"I don't need your lectures…I have a right to smoke in my own home!"

"You have a right to poison your son!"

"Oh, go ahead and make it sound like I'm killing him…you of all people!" Wendy screamed with her face turning red, she sat back further onto the couch.

"The doctors said to keep him away from all toxins!…I can keep him away from you, if I have to."

"You would smoke in front of him…if you smoked, so don't go there with me Bear!" Wendy huffed, folding her wide leg upon her knee.

"No, I wouldn't, so don't go there with me!"

"Wake up!" Wendy screamed reaching for her cigarettes. "The doctors say he needs a perfect match! My family has been tested…to bad they can't test yours because, who knows, maybe your father would have been a match…but we will never know because you killed him!" She shouted fueling Bear's anger.

"He was a piece of garbage! Just like you and your family…I wouldn't feed my son poisoned bone marrow if my life depended on it!"

"Yeah, well if I was a match I would clean up and you know it! Or we should have had another baby together! You left me Bear! You left me!"

David turned to the door and slammed it on his way out.

Conner was sitting in his father's truck. He didn't like it when his parents fought. Well, they will have one good thing come out of his death, they won't have to see, or talk to each other ever again if they choose not to, Conner believed they would make that choice in a heart beat. If the two of them would see each other in the grocery store they would just look away, perhaps pretend that they didn't see one or the other in the first place and the day would be none the difference.

David got into the truck; he slammed the door, and then turned the key.

"Conner I thought we had a good talk this morning, why didn't you insist to her that she go outside and smoke?"

"I didn't want her to get mad at me." Conner replied with a cry in his voice as he took his pack from his dad and set it down by his feet.

"I'll tell you what, how about we get you sighed up for school on Monday."

Conner's eyes grew wide as did a smile. "You really mean it!"

"I really mean it." David said with a smile, he reached over and tipped Conner's cap.

"So cool, thanks dad, can I call Sam when we get home?" "Of course you can, why don't you invite him over for pizza tomorrow night, we will have our own Halloween party."

"Oh, so cool, can we play space patrol?"

"We can." David replied as he pulled out onto the street. He just hoped that Sam would keep his religion and faith to himself, because, God wasn't going to save Conner, cancer does not lie; there is nothing to offer but false hope.

# *Halloween*

It was warmer than most, no wind, yet the ground, like most Halloweens was covered with leaves. The sun was setting, as Marshall pulled into the driveway of his grandmothers, he realized that, few, if any trick or treater's would come down this dirt loop road that really lead to nowhere but back to the main highway from which it came, yet he had a small bag of candy in his hand just in case. His grandmother told him not to bring anything, but himself for she was making chili for supper.

Marshall was a bit uneasy, Grandpa wasn't here, and he wasn't sure if he could entertain her by himself. What would he say? He had nothing in common with his grandma. Small talk doesn't last very long; perhaps she had a project for him, something that needed to be repaired, or something grandpa left un-done, yes that will be ticket, he will find something to do.

His grandmother opened the door with a wide smile on her face, and tears in her eyes she was filled with bitter sweet sorrow. "Hi Gram!" Marshall said with the same tears, they embraced in the door way.

"Oh Marshall, thank you for coming, I hope you like chili."

"I do, I'm not fussy Gram."

"I know you're not. Come, Come in, and make yourself at home."
His grandmother said proudly.

"I brought candy."

"Oh you didn't need to fuss with that, we don't get any kids at the
door around here." Marshall shrugged setting the bag of candy onto the
table.

"Is that why you came dear?"

"No Gram, I just thought you could use some company, and if you
get any pestering kids making noise next door I could chase them
away."

"Oh, they come from time to time, doesn't necessarily only happen
on Halloween, I wish someone would just take a torch to it. I thought
about doing it my self just to put that poor woman's soul to rest."

"Gram, do you think her souls in there?" Marshall asked taking off
his quilted jean jacket.

Beth shrugged, and then walked over to the stove to stir the chili.

"You don't think it is possible? Poor woman was beat and battered
every time that man stepped foot into that house. Does it matter that she
was still alive when she was taken out of that house? Like I said I have
always wanted to take a torch to that house, your grandfather would not
let me.' She said leaving Marshall somewhat surprised.

Marshall took a seat at the kitchen table.

"You can't do something like that Gram, you could start a forest fire,
and it could have taken your house with it."

"Oh, I would have been careful. You have to pick the right night for
it you know, what would have it hurt, can't wait for the state or county
to do it."

Marshall didn't think he liked what he was hearing, she couldn't

33

possibly be hinting, or silently suggesting to him that he should go out there and burn down the house of pain tonight.

"Well, Gram, you won't have to worry about it much longer. Come spring you will be living in town, with us. I don't know how long I'll be around, because I'm looking into a couple of different scholarships."

"That's wonderful dear." Beth replied taking a seat across the table from her grandson.

"I know I should let it be, but it troubles me."

"The house docs, Gram?" Marshall asked, he could see how much Grandpa's sudden death had aged her, just in this short time. "No, I suppose it is the side show, I don't care for it. I just want that poor woman to be at peace. Your mother and I tried our best to do what we could, when that awful man wasn't around.

"Well Gram, I can try to contact, somebody, the county, the state, I will see what I can do to get it tore down Gram, okay?"

"Oh, thank you Marshall. Thank you."


Sam was more than happy to accept the invitation. He did not mind the long drive into the city at all, in fact he enjoyed it, and it helped him clear his head some. He stood outside the Bear home with a plastic jack-o-lantern filled with trail mix, granola bars, and caramel apples. He knocked on their door, noticing no outside decorations, the only indication that they were excepting trick or treater's was the outside light that was left on.

Conner opened the door with a wide smile. He wore a ninja outfit that was a couple of sizes to small, in height yet fit his thin frail body just right

"Sam!" He called out loudly, he then looked down to see what was in Sam's hand, for he never came empty handed.

"Conner, how are you feeling?"

"Feeling like some treats, is this for me?" Conner asked keeping his smile.

"It sure is." Sam laughed following Conner inside of the Bear home.

"Thank you Sam. Dad is in the living room setting up Space Patrol."

"Well I don't know how to play Space Patrol, no fair you're a ninja tonight you will beat me for sure."

"Yeah, I probably will." Conner laughed, he felt younger tonight, and it was a good feeling to be an innocent child again, even if it were for just one night. If he were well, he may be at Jimmy's house, perhaps overnight to watch scary movies, that is if they were still friends, last year was, so long ago; even then Conner felt Jimmy slipping away from him for he had missed a lot of school. He had a nervous feeling deep inside of him for Jimmy hadn't called him, or tried to contact him in any way all summer. Friends come and go as they tend to do, oh what would his father do without Sam.


Conner took another bite of his caramel apple, why, he didn't know for his stomach was not settling right. He was enjoying watching his father and Sam sitting on the floor in front of the TV like children would often do. They were battling the aliens with the power of their remote control. He had his fill winning most of the games. He had his fill of this apple; in fact, he wasn't feeling well at all.

Conner stood from the couch and walked into the kitchen, he turned to see if they were watching before he dropped the half eaten caramel apple into the garbage. He then put stride into his walk, almost racing for the bathroom. His stomach was going to empty there was no stopping it.

Conner was swishing his mouth over the sink. He spit out the used mouthwash into the basin then ran the water and patted his face. He felt better now nobody would have to know.

"Conner...? He heard his dad's voice outside the door. Conner shook his head in disappointment

"Yeah dad?" he replied opening the door, all was well. He thought to himself looking up at his father.

"You got sick, didn't you?" David asked looking down as his sons pale face.

"I...ah...yeah sort of, I ate too much, that's all. Really, I feel better now."

Sam took it upon himself to see what was up. He walked up to the opened bathroom door to see Conner sitting on the edge of the bathtub with a thermometer in his mouth. David pulled it out, relieved at the results.

"No fever."

"I just ate too much."

"I'm sorry, that was probably my fault." Sam said then added. "It happens to thousands of kids every Halloween, Bear."

"I guess so." David scoffed.

Was this part of the denial process? He asked himself.

All evening, Conner wanted to set Sam aside and get his reassuring words that he would never leave his dad after he dies. The pizza and the games, it was all a fun time, but it was all for him. His dad made sure he wore his sweatshirt, and jogging pants to bed.

He supposed he would get a lot more chances for that. Conner snuggled up warmly in his bed while his dad turned off the light.

David walked back into the living room thinking it would be a good time to be left alone; it would be a good time for a drink. Sam would be leaving soon, course he had no wife to go home to any more. Sam was on the living room floor stuffing the game remotes back under the television.

David plopped down into his recliner.

"So, how have you been?" he asked Sam, with a sigh in his voice.

"Well, you know when it rains, it pours.' Sam replied standing up from the floor. He took a seat on the recliner.

"It's good to see you finally coming around; I think it's about time you throw your God out the window."

"This is not a perfect world Bear. He ate too much, and he is probably excited and nervous about starting school on Monday."

"Well, I had no choice, the environment he would have at school is a lot healthier for him than sitting in his mothers smoke filled house all day. She is ticking me off; I'm keeping Conner away from her."

"Bear, she has a right to see her son. If you feel they need to be supervised, then hang out with them."

"I don't have time Sam; I have a garage to run!"

"Then invite her over here, you may not care for her, but Conner loves his Mother."

"You shouldn't be to upset that you couldn't have any children, now you won't have to toss a kid around back-and-forth. It's not easy, believe me."

Sam nodded, if only he were able to give Mia a child, they may not be having this conversation right now. A child was what Mia had longed for, that longing was stronger than the love she had for him. Accepting it was hard, accepting Conner's sickness was harder.

"I have my kids, I feel like a father to a small handful of them." Sam protested, and then wished he would have kept that last remark to himself, for it may not be to much longer before Conner gets taken away from him. He hoped that Bear wouldn't take it to heart, and apologizing for words he hadn't intended to say in the first place was something Sam wasn't used to doing, perhaps it comes with the six years of teaching he had under his belt.

"Then, they're gone." David added.

"I'm here for you two, we will get through this." Sam said with his heart aching, he stood and reached for his jacket that was lying on the back of the couch.

"Hey, did you sell your house yet?"

"Yes, I did. We're closing in a couple of weeks. I've found an apartment too."

"You need any help with that?' David asked hoping the answer was no.

"No...thanks anyhow. I have it covered."

"What about your divorce, is it final yet?"

"No, November eleventh."

"Killing two birds with one stone."

"Yeah pretty much, a couple days apart."

"I saw her the other day."

"Yeah, where?"

"The shop and go, she was pumping gas."

"Was she alone?"

"I think so; I really didn't pay a lot of mind."

"You didn't say hi?"

"No…"

"Did she?"

"She waved.'"

"You didn't wave back… You should have at least given her a nod." Sam huffed walking toward the door.

"She left you Sam." David added, before Sam shut the door behind him.


Marshall was grateful his grandmother had found him a project, even if it was a cupboard door that did not want to stay shut. Grandpa's neatly organized tool box was set on top of the counter.

Marshall opened and shut the cupboard door several times, the clasp he tightened was complying He fixed it

"Got-err done Gram!" Marshall called out loudly; maybe she couldn't hear him over the television. Marshall put the tools back into the box as neatly as he found them.

Grandma was asleep, in her chair in front of the television. Marshall placed his hand over her hand as it was rested on the arm rest he rocked her hand with his, Gram woke,

"I fixed it Gram." Marshall said in a calming voice.

"Oh, you're such a good boy; I guess I must have fallen asleep. And look at you, you've grown so fast. Where does the time go?" She asked reflecting on her life. Marshall hasn't heard that phrase coming from his mother yet; he supposed it comes with age. Was it asked out of regrets for time less spent or did the elderly really believe that in the end their life is just the wink of an eye?

"I don't know Gram, why don't you go to bed; I'll lock up and let myself out."

"Very well, dear I am kind of bushed." She said lifting herself up from the chair, and she didn't mind at all getting some assistance from her grandson.

"Goodnight Gram." Marshall smiled giving her a hug. His grandmother patted him on the back.

"Good night Marshall I'm so glad you came to see me, let's do this again soon."

"You got it. We will."

Marshall turned off the TV, then the overhead light of the living room. He was glad he had come, and he did a much better job in entertaining her than he had thought he would. He was less worried about her, after tonight Giving his time to her eased his worries, he hoped she had felt the same way, he believed so.

She was right, not a single trick-or-treater tonight. From a glance out the window, the house of pain appeared to be silent. Marshall turned out the remaining lights, and then stepped outside with his keys in hand. The air was cooler than it had been much earlier.

He walked to his truck, detecting voices in the distance. The house of pain had company; apparently their vehicle was parked behind the house. Marshall's eyes peered as far as he could see; a faint light coming from the house. The voices were real, not just the wind, something was up.

Instead of walking across the brushy field in the dark, Marshall walked to the road. Angry at the situation, they are just kids having fun, he told himself, he and his friends considered checking it out more than just once, perhaps, if he hadn't had some pity on the woman and the boy who once lived there, he may have considered it, he had told his friends he wanted no part of it, and he didn't want to know what, or when they were going to do it. He was called; pansy, for his decisions. And He didn't rightly care just the same.

He walked up the Pane driveway wishing he had a flashlight, then thinking he should have just drove up in his truck. They must have pried the boards off one of the back windows that Grandpa had repaired time and time again. The male and female voices were getting louder as he neared the small one story house. They were screaming and laughing.

Marshall walked around to the back, near were a car was parked,

"Hey!" He shouted pounding on the side of the window where they had broken in. The loud voices were silenced; a flashlight shinned in his face. Marshall squinted from the light.

"It's just Perry." Tom boomed. "What do you want?" He added taking the ray of light from his face.

"I want you out of here, now!" Marshall replied

"Or what?" one of the girls asked with a smirk.

"Or I'll call the cops!"

"How about a beer, come on in, we can spare a couple."

"No…come on out…and get out of here before I call the cops…you guy's are all under age.

"Perry. You're getting soft on us, were not doing any harm, it's not like we are trespassing!"

"Come on let's get out of here Tom…This place is creeping me out anyway," One of the girls drunkenly replied.

"You are to trespassing!'

"Yeah…who's it hurting!?" Tom shouted squeezing himself out the window until he stood in front of Marshall.

Marshall never knew Tom Bentley as a bully even though Tom knocked a lot of guy's down; he is the running back on the high school football team.

"My grandma sent me out here; she wanted to call the cops on you guys. But I thought I would give you a chance to leave on your own."

"Oh, that's special, why don't you go back to your granny, and tell the old lady we left!"

Tom shouted in his face, while the others, one at a time, crawled from out of the window.

"I will, once you leave."

"Come on Tom, let's go." His friend Pete said, walking to the car with an opened twelve pack of beer in his hand. Tom stood his ground sneering at Marshall.

"I say we hog tie him inside of this shack!"

"The old lady, she'll call the cop's and he will rat on us, we don't want to be kicked off the team." Pete insisted. Big Tom lifted his eyes to the dark house.

"It's almost midnight, I say he is bluffing!…the ole lady is in bed, isn't she!?"

Marshall sighed deeply, now feeling a little frightened of this big oaf that stood before him. Tom took a piece of Marshall's jacket into his hands and lifted him slightly off the ground.

"Come on Tom, leave him alone, and let's get out of here." One of the girls pleaded.

"Are you afraid of this house punk?"

"Tom, leave him alone." The rest of them pleaded.

"No, I'm not afraid, get out of here.' Marshall panted.

Tom released his grip with a shove sending Marshall to the cold ground. He slowly got up while the four intruders got into the car. The car revved like the driver was sending a warning. He stood up brushing the damp leaves from his clothing. The car raced on out onto the dirt road.

The next day Marshall left the house early without telling his mother where he was off to, after all he was nearly an adult and had the right to come and go as he choose to. But if she had questioned him he would have told her where he was off to.

Grandpa had always repaired the house of pain before. He was only caring out his wishes, perhaps it was Grams wishes, but it was all the same to him.

Another overcast day it was, the cold drizzle bubbled onto his windshield as he drove down the; Loop road. He didn't want to alarm Gram in any way, so he decided to park his truck where the car was parked last night, hidden out of sight.

Marshall didn't believe Gram would hear him pounding nails into the old Pane house for it was much to cold outside for an opened window. Then there was that slim chance she had been looking out her picture window and seen him a split second as he pulled into the Pane driveway, just in case he was spotted, or heard, he would have to pay her a quick visit when he finished his job, if he had to explain, so be it.

He walked behind the ugly house of pain with a hammer and a bucket of nails in hand. He imagined that it was once all white and decked out in a bold black trim, now it was looking very wretched, the paint was peeling everywhere. It was on the ground and even blown by the wind scattered far and beyond the house. The busted two by fours were lying onto the ground. Big ole Tom must have ripped them off

43

with his bare hands. How so, he didn't want to know, just too grateful he didn't have to find out how strong he was on a more personal level.

Curious, he peered inside the wide open window. It smelled very damp and moldy. He believed he would have a strong argument with the city about this; it was a health hazard waiting to happen. There were beer cans and bottles scattered everywhere. It was a shame, what disrespect, granted ole man Pane may have been evil and if Marshall knew him personally he may have made it a point to spit on his grave. A woman was killed here, sure she didn't actually die here, but her soul had, could have disappeared little by little while Jack Pane thought he was the king of the world. He had his day, his day had come.

The reason why kids broke inside of this house could be debated. The fact that revenge had occurred was subtle for it was a failed attempt at saving a battered woman's life. The outcome was the same; it was death, and murder. David Pane should have just injured him instead; it would have been more justified. Ole man Jack Pane would have been rotting away in a jail cell with a bum leg, perhaps both of them.

Marshall had thought about going inside to pick up the garbage the kids left behind, but his mind was debating as well, could this be the ole mans real grave sight? He lifted a two by four, imagining how he could piece it together with out any fresh wood. He would find a way; he always made do with what he had. He began to drive a nail through the wood. If Jack wanted to see the light of day Marshall felt as though he had the power to deny him of it.

"This is for you Grandpa," Marshall said out loud. He was glad to be doing this chore, as he worked on it he thought about writing a letter to the mayor, certainly he had the power to get the ball rolling, sending this house to the ground. A true celebration.

# *School*

Last night Conner had set his bedside alarm. His excitement for school was already wearing down, and he hadn't even started it yet. Worries began to consume him. For he was bald, with no friends or the ambition to draw friends to him, instead he was tired, preoccupied, and uncertain if he was ready for school. If he wasn't now, he doubted he ever would be.

Did his last day of school pass him by without warning? Should he go today with the assumption that this might be his last school day, or would it be tomorrow? He had been yearning for this day to come for weeks and weeks, why wasn't he happy? Conner continued questioning his uncertainties as he dressed for his school day.

He did not want to go, and he didn't have the heart to tell his father. How could he, after begging and pleading his case for a small piece of normalcy. He wasn't normal, he could feel it, he could see it, and therefore it was time to believe it. His father would have to know there was something wrong, he always knew. He was just nervous, it should be very normal; it was something to hold on to, he had to. He just had to.

David was eating breakfast for Conner's sake, he was not hungry, Conner wasn't either he was doing the same for his father.

"Once we get you there and get you settled with your schedule it will be like ridding a bike pal, you will be fine." David said taking a bite of his toast.

"I know but I don't want Mom mad."

"You never mind your mom, she's made her own bed, besides she's happy for you." He said swallowing then he took a sip of his coffee.

"Do you really think so?"

"Course she is…now you have your house key on you?"

"Yes I do." Conner said picking at his scrambled egg.

"Now there is absolutely no smoking in this house, you make sure your mother is reminded of it, and I want to know if she does it anyway, you got that." David said taking notice of Conner's plate. He hadn't eaten much but he ate, probably just nerves.

"Yeah dad I got it."


After sitting in his new counselor's office for nearly an hour, Conner was given the list of his classes that was designed to fit his needs. He was grateful for the one floor arrangement; there would be no running up and down the stairwell for him. During that time his counselor had given him the permission to wear any cap or hat that he chooses to.

He walked into his second period English class wearing the cap his father had given to him. Bear's auto repair: it made him feel proud of his dad, and there was that little bit of toughness that came with it. All eyes were on him making him warm, but not good inside. He took his paper to Mrs. Smith who was sitting behind her desk; she was wearing a subtle smile.

There was no official welcome for him, after all this was junior high and not some grade school room you sit in all day with the exception of recess and physical education.

No one had to be extra friendly to him for there were other classes. Let the next teacher deal with his well being. She instructed him to take an opened desk, Conner did so.

Sitting in his fourth hour science class, Marshall was preoccupied with his pen, jotting down his notes during one of many of Mrs. Beamer's lectures. It was Ross's study hall hour. He had thanked Marshall for his promptness, and said he would take a look at his report this hour, what was he thinking about it, He asked himself, was he pleased? Marshall had to get that grade raised, he just had to.

He was no science wiz and didn't care to be, a passing grade was all he wanted from Mrs. Beamer. Like every teacher she had a handful of students that she had high hopes for, Marshall could only guess who those students might be, but he was sure; he was not one of them.

Marshall gathered his books from his locker slowly, wondering what happened to Luke for he had said earlier that he would like a ride home today. He probably met up with Cindy, he has been trying to get up enough nerve to ask her out ever since school started, and maybe he succeeded today. He didn't plan on waiting forever and he supposed he shouldn't be going on up to pester Ross either. He will just have to wait until tomorrow for the results.

He took his jacket out of his locker, put it on and at the same time pulled his cell phone from his inside pocket; he turned it on and rang Luke's cell phone.

"Hey, what's up?" Luke asked.

"What's up with you? You said you needed a ride"

"Oh…No dude, I got it covered, I'm hanging with Cindy, and we're on the way to the mall."

"What, you going out now?"

"Yeah…you can say that,"

"So you going to look at shoes and then go get your hair done together?" Marshall asked with a laugh in his voice while he walked down the hall with his backpack over his shoulder.

"Yeah, whatever dude, catch you latter."

"Yeah, you too, and thanks for letting me know that you didn't need a lift."

"Won't happen again…latter.'

He turned off his phone and slipped it back into his pocket. Very few students were left in the halls. The School busses were all departing. Marshall walked down the front stairway that led to the main exit of the building. He was surprised to see Todd Martin sitting down on the long steps inside the doorway. He found it odd; shouldn't he be in a hurry to get out of here? Surely he was in dire need for a cigarette. What was he waiting for, who was waiting for him? The thug looked like a mobster want-a-be with his long black coat.

Marshall made no eye contact with him as he walked down the stairs passing him. He stepped out side into the cool crisp air, finally, some sunlight it was almost blinding for he hadn't seen it in days.

"Marshall!" he heard his name called out from afar. He turned his eyes to the side of the building, back where the exit door was that many of the teachers used, for it was the closest to the staff parking lot. It was Mister Ross standing there throwing a wave at him.

He took the invitation and jogged over to him, this had to be good news: it just had to be. He did his best to keep the grin from his face, as he neared him; Sam opened up his brief case and pulled out his essay.

"You didn't have to run." Sam said with a smile handing Marshall his essay. Marshall took it into his hands, and then smiled widely.

"You understand I couldn't give you an A,"

"Yes, I know it was a redo; a B is great, thanks!" Marshall said with a wide smile for he knew it was A; material.

"Well. You did all the work, but good job Marshall..." Sam hesitated

"Remember last week when you had asked if there was anything that you could do for me?"

"Yes, its still stands Mister Ross."

"Well, I sold my house, and found an apartment. I could use a hand and your truck if you wouldn't mind."

"Oh, no, not at all, I'd be happy to give you a hand."

"Saturday sound all right?"

"Saturday works for me."

"Thanks, I'd appreciate it. I have a friend I would have otherwise asked, but he lives in the city, and he has a son that is sick...so I would rather not bother him with it."

"Oh, I'm sorry to hear that."

"It's just not a good time for him." Sam replied knowing that Bear had a hard time setting foot in this town in the first place. He would have come to lend his hand, yet he would have been uneasy and restless the whole time. No time was a; good time for him in this town.

Todd Martin had waited long enough, if Leo was looking for him here, he would have centennially given up by now. Todd stepped outside, looking about, there were cars and traffic everywhere, and Leo's car didn't appear to be in sight. He began to walk to where he had his car parked, near Hank's Bar down the street a couple blocks; he couldn't go home, Leo was sure to find him there. He messed up, big time; he didn't have Leo's money.

"I'm looking foreword to seeing your next report, no hurrying, you have until next Monday."

"I'll keep that in mind, I really have something cooking."

"Good, good..." Sam said with a smile facing Marshall.

He took notice, of the hard core student walking their way. He had seen him before, although he hadn't had him in any classes, he knew who Todd Martin was only because he was a bit notorious He didn't like the way he looked over his shoulder. Sam's smile slowly faded, he didn't like the looks of that silver mustang jacked up car crawling their way, with the opened window, the passenger shouted out the window.

"Martin!!" The horn honked repeatedly.

Todd paid no mind; he kept walking, passing Sam and Marshall without acknowledging anyone.

"Hey...Todd!" Sam called out to him walking over to him to Marshall's Surprise.

Todd was hesitant to stop, yet he did so. They watched the car pull away. "You in trouble?" Sam asked with his eyes moving about Todd's expressionless face.

"What's it to ya?"

"I can find a way to help you out."

"No I'm cool." Todd replied without conviction.

"Yeah…who thinks you're cool today…Those friends you had yesterday…Who thinks you're cool today?"

"You can't help me."

"Try me."

Todd still stood, fighting with the urge to walk away, and the need to stay in place for a moment longer, just as Sam was about to excuse Marshall in a polite manner.

"Umm…, Mister Ross…I'll see you tomorrow."

"All right Marshall, I'll see you tomorrow…Thanks again." Sam replied then turned his eyes back to Todd. Todd lifted his eyes to Mister Ross.

"I owe one of those guys fifty bucks."

"Was it money borrowed?"

"You can say that."

"How do you plan on solving this problem…Do you have a job?"

"No…" Todd said with a shrug "I'll figure something out" He added.

"I have a lawn that needs raking…Are you in for fifty bucks?" Sam asked as he reached into his back pocket and pulled out his wallet.

"Yeah…I'm in." Todd replied, puzzled; he took the bills from the teacher.

"How do you know I'll show?"

"You haven't given me any reason not to trust you."

Todd stood there dumfounded, while Mister Ross jotted down his home address. Handing him the piece of paper Sam turned to see if that

Silver mustang was in sight. It wasn't, he looked back at Todd who was shoving the money into his pocket.

"If you continue to hang with those guys it is going to land you nowhere, in jail, or worse, you know that don't you."

"Course...I...Just..." Todd shrugged having nothing to say.

"I would like it done by Sunday...Come any time. If I'm not home, I will leave a rake on the back porch along with some trash bags...bag them and set them on the back curb, all right?"

"Yeah, sure."

# *Mia*

Mia took it upon herself to be here. She held onto the inside of the empty kitchen cupboard while she knelt on the top of the counter; beside her, was a bucket of warm sudsy water. She squeezed out the excess water, and continued scrubbing. Some of her black curls dangled out from under her blue bandana scarf. This last minute cleaning was something she felt she needed to do.

It was after four, she wondered where Sam was, could he have found someone's shoulder to lean on so soon? Did he just not want to spend his leisure in this broken home? Mia did have to admit it; she herself was having difficultly spending her time here.

Sam was hesitant even before he stepped through the door, for Mia was here. Although this has been a friendly divorce, it was going to be hard putting up a front; at least he wouldn't have to tell her why he was late. He didn't have to tell her that he loaned a hoodlum fifty bucks to cover a drug debt on the sheer promise that he would come clean, do drugs no more. Sam didn't have much hope for Todd to fulfill his promise, but at least someone had given him the initial benefit of the doubt, for no good deed went unpunished. He had little time to prepare. He stepped inside his living room, nervous to be in his own house, everything in this house was emptier without her. From the décor to the environment that only a woman's touch could complete. Not every thing was absent today; sure the long leather couch has been gone for weeks along with a number of other items they had split up between the two of them, did he smell lasagna? Why on earth did she cook him supper?

Sam walked slowly into the kitchen, like Mia knew he would. She emptied the bucket of water into the sink, at the same time telling herself to keep her emotions at bay. She turned to him cracking a smile clutching onto a dish towel.

"Hi Sam…I'll be leaving shortly…I've just been tidying up some, and your supper is in the oven."

"Mia…you didn't need to do this."

"I wanted to…" she replied with a cry in her voice. "Don't you go shopping; you had barley anything in your refrigerator."

"I've been making do…Did you take the day off from work today?"

Mia nodded swallowing her tears. "It's my responsibility to clean this house too."

"You always kept it nice and clean, you need not worry…so how have you been?"

"Oh, all right…I saw David the other day."

"Yeah he mentioned that."

"How's Conner doing?" Mia asked with her eyebrows raised hoping for good news."

"He's still in remission…He started back to school today."

"Oh, he must have been so happy about that."

"I don't know I think he was nervous about it…"

"I suppose so." Mia replied replacing the ice cream bucket back under the sink while Sam stood behind her.

"Have you found a place to live yet?"

"Yes I have, it's on Hampton Street, it's a good size apartment, and did you find a place in St Paul?"

Mia turned to Sam, trying to keep her smile. "Yes, not to far from the office."

"Good…well…no more commuting in rush hour traffic. It's got to be a plus, what did it take you an hour, an hour an a half?"

"I didn't mind it so much." She replied finding it hard to keep her tears back.

Mia opened the oven door, and then shut it putting the oven on low. "If you need help moving furniture, I can ask Scott."

Sam shook his head with his hands in his pockets. "I have it covered…thank you."

Mia took her bandana from her head, her black curly hair fell down to her shoulders and onto her yellow sweater that Sam always complemented her on, her brown face blended so well with that sweater, she cracked a smile.

"Oh, did you ask Fred and Gary?"

"No…their going out bird hunting on Saturday, I've asked one of my students, Marshall Perry."

"Oh good I'm glad he's still writing. Is he the one who wrote that story last year about the homeless elderly couple who lived in a boy's basement, and hid them from his parents?"

Sam chuckled nodding. "Yes, same student…And how did things go with the Bender kids…were you able to place them together?"

Mia smiled widely and nodded.

"Yes I was…they went to a wonderful home, I think it will last for a while."

"Good…That's good news…" He added as the conversation slowed.

"Well…I best be going." Mia huffed with a sigh. "You probably got your own things to do." She added.

"Take care. Mia…"

"Yes you too Sam…I gave you my new phone number, didn't I?"

"Yes I have it…I'll call you when the papers are ready."

"All right, I'll see you then."

Sam wanted to stop her in her tracks and throw her into his arms as she walked by him. He was so grateful he controlled that urge inside of him. She spent her days helping others, tending to their needs so they could live happier; and here he was, miserable enough to hand a drug dealer, money for his debts. What was he thinking?

Mia dabbed her eyes with a tissue as she sat inside her car, she had hoped that Sam would have asked her to stay for dinner. It was a long shot, she knew, for she had been the villain in this seven year marriage.

Once they were so in love and so happy together sharing their evenings after a long day at work. The two of them took their worries and concerns home with them to talk them over, and they both listened to each other it worked for them, it kept their marriage strong and they had become friends in the process, for better or worse, but Sam couldn't give her what she wanted the most, a child together. After hours of doctor visits she went through asking why, why couldn't she bare a child? The doctors found nothing wrong with her. She then begged Sam to get checked out. The answer was with him, He was sterile.

It wouldn't have been the end of her world if Sam would have agreed on adoption. Sam has heard of the horror stories that come with adopting infants. A couple gets so prepared for the baby to be handed over to them, and the biological mother changes her mind. No, he just wasn't meant to be a father. It was not in Gods will.

Mia had enough; she had accepted Sam's faith to a certain extent before she had put her two cents in. "God gives us the right to make decisions on our own; we married under God why can't we adopt a baby under God…Is it God's will to punish me because you are too afraid of becoming a father…?"

Her arguments went on and on, Sam spoke little in defense.

"I can't do it…I'm sterile! You want a baby then leave me…have your babies…I'm not afraid, it's just not meant to be…"

Sam took the lasagna out of the oven; she had cooked so much, a whole cake pan loaded with his favorite cheeses. He should have at least asked her to stay to help him eat this, perhaps that was her intensions, but why, why now? Nothing could have changed, what was done was done. What was said was final, wasn't it? He questioned her visit.

Class by class Conner went though his day with little communication from his peers. Some of them he had known from last year. What happened to Jimmy? He wondered, it didn't matter just the same, for it would have been a big disappointment if Jimmy would have shunned him like the shunning he had grown to understand today. Now he lay there on his bed wondering what he had done wrong.

David had entered his home with his nostrils flaring. He didn't smell cigarette smoke. Wendy came before him and then leaned herself against the wooden table, leaving him in wonder.

"What's wrong…where's Conner?" He asked, standing in place.

"He's taking a nap…he's had a long day."

"What do you mean…long day, what happened?" David asked with concern for Conner didn't take naps, he wouldn't much approve of a well child taking a nap in the evening hours like this. David knew now; Conner's naps were just going to have to accepted.

"He doesn't want to go to school Bear…The kids at school don't treat him the same anymore…He wants to go back to staying with me." David shook his head.

"No. no…He's begged me to let him go back…you are just saying this so you can have him! It's not going to work…You are not going to twist the truth from him. He wants to go to school."

"He doesn't! He doesn't…Ask him yourself!" Wendy huffed, and then folded her arms across her wide breast line.

"Oh, I will…I don't need you telling me how to raise my son!" David shouted dropping his set of keys to the counter.

"Please stop fighting!" Conner shouted, now standing behind his mother. "Both of you stop!" he cried.

David reached for his chin and roughly stroked his short beard, and with a sigh, he looked over to his son.

"You feeling all right there pal?"

"Yeah, but I don't want to go to school any more, the kids are mean, I want to be with Mom and do my homework at her house." He cried…

"I told you so Bear…"

"Mom don't yell at him…please stop fighting."

Wendy sighed, and then put her arm around him holding him tightly. "Okay honey bear,"

After reassuring her son that all would be well to the best of her intensions, she had excused herself hoping that tomorrow would be a better day for him. Why couldn't David see that she was not plugging their son up with a list of dos and don'ts that would only be made to benefit her needs? She was no monster, but a mother that has to go day by day watching her son's health deteriorate.

Conner sat on the couch with his history book in his hand. Why did he have to do this dumb-ole homework anyway? It was like training a man in a wheel chair to climb a mountain, chances were he would never get to the top. He was losing hope for a recovery and it was getting harder and harder to put up this front. Today was hard; facing the real truth was hard.

David entered the living room with a blanket in his arms. He fluffed it out and laid it onto his sons lap.

"I'm not cold dad."

"I don't want you to catch one either…I'll call your tutor in the morning…Okay?"

Conner smiled, feeling no need for explanation and no need for apologies.

"Okay…Thanks dad…What's for supper?"

"Macaroni and cheese…sound all right?"

"Sounds all right, but how is it going to taste?"

"Very funny…" David replied then gently tugged on the bill of Conner's cap, leaving them both with a chuckle.

Marshall stood in front of the sink; he rinsed his plate clean under the running water.

"I don't know mom...I think it is strange too, a guy like him should have a lot of friends. I've seen him in the halls carrying on with Mr. Baker and Mr. Rothberg, seems like he would have a lot of help moving...Maybe he just didn't want to ask...He did say that he has a friend that lives in the cities...something about not wanting to ask him because he's got a sick kid." Marshall put his plate into the dishwasher while his mother scrapped her leftovers into the garbage.

"Sick? You mean terminal?"

Marshall shrugged.

"I don't know...kind of sounded like it to me.'

"That's to bad...Well don't take any money from him if he offers it to you."

"No.... I won't...Oh. By the way, I wrote a letter to the mayor today and sent it out." Gwen raised her eyebrows.

"You what...Wrote to the mayor, what on earth for?"

"Well...Gram wants the house of pain tore down...It's a health hazard...kids are breaking in there all if the time."

Gwen sighed. "I didn't realize it bothered her so much...we should have thought of this sooner...So you explained her case?"

"Yes...our case, I did get a point or two across."

"I believe you did. You are going to make a very fine journalist one day hon."

Journalist...it didn't seem to be a fitting profession for him, he would have to study politics, a never ending debate and countless arguments that may corrupt his brain and take away from his creativity to become the writer that he yearned to be. The time was nearing for him to make these difficult decisions. He loved his mother dearly, yet wished that she would freely allow him to make his own choices.

Gwen was back in her sewing room; her son's decision to write to the mayor was a fine one. She hoped for the best, having that house out of sight would benefit everyone; she changed the white thread back to the deep teal color, remembering that awful night that had changed her life forever. Her heart once ached for David, but as they say; time heals all wounds. It's been a long process, and now all that was left was that house still standing as a reminder. Once it was gone perhaps she could get David out of her mind for good.

# The Failed Attempt

Sam carried his empty dresser drawers down the stairs. There wasn't a whole lot left to transfer to his new apartment down the street, just the big items that would require some assistance. His dresser, bed, a couch and chair and the kitchen table, the rest he managed on his own, all week he has been slowly empting out the broken home and filling his new apartment with the old memories. Everything was already a reminder of his failed marriage. He hoped that Mia was finding peace with the divorce; he hoped she could move on quickly, and soon start dating again, for her biological clock was ticking.

Marshall had driven by this house many times before without knowing that it was his teachers. He tapped on the door and then rang the door bell. After a moments time Sam opened the door wearing a Green Bay Packer sweatshirt and worn out blue jeans. Sam still had hopes that Todd would show to fulfill his end of the bargain, so he was a bit disappointed to only see trusty Marshall at the door.

"Hey…Marshall…Thanks for coming…come in…Shouldn't take us no more than an hour or two," Sam replied addressing him with a fake smile. Marshall saw right through it, the guy looked exhausted and bummed out. He supposed there was no reason to pretend for it was the truth. Marshall nodded and looked about. The house was nearly empty. He searched for words to say.

"No problem, I have all day if you need me."

"No…Not going to be tying your whole day up."

With the tailgate down, Marshall had his truck backed up near the front door that was left wide open. The cold November air was cooling off the house. Sam was slowly stepping backwards, stair by stair, with one end of the large oak chest dresser in his grips.

"You got it?" Sam asked with a grunt. He stepped down anther step.

"Yeah…" Marshall panted. This dresser was heaver than it had looked. His grip was slipping.

"No…I…"

"What Marshall? You don't have it…?"

"I have to…"

"Set it down!" Sam panted, finishing Marshall's statement, holding his end of the heavy dresser.

"No…I. Got it." Marshall replied getting his grip back. Sam was grateful for that; he stepped down once more, it was too long of a step. The heel of his boot was completely off of the carpeted step.

In that spilt second Sam fell backward. A rush of anxiety flooded Marshall's body, he had to hold onto this dresser all by himself, but he couldn't. His hands clutched onto his end of the dresser, as it slid away from him, in that split second.

"Watch out!!!" Marshall screamed.

Sam was on the floor at the bottom of the stairs with the dresser slightly toppled over him.

"Mister Ross!" Marshall screamed scampering down the stairs…Mister Ross!"

Sam gasped. Lifting his arm out from under the dresser, it was taken as a gesture. Marshall reached for his wrist.

"Pull…" He gasped, and then groaned. Marshall did so. Sam's chest was throbbing, his leg paining him something fierce. He was freed from the weight of the dresser, but the weight on his chest remained. He continued to gasp; it was somewhat familiar to him. Marshall was more than concerned, he wasn't all right, and he didn't look as though he was getting air.

"Marsh-…" He gasped harder and deeper.

"I'm going to call the ambulance! Mister Ross hang on…Hang on!" He called out reaching for his cell phone from inside his jacket pocket. He dialed 911.

"Yeah I need an ambulance…my friends been in an accident, he's having difficulty breathing. We're on Pine way…32…3233 Pine way…"

Sam couldn't breath, he needed to breath. "Mar…shall?" He gasped and wheezed. "I…need…"

"Help is on the way…Mister Ross…Hang on…hang on." He huffed looking down on him. Sam attempted to lift himself from the floor.

"Stay down…Please…" Marshall pleaded taking off his jacket for the inside of the house was cool; he draped his jacket over Sam. He was trying to say something and Marshall didn't want to listen to perhaps Sam's dieing words.

"Help is coming!!" He assured listening for sirens in the distance, but he didn't hear any yet.

"Where are they!!?" He cried as his own heart raced.

"My…glove…box…" He wheezed fighting for air.

"Your glove box?" Marshall questioned. Sam slightly nodded as he laid there helpless.

"Ple...please..." he gasped.

Marshall scampered out the open door, and nearly jumped over his tailgate, to Sam's car. He flung open the door and then the glove box not knowing what he was looking for.

"Oh thank God!" He panted grabbing hold of an inhaler from inside the glove box. He's got asthma, he wasn't dieing he has asthma. Marshall rushed back into the house with the inhaler in his hand. Sam was still wheezing still gasping. He dropped to the floor placing the inhaler into Sam's hand.

"Here...Here!" Marshall stated with urgency.

Sam took the inhaler to his mouth with his trembling hand and pumped it into his lungs almost immediately, Sam's heavy gasping ceased. He pumped the inhaler into his lungs once more, until he laid there catching his breath. Marshall too, let out a huge sigh of relief.

"I thought you were dieing...I didn't know you had asthma...You're going to be all right...You are all right aren't you?"

"I don't feel so well...but I'm not dieing." He panted. "I think I have...A couple of broken ribs...And my leg..."

"I'm sorry...I couldn't hold it."

"It was my fault Marshall...I slipped." Sam replied still very much catching his breath, as the sirens wailed in the distance.

"Well...Help is coming...What do you want me to do?"

"Go...Home...I'll, figure something out." Sam panted.

"No...I can get my friend Luke to help out. But I want to make sure your going to be all right first...Can I call someone for you...Your wife...anybody?"

"No need, for that…I'll be all right…Just lock up for me." Sam replied as the paramedics rushed inside through the open door.

Marshall stood by while they talked with him and accessed his injuries through his words and his vital signs. Shortly after, he was placed on a stretcher, with his leg in a brace.

"Which hospital are you taking him to? " Marshall asked, hoping that he wouldn't be told; to the city for it would only mean that his injures were much more serious than Sam believed. Sam too, was waiting for that answer as he lay on the stretcher with an oxygen mask on. He could breath so much better now, he felt comfortable and a bit groggy. They gave him something, but he didn't know what.

"Here…Memorial." One of the paramedics replied, before they wheeled him out of the house and into the ambulance.

People were gathering outside, some were curious while others knew and cared, some rushed up to Marshall who stood outside. One woman was frazzled; she had a frightened little girl in her arms.

"What happened!!? What happened?"

Marshall explained to her while he stood chilled and worried. As the ambulance drove away he took a moment to catch his own breath, disregarding the small crowd he stepped back inside of Sam's house. He was to lock up, keys, keys where would he find them? He had hoped Sam didn't have them in his pants pocket. Pocket, right…He thought to himself, looking about he spotted Sam's brown leather jacket hanging high from what appeared to be a closet door. He reached for the right hand pocket, it had a snap for looks only, he unzipped the pocket, no keys just a slip of paper. He asked himself why he was pulling it out when he was searching for keys only. The small piece of paper had a phone number on it, with the name: Mia, above it.

Mia was his wife's name, wasn't it? He questioned himself, he thought so. Again, he questioned himself, Sam didn't want him to call his wife, and he should respect that. Sam could change his mind, and what if his condition wasn't so good after all? Marshall tucked Mia's phone number into the pocket of his blue jeans. He reached for the other pocket and was grateful to feel a set of keys inside. He pulled them out into his hand, and jogged over to the door with them.

Which one could it be? The key needed to be used to lock the door. He stood outside trying one at a time from the handful to choose from. One finally worked, he turned the door knob to be reassured that it was indeed locked.

"Marsh...?" Becky eagerly called out racing up to the porch beside him. He shouldn't have been surprised to see her there for she only lived a half a block away. "Mister Ross...What happened to him! My brother said he..."

"He's all right...Some broken bones...He fell down the stairs...We were hauling a dresser down and it kind of got away from us..." Becky's eyes widened. "What, He's moving?"

"Yeah...we didn't get very far...I got to go Beck...I'll talk to you later." He replied walking away from her, he then lifted his tailgate back up, and it slammed it shut.

"Let me know...Please Marsh!" She cried. Marshall nodded.

"I will."

Marshall got behind the wheel of his truck and reached into his own jacket pocket, now two sets were inside, He pulled out the wrong set, Mister Ross's set, The key chain was odd, somewhat interesting, It looked hand made, puzzled, he sat there observing it. Oval shaped and incased inside and under what appeared to be some kind of plexi-glass was a small yellow seed. He found it very odd. He turned it over, looking at the back where there was an inscription in small print, it read: Have faith as small as this mustard seed and nothing will be impossible onto you.

He understood it; it came from a verse in the bible somewhere. Wow, he didn't know that his teacher was a religious man; course teachers aren't supposed to disclose their beliefs to their students. As a young boy his mother had him enrolled in Sunday school. Some Sundays Marshall went, and others, he got away with bowing out. It wasn't long before he quit entirely, mom didn't seem to care much; it was when she and Marshall's father were in the process of their divorce. So much for his teacher's faith, it didn't save his marriage.

Marshall pulled away from the driveway with Becky standing in place solemnly waving him off. She wasn't so bad, perhaps time would heal the issues that she had for herself and others, just the same; he didn't want to date her.


Gwen was inside her sewing room, she had little time left to finish these brides' maids' dresses and the hem on this dress was to uneven for her standards. She began to carefully rip it out. She liked how the white sash accented the beautiful teal color. The phone rang, she choose not to ignore it and reached across her sewing machine.

"Hello…Marshall, what's wrong?" She asked for she knew when her son was upset.

"Oh dear god…Well I certainly hope so…Are you all right…Were you hurt?' she asked in concern.

"I'm ok mom, I was wondering if I should call his wife."

"Their divorced aren't they?" Gwen asked as she ran her fingers through her hair.

"Well yeah, recently…I have her number." Marshall replied stopping at a red light, at the last second, a loud truck roared by him.

"Are you driving?"

"Yeah, I'm sorry mom, I just had to talk to someone, but I'll let you go."

"Call me back when you're at the hospital, and let sleeping dogs lie Marshall, don't call his wife leave that up to his family, or himself when he is able to call her he will, if he wants to."

He supposed she was right; he took that thought with him into the hospital, deciding to wait to call his mother back after, for what more could he say to her. He walked up to the front desk inside the emergency room, and then was instructed to wait in the surgical waiting room. The nurse probably thought that he was his son, He guessed that Sam was much too young to have a son as old as he was, pushing eighteen an all. No, this wasn't right, something was wrong with this picture.


Holding a small paneling nail in place, Mia pounded the nail into the white based wall, still wearing what she had wore to bed last night, her blue flannel pajamas Her living room needed some cheering up as much as she did, to put this picture of her mother and father on the wall may give her that sense of home that she longed for. She placed the eight by ten onto her wall. Her mother was African American, and her father was as white as could be. They are a happily married couple and always have been, if only they didn't live so far away. They both were disappointed to hear about the divorce, yet they understood her reasoning for she wanted a child more than anything.

Mia shook her head, no this didn't make her feel better at all, this apartment, this busy city is not what she had intended for her life at all. She would have to try harder, soon she would have to venture out, and could she find a good man at a new church? Perhaps she can, tomorrow she will go to church and attempt to start a new life, she told herself as she grabbed a telephone book and then sat down on her loveseat in her small living room, and she opened the thick book to the yellow pages and looked under churches. Sam had preached very little to her about God and his beliefs, perhaps just the ten percent that he believed should be given. He say's that if everyone was to give their ten percent the world would be a better place.

She had a few churches in mind already, some were circled. She pondered another when her phone that sat on her small coffee table rang. Mia reached for it quickly looking at the caller ID screen. Her heart skipped a beat when she read: Hudser Memorial.

"Hello?" she eagerly questioned.

"Yes is this…Mia?" Marshall asked nervously.

"Yes! What's wrong? Is he okay?" She questioned assuming that Sam, more than likely had an asthma attack. He hasn't had a major attack in so long that she knew of, but the stress of the divorce, and with Conner's health, one was about to flare up.

"My name is Marshall Perry, Sam had a fall down the stairs…He's got a broken leg and I guess a couple of broken ribs, he is in surgery right now." Mia had her hand to her chest; her eyes closed briefly

"I just thought you ought to know ma'am"

"Oh, no…thank you so much for calling…Thank you Marshall."

"I'm here by myself, and I didn't know who to call, so could you relay this message to his family?"

Mia nodded." I will…I'm on my way…He's there at memorial in Hudser?"

"Yes ma'am…"

"Thank you again Marshall." Mia replied closing the line, she dropped the phone down onto the loveseat next to the opened phone book and then jogged into her bedroom to quickly change her clothes.


His family, Sam had no immediate family besides herself, and that was about to soon change. The thought of it made her tear up as she began the thirty minute drive to Hudser. What was she doing to him? Didn't she know that he was a fragile person, and not the strong man he tried to portray? She has forgotten why he had his fears of becoming a father, maybe Sam was right, maybe god didn't intend on him to become a father. She felt so selfish right now.


Marshall stood in the hallway dropping his coins into the pop machine and selected a coke, it dropped down. He picked it up and decided to wait a moment to open it. He lifted his eyes to the approaching slightly familial faced woman with the beautiful light brown complexion. He remembered her as polite person who didn't mind meeting and greeting her husband's students last spring at the

71

annual drama play. Was it all a put-on? Did she have divorce in her vocabulary at that time? He questioned, she had seemed nice enough on the phone, but most of all she was here.

"Marshall?" She cried out, seemingly knowing that it was him. "Is he still in surgery?"

"I guess so…I haven't heard anything other."

"What did you say, he fell down the stairs?"

They both walked back into the waiting room while he filled her in to what had happened. Mia had listened as she dabbed her tears with a tissue.

David poured some whiskey into his empty glass; he didn't expect Conner home from the evening movie for at least another hour yet. It was his mother's idea, and a good one. He enjoyed movies and popcorn, and he was enjoying this drink right now too. Conner may be tried from his long day and with any luck, he won't notice that he has been drinking. He wouldn't have to give his son a hug goodnight latter on, he has been reminding him of his age and twelve year olds don't give goodnight hugs. David sat down in front of the television. A science fiction movie was playing, he sipped his whiskey.

Mia was sitting at Sam's bedside quietly waiting for him to wake. She was informed that when he did, he would be groggy. An oxygen tube was making his breathing much easier. His leg was in a cast and his chest, tightly wrapped. She wanted him to know that she was here. As subtly as she could she placed her hand over his, not necessarily wanting him to wake because of her gesture, she just needed to do so.

Sam slowly opened his eyes feeling the numbing pain in his body. He turned his head to see Mia sitting beside her she had tears in her eyes, why was he dieing?

"How are you feeling Sam?"

"I told him not to call you," he muttered in disappointment.

"I thanked him for it…I care Sam."

"I took a clumsy spill…No need to fret about it." He replied lifting his head to notice his leg in a cast. His chest ached. He dropped his head back down in defeat.

"You broke it in two different places and you have two cracked ribs. It's what probably brought on your asthma attack."

"Ohhh…He told you about that too…" Sam sighed, and then finally felt her hand over his; she then brought it back to her lap.

"You had him real scared for a while."

"Mia…this is not how divorces are supposed to work…You shouldn't have come…and you shouldn't be making me meals…I can take care of myself…even when I get out of here…"

Tears flooded Mia's eyes, she thought he was supposed to be groggy, somehow she wished it were so right now, her reasoning for being here would have been more justified if that were so.

"You can't expect me to stop caring at the drop of a hat."

"The hat has been dropped months ago Mia."

"I'm not to stay long anyway…You get some rest." She cried raising herself off her chair without another word she left the room, leaving Sam with a cringe of pain that was inside and out.

Marshall sat on the edge of the couch with his hands folded over his knees. His mother sat across from him in her favorite padded chair. She had left her work in her sewing room where it belonged here and now.

"Yeah I called Luke, and I guess he is going to help out tomorrow, he says he's going to ask Donny too…So I'm going to have to see or call Sam tomorrow to get his apartment address that we never got to…I would have gone to see him after his surgery but they said he would have been kind of out of it. Mia went in to see him…then again who knows, maybe he will be released tomorrow…I don't know who's going to bring him home when he does"

"He's got to have someone…Some family or close friends around here besides his ex wife."

"Well there is that friend that lives in St Paul."

"Right…The one with the sick child."

"I don't know Mom…Mia kind of implied that she was his only family just by not saying anything…Then again, maybe Sam just isn't from around here"

"Sam, now is it…Marshall?" His mother finally smiled though this sad story.

"Well…It's easier to say sometimes…"

"Could it be you're becoming friends?"

"I don't know Mom…I don't think he is too happy with me right now…I dropped a dresser on him…and I called Mia after he told me not to."

"He will get over it hon…Just be careful tomorrow okay."

Conner retuned home with a chill, he kicked off his boots and kept his knitted hat and jacket on. His father was brave enough to leave his empty glass on the top of his TV tray.

"How was the movie?" He asked Conner, watching him plop himself onto the couch. Conner was keen enough to hear the hidden slur in his words.

"It was all right."

"Yeah, what one did you go see?"

"I already told you…The pole sitters…And you have been drinking…" He replied taking the blanket close to him and wrapping himself up in it."

"So I had a drink…Don't you talk down on me…How are you feeling…Conner?"

"I'm just cold." He complained clinging onto the blanket. David got out of his chair and walked over to him touching his son's forehead with the palm of his hand.

"You don't feel warm."

"That's because I'm cold."

"Well it's cold and damp outside…Maybe you should just take your pills and go to bed."

"Why? So you can drink yourself to sleep." Conner remarked with sarcasm. His dad backed off not happy with his words.

"No…So you can get your rest so you don't get sick." He replied as the phone rang.

He shook his head at Conner, and then went to answer the phone.

"Hello…"

Conner laid there listening to his dad talk on the phone.

"You're kidding…" He scratched his forehead with a heavy sigh.

"I know you don't care to step foot in that town, but he really needs your help Bear. He's got one of his students helping out, and possibly another, but if we had your truck there, and you...it would help so much."

"We...Mia?"

"You...Them, whoever...I would just be in the way, all he has left is the heavy things...So, will you be there Bear?"

"Of course I will...What time?"

"Oh I don't know it won't do you any good without the keys. I have his student's phone number."

Conner was now very curious about the phone call. His dad was talking to Mia of all people. Something was wrong. He was now writing down someone's phone number.

"All right I'll give him a call...He's fine...just got back from seeing a movie, he's a little tuckered out, but feisty enough...All right Mia...Thanks for the call...Bye." David set the phone down with Conner staring at him.

"What happened? Something happened..."

David nodded then sighed. "Sam had a fall down the stairs...He broke his leg and a couple of ribs...But he's okay. I'm going to go into Hudser tomorrow to help one of his students move him out of the house and into his new apartment."

"Can I come?"

"I think I should just drop you off at your mothers."

"I want to see Sam...I want to help!" Conner protested."

"I don't think you are felling very well pal."

"Please...I want to go...I want to see Sam."

"Sam is in the hospital Conner. He's all right, but I don't know if he will be up for a lot of company and I can't stay long, we have work to do."

"Then leave me with Sam, at the hospital…Please Dad?"

"We will have to see how you are feeling."

Conner pleaded his case long enough; he did what his father had asked of him by taking his pills and getting himself into a warm bed. It would be different visiting someone else in the hospital for a change; Sam had always come to see him when he was laid up, whether he was in the hospital feeling ill or at home. He felt he needed to pay back some of the kindness.

David poured some whiskey into his glass and quickly drank it down. He picked up the electric bill envelope with Marshall Perry's phone number scribbled onto the back, then sat back in his chair with the phone in his hand. It appeared to be a cell phone number, he dialed it.

"Hello?"

"Marshall Perry, Please?"

"This is."

"Hi, I'm a friend of Sam Ross; I believe he is your teacher."

"Yes…"

"Well, ah…my name is Bear, and I'd like to help you out tomorrow."

"Great…" Marshall replied wondering what kind of character he was talking to, the guy sounded drunk. Was this the friend with the sick kid?

"What time are we meeting?"

"What ever time is good for you. Are you coming from St Paul?"

"Yeah…I might be stopping by to see Sam first, my son wants to see him, and if it's okay with Sam, I can leave him there for a couple of hours or however long it will take.

"It shouldn't take us long at all; I got a couple of friends helping out."

"Good deal…does eleven sound all right with you?"

"Yeah, that works for me."

"All right see you…ah, at the house."

"Okay…Goodbye."

"Goodbye."

Marshall raised his eyebrows shaking his head. He wondered what these two guys could possible have in common.

# *The Moving Day*

David was so not looking forward to this. His head ached and it was easy for him to make his own excuses for the reasons why. Frustration and anger, why doesn't anything ever go his way, why doesn't he ever get a break? Of all the places Sam had to land a teaching job in Hudser. It was so much easier when he was here in St Paul. David fumbled for the aspirin on the top shelf and vigorously opened the bottle, he spilled three of them in his hand and popped them into his mouth, and dry swallowed them. He began to start the coffee.

"How's Sam doing Dad?" Conner asked still wearing his sweatshirt and sweatpants that he wore to bed last night.

"I don't know I didn't call him yet, I wanted to see how you were feeling first."

"I feel okay...I want to go with you...and maybe I can stay with Sam...I can just sit there and watch TV if he doesn't feel like talking."

"You know Sam always feels like talking, I'm sure he wouldn't mind, otherwise you can tag along with me. Just stay out of our way, now go on and get dressed."

Conner walked back into his room, he would get his chance today, his chance to talk to Sam alone, it wouldn't matter if he was laying there all broken he would listen, he would promise him that he would take care of his dad when he dies. Conner just knew it. He trusted him and believed Sam always when he talked about heaven and angels, and with his dad not there, Sam will probably tell him another story about heaven, why can't his dad see that these stories make him happy, he didn't really want to die but when he does, his dad should be comforted in knowing that he went to such a beautiful place.

Sam was now in a lounging position, yet feeling so contained to this bed already. He no longer need the extra support from the oxygen that he so welcomed yesterday. His breakfast tray was in front of him with the round tin cover placed over it. He questioned himself if he was too hard on Mia last night; he was finding it difficult accepting her visits as friendly jesters. He supposed these visits would slow to a stop one day and then it wouldn't be long after he could send a nice card congratulating her and her new husband on a long and healthy marriage together.

Marshall walked into the open door of Sam's room, interrupting his thoughts. Marshall smiled nervously.

"Hi…how are you feeling Mister Ross?"

"Fine…Thank you." Sam replied with a serious face, not even attempting to crack a smile sending a hint of hostility Marshall's way.

"Mister Ross…I'm sorry…I had to call someone, and I found Mia's number in the pocket of your jacket."

"Oh, no worries…I understand…say do you have it with you?"

"Yes I do." He said then pulled it out of his pocket and handed it to him. "And I'm sorry it took me so long to get the hint yesterday."

"Marshall you can stop apologizing any time now, you had no way of knowing."

"Yeah…well I'm going to make it up to you today; me and a couple of my friends are going to help your friend get you moved in."

"What?" he asked puzzled.

"Ahh…Bear he called himself, your friend from St Paul."

"Oh…okay…Mia must have called him." This didn't set well with him either, did she ask him? Did she beg him, or did he just take it upon himself to set foot in this town because he felt he had to on his own.

Mia had dressed herself conservatively, wearing a white sweater with her long black skirt for she didn't want to send the wrong message at her new church, if she was going to agree with the pastor and if she felt the welcoming that she was looking for.

She sat in the pew, while the choir sang in unison, the familiar hymns and some she had grown up with, most of the congregation was singing along as they were encouraged to do. She looked about at the happy satisfied with their life people, most; were couples young and old. She tried to sing but didn't feel any strength behind her lungs; Sam wasn't beside her because she abandoned him. She suddenly didn't feel worthy of this church or any other for that matter, it may pass, she told herself, it may pass. Sit through the message and it may pass.

Marshall held Sam keys in his hand, he let himself in, and again curiously studied Sam's key chain, the incased mustard seed that symbolized his faith, faith in miracles he supposed; and look where it has gotten him, he thought to himself.

Inside it was chilly, and after walking over to the thermostat on the wall, he understood why. Sure, why heat this big house if you are not living in it any way? He left his jacket on and accessed the damage to the dresser at the bottom of the stairway, he wasn't sure if he found any except a few scratches on it and how could he be sure if they were there in the first place. The wall had a dent from where the dresser hit making him wonder if this could have been a miracle in itself, how can one be sure, where does one draw the line? Did Sam think it was, and would he ever confess to it? He seemed to be a very private person that he himself was just beginning to understand.

As he lifted, and managed to get the dresser upright he saw someone walking outside through the back window, Marshall walked though the living room and to the back door. He pushed the sheer curtain aside, and peered out. Someone was walking though the lawn with a leaf rake in their hand. It was taken from the porch. Quickly he opened the back door, getting the thief's attention.

"Hey!!" Marshall bellowed.

The guy turned around with rake in hand revealing his identity to him. It was Todd Martin. He flung out his arms with his long black leather coat wide open disclosing how tough he was in this cold November air. "What?" He shouted, walking back up to Marshall

"What are you doing?"

"What does it look like I'm doing…You dork! I'm going to rake his lawn."

What on earth for, he questioned letting himself out, he stepped up to Todd. Todd met him in the center of the lawn that was covered in leaves.

"Did Mister Ross ask you to do this?"

"No…I thought I needed the exercise!! What do you think…You duffiss?" Todd shouted back.

Not offended by Todd's words Marshall was beginning to understand.

"Oh…all right, well thanks…"

"I don't need your thanks…He paid me to do this…go ahead, ask him?"

"No…I believe you…So just do it"

"I think it's a waste of time and money if you ask me…because they just rot any way, and come spring their gone."

Marshall knew where he was coming from, he never raked his own lawn, his mother never requested it; they just rot away anyhow, she would say. No need for that Marshall.


Sam was asleep, the TV tuned on to the Sunday morning politics program when David and Conner walked in.

"Can I wake him up?" Conner whispered to his father.

"Go ahead." David replied with a shrug for he couldn't wait around to long, he was expected to be somewhere, and he just wanted to get it over with so he could get out of this town. David leaned against the wall and folded his arms over his waistline.

Conner knew that Sam had broken bones so he touched his forearm and nudged it ever so gently.

"Sam." He called out with a raised smile, Conner felt special he was the surprise, always in Sam's eyes. And Sam opened his eyes raising his smile.

"Conner…Hi…" He replied waking himself to his fullest to gaze across the room where Bear stood. "You guy's didn't need to come,"

"We wanted to…I'm sorry you fell…"

"Oh…Conner, it was just a clumsy mistake…You got to be careful when you're going down the stairs backwards with a dresser in front of you."

Conner chuckled, "You broke your leg?"

"Yeah I'm afraid I did."

"Are they going to spring you today?" David interrupted, at the same time he wondered if he were supposed to haul him home when it was time.

"I don't believe so…The doc was here a bit ago and said they were going to set me up with some crutches today…and take some tests."

"Well, Dad's going to help you move, can I stay here for a while? Until he gets back…if you want to go back to sleep, or if you go down for tests. I can just watch T V for a while."

"Or—I can take him with me."

"No, no he can stay here with me Bear…I appreciate this, big time…yeah…We can shoot the breeze, I'm bored out of my head anyway."

"So where is this new apartment of yours?" David asked unfolding his arms bumping himself off the wall, until he stood straight up.

"I've given the address to Marshall…He should be at my…the house right now…It's just down the street a few blocks."

"All right, I'll get a move on then, are you sure you're up to this kid's company?"

Conner wanted to take it as a joke, but he wasn't so sure he should under these circumstances.

"Oh no worries…I think he will be all right with my company. And thanks again I owe you one." Sam replied with a smile.

"Sam…" Conner chuckled, waving at his dad before he left the room. He turned his attention back to Sam, whose smile was wearing down for he felt discomfort inside and out. He was hoping Conner wasn't going to ask for a story, he didn't feel much up to it at all.

"Are you hurting Sam?"

"No, not much, I'm on some medications that numb me for a while…So how's school going for you?"

"Well…" he replied then bowed his head slightly. "It's kind-a-not going…I went on Monday, but didn't…I just…"

"You just what Conner…Come on lift your head and look at me."

"I…just…" He said lifting his head with tears welling in his eyes. "It was different."

"Why is that? Tell me about different."

"You know…Not the same."

"Not the same as last year?…Conner you're not the same as last year…You have grown up, and you're friends are the same…Some kids grow up fast, like you, and other's got a lot more learning to do."

"What do you mean?"

"I mean you are a smart kid." Sam replied, stifling himself, where was he going with this, he couldn't say.

"I'm not that smart…not like I'm supposed to be…and I don't see no point in it…Sam I haven't been there since Monday, and I'm not going back…the kids are mean and I'm dumb!" He cried out loud, and then took it upon himself to lay his head on Sam's shoulder where he cried harder. Sam patted his back. Could life get any worse than it is right now? This was far beyond; raining and pouring, it seemed more like a doomsday to him.

"Shhh…its all right buddy I'm here for you." Sam cried, not wanting to prepare him for heaven at all yet, there was still hope. There was still hope. Conner lifted his head, with despair written all over his face.

"Sam…if I die my Dad won't make it with out you…He'll drink and drink and he'll probably lose the garage…You won't leave him will you…?"

"Oh…Conner no…and you won't either…you wont!" He cried, with his tearful eyes closing tight, the heartache was so much to take in, as if his chest were to explode. Let it happen now, no…not now, he couldn't leave Conner now…not like this…Oh God help…he silently asked.

"That's what Dad says, but what if I do?"

"I promise you…We're going to be okay."

"You promise?" Conner asked starring him down, Sam closed his lips tightly, but they quivered anyway.

"I promise." Sam replied; for it was all he had to say, he had no more words, immediately he regretted giving broken promises, but what was he to do, stomp on hopes that could yet be? Conner laid himself back on Sam's shoulder; Sam searched his mind for comforting words as he cringed in pain.

"Conner It's a new school…You got a late start, I think you should consider giving it another shot."

Again, Conner raised his head; he wiped his tears with the back of his hand.

"Dad say's its up to me, I can stay home…my tutor still comes."

"It is up to you, But don't make these decisions based on fear…or you might be asking yourself…what if…what if it wasn't as bad as it seemed at the time…what if the next day worked out better for you.?"

"Well…I do want to have friends again." He said with that sigh that comes after a hard cry…that accepting problem solving sigh.

"I guess I can go back, but Dad will think that I can't make up my mind."

"Your dad and mom want to see you happy." Sam replied, at the same time wondering where Mia was this morning, she hadn't answered the phone, was she there but decided not to pick up? Was she finally letting go?


I owe you one, thought David. Sam has said many of times before; sure they both had exchanged favors regularly as friends tend to do. David was Sam's mechanic and trouble shooter, and Sam was always there with a helping hand when ever it was needed, he could not argue that he has always been there for Conner as well, even after he moved out of the city to this dreadful town.

It was the big favor that gnawed at David's consciences, the one that Sam had referred to as a Godly deed and it wouldn't go unpunished, and here's Sam, telling him that God owes him one. David didn't believe that at all, the big one was payment; he had made his amends, and apparently, the big favor wasn't enough, Conner illness was the proof.


He was only at this house once before, the day Sam and Mia moved in Five years ago, it was a hot summer sunny day, and he was as nervous as could be, and right now his nerves were on edge. This town never felt like home, nothing but terrible memories here, and he could not escape them, not today anyway.

He tapped on the door and let himself in. a couple of high school boys were inside leaving David to wonder why he even had to be here, just the same he questioned if they were trustworthy enough.

"Hi..." Marshall replied with a smile. "You must be Bear." He added stepping up to him with his hand extended.

"Yeah...Pleased to meet you." He nodded, taking his hand briefly.

"Well...these are my friends, Luke and Donny."

"Hi..." they said in unison.

"Let's get this show on the road..." David said eagerly.


Marshall took it upon himself to pair up with the man he knew as Bear, although, there was work to be done, he didn't find; Bear very friendly, and in the back of his mind he wondered how two completely different people could be friends, then again Todd Martin was out back raking the leaves. there was so much he didn't know and completely understand about his teacher. The two of them had loaded the couch into the back of Bears truck where Marshall had read the painted advertisement. Bears Auto Repair...

Once the couch was settled inside, Marshall felt the need to break the ice.

"You're a mechanic hah?"

"Yep..."

Marshall shrugged it off; they went back inside for the table.

Conner sat inside Sam's hospital room by himself, he flipped the channels, nothing was on that interested him. The bedside phone rang. Should he or shouldn't he, he asked himself then picked it up.

"Hello?'

"Oh…I'm sorry I must have the wrong room number."

"Are you looking for Sam Ross?"

"Yes…I am."

"Yeah…he's having some tests done right now, this is his friend Conner"

"Oh…" The voice on the other side of the line remarked curiously. "Well, this is his uncle Larry…How's he doing?"

"He's okay."

"Could you tell him I called, and that I will call back later?"

"Sure…" Conner replied.


With a bag full of groceries in her arms, Mia shook off the chill and kicked off her shoes at the door. She was not sure if she was going to go back to that church or find another, she had time to decide yet. She set the bag down onto the counter; the small red flashing light was blinking on her answering machine next to her phone. She pushed the button to hear the message.

"Hi Mia…It's me, Sam…I…was a little testy last night…I'm sorry…Take care…bye."

"I'm sorry too…" Mia cried out loud. She never thought this divorce was going to be this hard on her, she had been so angry with him for dismissing her need to adopt a baby, though he gave his reasons, she didn't stop to rethink deeply as to why.

# *The Find...*

The apartment was one of four inside the large brick building, they were all happy in the fact that Sam's was one on the main level.

"Hey Marsh...you want to go over to Ted's with us...He's got this super cool new game on play station, called Road Rage."

"Take a jaunt in the city..." David scoffed, as he placed the last kitchen chair down beside the table. "I got-ta run...It was nice meeting you all, and thanks for your help."

"You too, Bear." Marshall replied.

"Yeah nice meetin-ya." Luke added, and then waited for David to walk out. "He seemed aright, a little strange, and speaking of strange...what's with Todd Martin raking the leaves, at Ross's?"

"Well he sold the house I guess he just wanted the yard cleaned up."

"So he hired Todd Martin...How much is he paying him?"

"I don't know...you know Ross. He's a softy...Guys, it's no big deal."

"Yeah, but he could have hired me...and here we are working for nothing."

"You're done...leave!"

"Hey what's with you? We're done...let's go."

"Yeah...come-on." Donny added.

"No…I'm going to hang out here for a while and see what needs to be put together…His bed is in pieces…He can't be messing with it when he gets out of the hospital."

"Teachers pet…You think it's going to get you that A?"

"Cut it out Luke…He's all busted up."

"Then why didn't his friend do it?"

"He's got a sick kid…Just go."

"A likely story…His kid has got the flu." Donny snickered.

"It's not the flu…I think it's terminal…or something I don't know…!"

"Don't need to have a bird Marsh…What…he tell you?"

"Yeah…Something like that…"


Feeling tired himself, Conner sat there while Sam was wheeled back into the room, and Sam grimaced in pain as he spoke,

"Oh…the packer game…What's the score there pal?"

"Packer's are ahead…21 to 14…"

"Sorry about that…but I can't say that I don't mind a bit." Sam replied with a smile as the nurse turned to Conner.

"Do we have a Viking fan here?" She boasted, taking notice that this boy was bald under his cap, yet she tried to keep her smile for she was no stranger to such a sickness as cancer, and at the same time so grateful she didn't have to see young cancer patients every day.

"Yeah…I'm a Viking fan, cause I live there, so close to the metro dome…but the Packers can win today because they are playing Atlanta."

"You got-ta love him!" She giggled before she left the room.

"Sam…Your Uncle called…Larry…He told me he would call you back."

"Oh…okay." Mia must have called him. He thought to himself.

"Sam…Where's your Mom and Dad? Did they…"

Sam sighed, not wanting to explain. "My mother is gone…Didn't really know my father much…"

"Sorry…what about…do you have any brothers or sisters?"

"No…I, don't."

"I wish I had a brother or a sister…Then you know…"

Sam sighed again, he knew. "So…When do your Vikings play?"


Marshall found a tool box stuffed inside the broom closet near the back door. He had it on the floor, next to his feet as he lay screwing the bolt into the bed frame, there was no way Sam could do this in his condition, and he hoped that his teacher wouldn't favor him more as a student for this kindly gesture, he wanted honest grades, and he assumed that's what he would get. He did find it odd; that he was here in-the-now, doing this, yet so glad he could be of help. Things weren't going to be the same at all in his class. Who would take over while he was laid up for who knows how long? His mind pondered these questions while he finished putting the bed frame together.

He wrestled the Queen sized mattress and dropped it onto the box frame. There, it was done, would he go as far as to make his bed? He thought not, it was just a guy thing; maybe he would, but not now. If he were to take him home from the hospital, or stop by to lend a hand whenever that may be, he could always offer to do so.

He supposed he did enough yet found himself searching for

something else to do. Walking though the short hallway, he stopped at a second bedroom that looked as though it were possibly his teachers office space, yes there was work in here that could be done.

The computer sat on desk the top with all the wire cables and connections rolled in a ball. He should give him a call to ask if he could set it up for him, he has learned enough from his teacher to know what the answer would be, and he knew he wouldn't get scolded for it either.

One more stop; pick up Conner and get...out of Dodge. David thought to himself before he entered the room.

"Packers won." Conner replied looking up at his dad.

"Oh...You all set?" He muttered and then added. "So when are they springing you...Have you heard?"

"Hopefully tomorrow...No worries, I'll get home."

"Yeah you got that, student of yours."

"Perry...Marshall, yeah I can ask him, or maybe I'll give Mia a call."

"You're not serious...Sam you got to break away."

"I will...we are still friends."

"Well...I don't get it, but, whatever, you know I would, but Mondays are busy at the garage."

"And dad...I...Want to start back at school again...I got to try one more time."

"You put him up to this?"

"Dad...you said it was up to me."

David sighed. "If that's what you want." He replied shaking his head at Sam.

"It's what I want."

Marshall did not turn the computer on, but he believed he had it set up correctly, just the same. He has done enough, no need to over-do it; well, he could hook up the printer that sat on top of a box on the floor. He lifted it from off the pile of what appeared to be, books? Not just a book that caught his eye, but a spiral hard cover note book that sat on top of the box. He set the printer onto the desk and then turned his attention back to the box on the floor. It looked like one of his yearly grade keeping logs, or something very much like it. It was plain and brown, just like the rest. He wondered if he was his best student, he had to be close, was this one from last year? There was only one way to find out.

Marshall observed the silence around him, it would never tell. He sat on the carpeted floor beside the box and picked up the notebook, taking it onto his lap, the opened it. Much to his surprise, it wasn't what he thought it might be, not a grade keeping log at all. Far from it, instead he looked down at the typed out page that read one single word in the center...SANITY...

Sanity, he questioned in puzzlement, he turned the next page. This page was dressed in one paragraph. He read:

: If there is one thing I learned in my young life, it is that everything is temporary. Taking my entire childhood to finally realize it was the hard part. I suppose I was one of many children who hadn't stopped to look at the big picture, although I was told to, in many different ways. I was like many...stuck in the moment, my moments...My cup runith over...This is my story...and my search for sanity...SAM ROSS...

Marshall shook his head, with his jaw dropped. "No way…" He whispered to himself, he so wanted to turn the next page, and told himself not to. He closed the book and set it back onto the box and then looked at his watch, it was a quarter-to-four. He should go, he should, it wouldn't be right hanging out and reading a personal document such as this, not right at all.

His teacher had wrote out his auto biography, for whom to read? If that's what this was, it surely appeared to be so, down right absolutely. Books are written to be read, he's said so himself. One has to give themselves away in their words, and in their characters, he's said so. Marshall sighed sitting there with his uncertainties. He picked it back up into his lap and swished though the pages. The note book was filled with the typed out words of, his life story, one that he wanted to read.

He took the victory and the note book into his hands. He can take it home, and read it there, he will bring it back and no one will ever have to know…no one.

If the cats away why can't the mice play? There is no harm in that, after all, curiosity killed the cat…

Conner reached for the stereo volume control, and turned it down stifling the classic rock station, and Tom Petty's song, living like a refugee; they were leaving the outskirts of the town his father hated so much. He knew why, for his mother had told him what his dad had done, so many years ago, and it was no secret that he knew, yet there was so many questions he still had.

"Dad…what happened to Sam's parents…His mother?"

"She died long time ago."

"She wasn't…you know…"

"No of course not…"

"How did you and Sam meet?"

"Hey, what do you say we pick up a pizza for tonight, to celibate you going back to school tomorrow…Sound like a plan?"

"Sounds like a plan." Conner replied then turned the song back up. Tom Petty sang, you don't have to live like a refugee.


It took Mia a couple of hours before she had gotten up the nerve to phone Sam, and now with the phone to her ear, she wasn't about to hang up and back out now.

"Hello?"

"Sam…Hi it's me I got your message a while ago, how are you doing?"

"I'm doing…With any luck I will be sprung from this joint tomorrow."

"I suppose you won't know until tomorrow."

"No, I don't believe I will."

"They are not going to let you walk out of there on your own…Would you like me to pick you up? I could take the day off, I'm sure your apartment is in shambles."

"I can't ask you to do that Mia."

"Okay…how about if you don't ask, and I insist, would that arrangement suit you?"

"I suppose we can make an exception…I appreciate this Mia…"

"It would be my pleasure, regardless; I will take the day off, to get your apartment in order…I will see you tomorrow Sam."

"Thank you Mia…" His voice cracked some before he hung up the phone.

Marshall pulled into the short drive way, his mothers van was gone, oh right, she had a day planed with Gram. This was working out just fine for the moment, he wouldn't have to tuck Sam's book under his jacket. He carried it freely inside the house, it's been a long day, he needed to relax, unwind, and perhaps he could read this story. He walked into his bedroom and shut the door with book in hand he flopped himself down onto his bed and opened it; he passed up the very first page that he had already read.

I am alive today for a few different reasons, but I won't get ahead of myself just yet. My father picked me over my baby sister; I may never know the real answer behind his choice. Did he favor me because I was his son, or was I just the closest to his reach? I stopped asking myself these questions years ago. I can't change the past, I can't justify it either.

I don't remember going to bed that particular night, if I knew what the morning would have brought I would have kissed little Angie good night, she's in heaven now and I'm sure she found balance in her walk, and spring in her step, yes she can fly now.

It was a freighting experience at the tender age of five, waking in the hospital and not knowing how you had gotten there in the first place; an oxygen mask covered my entire face. Thank God my mother was there next to me, but that small comfort only lasted for a brief moment, for she was stricken with grief and sorrow.

"Angie's dead!!" She cried out loud to me.

I remember the funeral; I had just made it from out of the hospital that very day. I sat in a wheelchair hooked up to an oxygen tank, it was a warm sunny day and I felt to warm, just thinking of my little sister in that little box, my mother was crying so hard that everybody was around her. A woman took my hand in hers, and she knelt down beside me.

"Hi Sam…How are you feeling?" she asked.

I said nothing, for what kind of question was that. There were others, relatives, and friends of my parents that I paid no mind to, I'm sure they understood that I just didn't want to talk.


I had also forgotten what the average day in the life was at home, the home we no longer had, I wasn't the same, my lungs were sickened from smoke inhalation, my chest was tender, I wheezed quite often. It would have helped a great deal if someone were to comfort me, but my father was just to ashamed of himself for not running back into the burning house to fetch little Angie, and I know now if he had he wouldn't have survived for the house blew, so I gathered from one of many of Mom and Dad's arguments.

I'd lay there in bed at night in our new home listing to their threats and accusations of who was to blame for the fire, it was someone's lit cigarette, and my mother testified over and over that my father was to blame. My father would plow out of the house making extra sure that the door slammed so hard that it would shutter the front windows.

Like many nights to follow my mother would take three or four tranquilizers and then go into her bedroom to cry out loud.

"My Baby…My Baby." My tears followed, for I didn't know what else to do. I wondered if Dad was disappointed in his decision to pull me out, instead of baby Angie, I can't say that I was glad to be alive, but I would just have to deal with it. Maybe find a way to make her happy, so she could be a mother to me again. There was always my very first day of school that was promised to start in a few short months.


If this tragedy hadn't occurred, I may have been outgoing, happy and well liked. But it did, it molded me into a quiet, shy, secluded, asthma ridden boy with an inhaler in my pocket for comfort. I'd let my class mates do there own thing without any regrets what-so-ever, I'd look away when I witnessed two or more sharing secrets, candy, and lunches.

One day, I no longer needed the map I used to find my way home from school, from my city of Springfield Illinois. I walked alone, because I did not favor nor did I seek anyone's company. I thought I was doing well for myself, throwing my wrinkled old map into the garbage can after I entered my house.

"Sammy…Come in here." My mother cried from the kitchen.

"What?' I asked wondering what I had done wrong, for she looked stern and angry.

"Your teacher called me today…She says that you are not getting along with the other kids…Don't do this to me…I have enough to worry about with your dad leaving me and running around with other women!"

"Dad is leaving?"

"Yes...He's leaving...and good riddance to him...Now stop fighting with the other kids! I mean it! I will tan your hide if I have to go to that school to talk to your teacher!"

"I'm not fighting...Why is Dad leaving?"

"Are you trying to call your teacher a liar? And quit your shouting...You talk too loud...it ether means that you are hard of hearing or you're mentally retarded!"

"Why is Dad leaving?" I shouted as my chest started to tighten, and my breathing became shallow, I wheezed taking my inhaler from out of my pocket, and pumped it into my lungs.

"Oh...Stop that! Just be glad that you can breathe at all...your baby sister can't...!"

I asked no more questions, but went into my room and cried. I wished that my dad had picked little Angie instead of me.

The following night my father woke me, I hadn't seen him for days, He and mom must have really hated each other, for him to come in the middle of the night for his belongings like he was.

"Sammy..." He called out as knelt beside me.

I had smelled the alcohol on his breath; I looked at him with much anticipation.

"What Dad?"

"I'm leaving...I have a job lined up in Chicago...I'm going to want you to come visit me next summer, I'll call you then...okay."

"Okay..." I whispered.

"I love you Sammy"

"I love you too Dad,"

It couldn't have been a dream, for the rest of the night I lay there awake, re-counting his words, and almost sorry I hadn't begged for him to take me now, that very moment with just the pajamas on my back like he had a few short months ago.

That morning I told my mother nothing of my fathers visit, it wasn't a dream, he really wanted me, I was not so sure my mother did, next summer I could be with him. She had only one thing to say to me that morning before I headed off to school on my own.

"Now you be good! And no fighting with the other children."

She misunderstood, now years latter I ask myself if she lived her whole life that way, or did she lose her grip on comprehending since baby Angie died, I suppose I was too young to pay any matter into that question.

I thought I went to school to learn, and not to please the teacher, and how was I to communicate with the other children when they were not paying me no mind to begin with. For that I had some resentment towards my kindergarten teacher, all in all I had graduated from her class without any further complaints.

Summer had come and gone with much disappointment, there was no phone call from my father, at least none to my knowledge, and I found it more successful getting an answer out of my mother when she was drinking her beer.

"Where is Dad living now?"

"Chicago…And he had better send me some money soon…" She bellowed before she popped another beer can open. "These welfare people think am getting enough to support you…they are crazy! I don't know how we are going to make ends meet."

"What is he doing there?"

"I don't know…Hustling…that's what he does the best."

"What's, hustling mean…Mom?"

"It means he is a smart robber."

"He's not a robber…you mean he steals?"

"Anything he can…and don't call your mama a liar…you hear me Sammy!"

"Sorry…but he has a job…don't he?"

"As long as he sends me money I don't care what he does…and you never mind him just because he pulled you from that fire don't make him a good daddy to you…now go to bed."


So many nights I would wake in our run down trailer house, to the sound of my mother bawling her eyes out, before her tranquilizers kicked in with the words. "My baby…my baby…oh God why did you take her from me?"

She had never thanked God for what she had, yet it came so easy for her to blame him for what she didn't have. It made me question my worthiness and ask myself what I had to be thankful for; I couldn't find anything…anything.


I carried the hope in my heart that my father would call, or come for me, not that I disliked my mother, but I really didn't care for her. I just wanted a change, and I was beginning to forget his voice, and what did he look like now? Was he even thinking of me? Maybe my mother was right about him after all. That night he left me for good may have not been my dream, but his. His intensions were in the right place, I had to believe it, and I had to give him the benefit of my doubt. It was all I had to give.


As we age our innocence wears off, I was seeing it in myself as well as my classmates, now in the fifth grade, I felt the pressure of belonging somewhere, I began to realize others like me were getting bullied and kicked to the curb, just because they didn't fit in, I couldn't speak for the bullies victims, but, I, myself didn't want to fit in, and I wouldn't take to kindly for being punished for such a decision.

There were clicks forming, I didn't have a name for all of them, but they were there. Except for the bullies' attention, the loners went somewhat un-noticed, like me. There was a group of three girls in my class who formed their own click, it took a while for them to get their name because they kept to themselves, but they followed me through my grade school years. Last year some of the teachers started to call them; The Three Musketeers. It grew on them and by the end of last year's school year, even some of the kids were calling them by that name. Theresa, Cheryl and Brenda were inseparable until now. Cheryl moved away shortly after we started the Fifth grade. The Musketeers lost their name, and now it was just Theresa and Brenda, but Theresa was sick with some kind of cancer. She missed a lot of school. One time it was as long as a month, and it that time Brenda was a loner just like me. I wanted to talk to her, to try to cheer her up, but I never did.

Theresa came back wearing an oversized wig. I thought it was a bit un-suitable for a school girl. No one laughed. They just stared and kept their distance, even Brenda had for the first part of the day. The next day at lunch they both brought each other a piece of cake and laughed at their Mother's gestures. I sat next to them wanting a piece of that cake.

I kept my distance at recess, doing what I had always done before in this school, sitting inside the library room reading a book where no harm would come to me, getting lost with Huckleberry Finn and Tom Sawyer, they were my friends; I was one of their Musketeers. I let my imagination run free with them, one time I truly did get lost. I felt a hand on my shoulder.

"Recess is over…" the principle of the school noted then added. "A half an hour ago."

"I'm sorry sir…" I replied then stood from my chair.

"You didn't hear the bell?"

"No, really I didn't…I'm sorry."

The rising smile on his face let me know that he believed me; he may never know how much it meant to me at that time, And for the break from my daily life to be swept away to a peaceful place where I ruled for a half hour longer was just priceless.

Settling back into the here and now was not where I wanted to be. Returning home on a cool spring Friday, when I'd much rather go to school for the entire weekend and into the summer, I had my books to protect me, of course I didn't always work that way. My mother was steaming mad, banging pots and pans. Her red hair was a mess and her demeanor frazzled.

"Job search…They want me to find a job…I can't work I have no education! I was to busy raising you to get a degree…And your dad…Forget about your good for nothing Dad…He's in prison…or soon to be! "

"What?"

"You heard me!! Embezzlement…I told you so…A hustler and Con-artist."

"When did…what did he do?" I asked in shock.

"Did I stutter!!? Oh I wish I would have sent you off with him when I had the chance…I could have gotten that education."

"What!!! You mean…You mean he called?"

"Yeah he called…A few years back."

"And you didn't tell me?"

"He's good for nothing…you would have wound up back here anyway!"

"You're good for nothing…" I shouted feeling anger that I never felt inside before.

"Watch your mouth!" She bellowed drunkenly.

"No…I don't have to, I hate you…I hate you!"

She swept her hand across my face, it stung some, but it didn't compare to the sting I had deep inside of me, I couldn't ignore the tightening in my chest. As I walked away, I reached inside of my pocket, and pulled out my inhaler. She followed me steaming mad.

"You take that back now Sammy…I mean it…"

I slammed my bedroom door behind me taking a hit, and welcoming a hint of relief.

"Take it back!" She screamed again entering my room, just irate she was when she gave me a shove, my mother never attacked me physically before that day, and feeling somewhat responsible for the onset, I apologized, and she left me alone, in my room, where I stayed the rest of the night.

I woke in the morning hating my life and adulthood was so far away yet, I took my Tom sawyer book into the living room and sat on the couch to read, when my mother gets up maybe she too, will apologize, and all will be semi well, or as much as it can be around here. Again I let myself get lost in the dream of being with them into there adventures where boys are men, at least in this dream.

I had finished it, and it was half past one-o-clock, I found it odd that my mother wasn't up yet, she never slept this late. I walked up to her closed door and put my ear up to it, didn't hear anything at all, no radio, no TV. I grew worried thinking about all those tranquilizers she takes when she was in one of her moods, last night sure qualified as one, and she had plenty of beer that I knew of for sure. I knocked on her door.

"Mom…Mom!"


A knock on the door startled him.

Marshall jumped up from his bed, closing Sam's book.

"Marshall!" his mother's voice called out from the other side of the door.

"Yeah…" He answered stashing Sam's book under his bed, he opened up the door and stood before his mother with wide eyes.

She gazed at him curiously, peering in enough to take notice that his computer was off.

"Were you sleeping?"

"No…I was just vegging-out."

"You sure…You feel all right? You look pale."

"I'm fine."

"Well I picked up some chicken from, Land and Sea, are you hungry?"

Marshall was very hungry; he had realized that he had been working most of the day on a single pop tart that he had eaten hours ago.

"So how is Mister Ross?"

He shared conversation with his mother as he always did, withholding some information, he could never tell, he was so glad he didn't have a mother like Sam had, probably no more, was she dead inside of that bedroom? Was his story for real? Oh the heartache, and it had just begun, surely things were to start looking up for him.

"Marshall...hon?" Gwen called out looking at him oddly, for he was holding a chicken drumstick in his hands without any movement, he lifted his eyes to her. "Look at you; you're a million miles away."

"I'm sorry what were you saying?"

"Never mind that, and tell me what is weighing heavy on your mind."

"It's nothing Mom, really."

"Well, I don't believe that for a minute, but please if something is bothering you and you think I can be of some help, for heavens sake let me know."

"I will Mom."

"Is it Mister Ross...A girl, that Becky girl?" Gwen continued to pry.

"Mom, it's...Well, I'm just kind of ticked off at Carl, I mean Dad...Mom I don't even want to call him my dad."

Gwen's heart pattered out of sort, in her chest. "He's been out of the picture for so long...what brought this up?"

"Rejection, I guess...I mean how would you feel if Gramps walked out on you when you were ten?"

She asked for it, she should have known it was coming. "It was my fault...we didn't separate on good terms hon, he never was much of a father to you and for that, he has himself to blame...you don't need to refer to him as dad or father, you have your role model…your mentor, even if he is going though a divorce, most couples do."

Gwen was so glad another "Dad" speech had passed, hopefully this was the last, oh lord, let it be the last. She couldn't bare telling him the truth now, maybe she could have ten years ago, but it was always one more day, one more week, one more year, and now she was afraid that the truth may cost her, her adored son. Yes it was best to just let sleeping dogs lie.

"So how is Gram doing?"

"I would like to say she is adjusting, but she seems so sad, and I am so busy with work to be with her more than, a few hours during the weekends. We did some shopping today and picked up some Christmas colored yarn, I asked her for a new throw for the couch, so, hopefully she will get back into knitting."

"Did you mention to her that I wrote a letter to the mayor, about having the house of pain tore down?"

Gwen nodded wiping her mouth with the napkin. "She had said you were going to do something like that, and I did tell her what you did, She is happy about it."

"Well it is the least I could do, who owns that land anyway…Mom?"

"I don't know the city probably. I'm sure the taxes hadn't been paid, and it just got turned over."

"Yeah, I don't suppose David Pane would have wanted to make a go out of it; don't you wonder where he is now? I know you were disappointed in him, for what he had done, but—"

"What was done was done Marsh…"

Marshall nodded, knowing that she was tender on David, although she has never said so herself, but Uncle Tony had. His mother did a lot for him, helping him with his homework, bringing over some food When there was more than enough to go around, but one thing she would never do was to step foot into that house when, ole man Jack Pane was there.

There was not much cleaning up to do, Marshall quickly wiped the table down while his mother reported that she had some work to do in her sewing room, they both scattered into there rooms. Marshall, again shut his door and then turned his computer on, just for show, before plopping himself back onto his bed only to reach for Sam's book he opened it and found where he had left off.

"Talk to me Sam…"


"Mom…" I called once more; I needed my inhaler before I opened that door. I just knew something was very wrong.

"Mom." I called out once more as I entered. She was there, on the bed, looked like she was sleeping, but I knew better. "She's not dead…she's not dead," I told myself

The afternoon sunlight shinned on her face, it would have been almost blinding, even if she were sleeping, one would want to roll in the opposite direction. I had my doubts even before I touched her shoulder, just because she looked to peaceful, looking that peaceful, she must have not been in there at all. It took the fear out of me. I nudged her with no tears, she was dead.


To my surprise; I could breathe when I made the phone call, perhaps I was a bit numb yet I can not recall it, for I felt calm, as though a weight were lifted from off my shoulders, so wrong it was for me to feel that way, so very wrong.

It wasn't like I was jumping for joy, or were even the slightest bit happy about her death.

There was just finality in my mind that played over and over again, No more would she be calling me or someone else a liar, no more would she be twisting people's words just to allow herself to feel better about her own self. No more would I have to hear her crying at night, no more…

Then there was that selfish question, what was to become of me now, I asked myself that while I sat in a waiting room at the police station, it wasn't long before a woman and a man had walked in claiming to be social workers. They had pity all over their faces, if I ever saw it. Which wasn't a bad thing, I'd take their charity, and what they had to offer me, because if I didn't I would only be pitying myself.

That night I slept the lady social workers couch. I'm sure she had told me her name but I didn't remember it at the time, for in the morning my uncle was to come and she would be just, what she was, there to help fill in the gaps for this poor homeless child. I suppose my uncle Larry had seen me once before at my baby sisters funeral, but I didn't remember, I've heard my mother talk about her brother once or twice before, I knew he was a police officer, and my mother didn't like him.

I was just finishing breakfast when he came to the door; he was greeted by the lady social worker.

"Hello, Larry Casper, I presume…"

"Yes ma'am,"

"I'll let you two chat I'll be in the other room if you need me."

"Thank you, ma'am." He said standing tall and broad before me. "Samuel…"

I just nodded while he took a chair on the opposite side of the table. He sighed heavily, I could see he had been crying, if I could read his mind at that very minute I would say he was disappointed in me. But instead I was noticing the resemblance, for he looked very much like my mother had, except his hair was a little blonder, didn't have that red tint like her.

"I'm your Uncle Larry…How are you doing?" he asked studying my face, folding his hands onto the table before him.

"I'm okay."

"Your okay? I'm sure it must have been an awful experience for you…finding her like that…Did you know that she took a lot of tranquilizers…Do you know that is what killed her?"

"Yeah…I figured it was that, she was very, mad about…my father, he's in jail, in Chicago."

"He's in Stillwater Sam; he was sentenced to ten years in prison. You will be an adult when he is sprung."

"She never told me, until last night. She doesn't tell me anything."

"She didn't Sam, she didn't tell you anything…Do you think she may have been trying to protect you?"

"No…She doesn't care about me," I said calmly.

"She did care about you…Sam It's okay to be angry with her because she took to many pills, but she cared."

"You're a liar…You don't even know her, and you don't know me either,"

He sat there sighing again, shaking his head wondering what he was getting himself into. I wanted to say more, but I didn't, because I was getting the hint that he was going to be taking me in, and for that I had to make amends quickly.

"I'm sorry sir."

"I know we barley know each other, I live in Minneapolis, quite a ways from here…and to be honest your mother and I hadn't seen eye to eye on a handful of things…There is no doubt your life is going to change from here on out…You will be coming to live with me and my family…And you will follow the rules of the household…Do I make myself clear Sam?"

"Yes sir." I replied sort of liking this guy, from my first impression. He was very soft spoken, very different than my mother's high pitched voice.

He took me back to my house where I gathered the belongings that I needed. I was embarrassed; the trailer house was in shambles, what little respect he had for my mother, he may have lost it after seeing what we called home, I hoped his home was a real one, one with an upstairs and two bathrooms.

I didn't realize, that I wasn't conducting myself in a predicable manner at the hotel where I had to meet, Uncle Larry's wife, Mae, and their three children, nine year old twins James and Josh, and there two year old sister Jeannie. I went into the pool with them and then they ordered pizza, it was such a good change from hot dogs and pasta.

I kept getting the twins mixed up because they were identical, but by the time my mothers funeral was over and we headed for Minneapolis in uncle Larry's suburban, I found the differences in their personalities, Josh had a gap between his teeth, he was the trickster while James was more conservative.

A portion of the twins bedroom was set aside for me, they must have went out and bought a bed that day they had gotten the call that my mother had died, and it was a real two story house, I did feel welcome for the moment, yet it was going to take some getting used to sharing a bedroom.

My first supper with them was very different than I was accustomed to from the start; they bowed their heads to pray. Like the Walton's, only we didn't have to hold hands, Mae thanked the lord for the meal they were about to receive. I didn't get it, she was the one who cooked it, and Uncle Larry was the one who went out and risked his life to save this city from the robbers and killers.

Their lack of conversation made me feel a bit uneasy, chaos would have felt more like home, I could just block that out, but how do you block out silence? Is this how they had always eaten their supper at home? It wasn't like this at all last night in the restaurant. The twins were all excited about summer vacation and how they were going to spend it, skateboarding in the park. Mae had even offered to buy me one; Larry had smiled and said that it was a good idea.

Ahh, finally something, Josh crossed his eyes at me and opened his mouth that was full of food. It did not go unnoticed.

"Josh!"

"But Dad…He's staring at me."

"Apologize right now!"

"Sorry!"

"I'm sorry too." I said, and then kept my eyes to my plate.

After dinner I helped Mae clean off the table while little Jeanie sat content in her highchair, she thanked me, and then it hit, the tightening in my chest grasped me, brought me to my knees, I reached for my inhaler and pumped it down my throat. It just wasn't enough for me, Mae picked me up.

"Outside...Come...Larry!" She bellowed, guiding me outside onto their patio.

It helped some, but it wasn't enough for them to see my breathing finally returning back to normal in the slow pace that it always had.

Larry drove me to the hospital, even though I insisted that I was fine.

"You are not fine, not one tear did you cry for your mother...it's not normal...you are suppressing. I didn't take you in blind, for your information, you are going to get checked out and then we are going to set you up with some counseling."

I wasn't normal; it was no big surprise to me.


Marshall's cell phone went off taking him away from Sam's story; he shut the book and answered.

"Hello..."

"Marshall, It's me Sam...I want to thank you for your help this afternoon."

"Oh...glad to help, we got it done in no time."

"Hey I'll give you a few bucks for it; you can split it amongst your friends."

"No...No, we don't want to get paid, really Sa-, Mister Ross."

"That's all right...you can call me Sam, as long as were not in the class room...Hey I appreciate this big time."

"No problem...All right then, oh...I saw Todd Martin today, he came to rake your leaves out back."

"Is that right, well I'm glad to hear that…real glad, thanks for the info, hey, by the way do you think you can run my set of keys by on your way to school tomorrow?…Mia wants to tidy the place up you know…Marshall?"

"Oh, sure, no problem, I can do that, how are you doing?"

"Not bad, walked around some today, I'm ready to go back to class."

"Yeah I wish you could, who's going to replace you?"

"I'm not sure. I've already made some phone calls, could be a woman, she's young, and a bit short of her teaching degree, but fits the criteria, I shouldn't be off for more than a couple of weeks, hobbling or not I will be there."

"Works for me."

"Well in the meantime, help hold down the fort, I'll see you in the morning?"

"Sure thing, Sam."

Marshall hung up the phone, with a feeling of urgency, he shouldn't be reading this story without his permission in the first place, but it was too late for that now, he had already started it, and he intended to finish. Get it back inside of his apartment before he stops at the hospital, a tight schedule, and he will feel bad about it for a while, then again, he can consider it as payment, for all the chores he has done so far, besides, who was it hurting?

He set his phone down onto his night stand and once again, finding where he had left off, opened the book…

The Casper's were afraid of me because I hadn't cried over the loss of my mother. I had already known that I wasn't normal. But wasn't that my problem? What, did they think, I was evil? As I sat there on the couch, waiting for the doctor to come in the room to decide if I was evil, or just not normal, I thought of the Omen, and evil Damien who had 666 etched somewhere on the back of his head. I found myself feeling the back of my hairline for such an engraving, when the doctor came into the room.

She was a woman, not what I had expected, she looked to thin and old to be sitting in front of someone who was not of sound mind, what if one were evil and hostile? I didn't believe that I was going to turn a demon loose on her, but what about the others?

"Hello Samuel…Or would you prefer I call you Sam?" She said as she sat down in a chair beside me.

"Sam, please ma'am."

"Very well, I'm doctor Albey; you can call me Grace if you choose. Sam, do you know why you are here?"

I nodded knowing that I had better start crying before I get thrown in a mental institution. She looked old and wise, would she see right through it if I could produce tears?

"I'm sorry to hear that your mother had passed away…This is a big change for you, moving away from your home and into a strange city with a family you barley know…And leaving your friends."

"I didn't have any friends."

"I'm sorry to hear that too…Did that bother you…upset you in any way?"

"No…not really, I can't play baseball, or kick ball…I have asthma."

"What kind of exercise do you get Sam?"

"I walk home; I walked back and forth from school every day…I live, I lived a mile away."

"Fair enough, you got your exercise…and I suppose you had a list of chores to do."

"I took out the garbage, and cleaned my room, some times I washed the dishes when, well, when they were all dirty."

"Did your mother ask you to wash the dishes?"

"No…"

"You just took it upon yourself to wash them?"

"Yeah…it was that or eat out of the pan…sometimes she would just wash a plate for herself, and hand me the pan to eat out of."

"Did this make you angry?"

"It made me wash the dishes."

"Were you angry about it?'

"Well, I guess it was my chores, to wash the dishes. She yelled a lot, said she couldn't do everything."

"Did she yell at you?"

"Yes…I was the only one there."

"Did it make you angry?"

"They're just dishes."

"What else made you mad Sam?"

"Nothing…"

"You are not angry with her right now…Sam?"

I just looked at her now thinking that maybe I could cry, and get this over with, she would let me go with a cleaned-up bill of health.

"I told her that I hated her…the night before she…"

"The night before she what…Sam?"

"You know…the night before she died."

"But you didn't hate her…You're eleven, many young children say things they don't mean, and what you had said to your mother, was fueled from anger, like many, even us adults say or do things we regret latter on…Do you regret what you had said to her that night?"

I nodded with the numbing heartache coming to life inside of me. "Course I do…It's probably why she took all those pills."

"It's okay…Go ahead and cry."

I fought it for a moment, and then she sat beside me and took my hand, then my arm, then me, I was crying like a baby with my head on her small, frail chest, I hugged her as tight as I could, and she did the same for me.

How did she know these things? She was right about my father; absence does make the heart grow fonder, even if it is for the wrong reasons, I was being too hard on myself by being to easy on others. I no longer cared for my father, yet I wished him well. I walked out of there grieving for my mother, and I know Grace told me that it wasn't my fault my mother had died, I just couldn't see her reasoning behind it. I suppose it would make her feel better if I believed it, and I told her I did. I lied.

I should have known they were church going people, and I didn't believe that I had a choice one way or the other. I was tired, I had a rough night, and I'm certain that if I had asked Mae if I could stay home because of it she would have said no.

Mae took her children and me to church, while Larry was working. I never had been to church before that Sunday. I didn't understand anything that the preacher man was saying. He was damming us all to hell, because we were sinners. Talking to me probably, sure couldn't be talking about all these nice people in here, they are here because they want to be. Why did they come just to be dammed for it? And why doesn't this preacher man take his sermon to the prisons, I just didn't get it.

James nudged me before he stood up, I lifted my head, noticing that everybody was clearing the church, I followed him down the aisle, and there she was Grace Albey, standing in place talking to Mae. She saw me and cracked a smile; I made my way up to her feeling a little embarrassed about the other day, how tightly I held onto her, not wanting to let her go.

"Sam, how are you doing?"

"Okay."

"Just okay, I tend to hear differently…I live nearby, would you like to come over for a visit?"

I shrugged my shoulders and looked at Mae.

"Go ahead, just call when you're ready to come home. I will pick you up," she said, adjusting little Jeanie in her arms.

"Oh no need for that Mrs. Casper, I'll bring him home."

"Very well."

I didn't know what this was about, I thought I was healed, what more did they want? Does she know I lied to her, how could she? Living was so much easier when I didn't have people pestering me.

I heard her music station, it was a religious song, oh no; she was going to preach to me.

"Put your seat belt on Sam," she said locking her own into place. "I just live a couple of blocks away; I don't know why I don't just walk it now that spring is in the air."

She kept her one sided conversation going, all the way, and as we entered her beautiful home. I had questions I could have asked, but choose not to.

"Have a seat Sam, make yourself at home."

I did so with my eyes on the piano she had centered in her living room. It wasn't a school room piano, more like one of those you would see Elton John playing.

"So, you had an asthma attack in the middle of the night, did you?" She asked sitting herself onto the couch beside me.

I tried to be as quiet as I could, because I wanted to keep my privacy, I thought it went unnoticed; so much for that.

"You know your attacks can be brought on by stress…Did you have a bad dream?"

"I don't know." I muttered catching her expression; it appeared to give me the idea that she didn't believe me. I gathered real quickly that there was no fooling her, and perhaps I was insulting her intelligence. "Yes I did, but…"

"But, you don't want to talk about it?"

"Right."

"Perhaps, getting it out in the open will prevent further, bad dreams."

"Well…I dreamed, that I was in the fire, and I was…running through the house trying to find my baby sister…And my mom was crying; my baby my baby…but I could not find her…"

"You can't change what happened that night Sam, and it is not your fault that it did happen…You realize that don't you?"

I nodded. "Yes…I guess so."

"How is it going with your cousins?"

"I get along with them, mostly James, but they are younger than me, and we don't have a lot in common, they ride skateboards, and I, just rather not, Mae was talking about buying me one yesterday, and I don't know."

"It sounds like fun if you ask me, with summer vacation here, you should give it a shot, what about a bicycle, do you have one?"

"No, a couple of years ago my mom was going to buy me one for my birthday, but I asked for a guitar instead. It was just a beginner's guitar; it came with the song book and stuff, and I learned how to play some songs by myself."

"Good for you, do you still have it…Sam?"

"No, it got busted…My Mom was mad at me one day and threw it into the wall."

"I'm sorry to hear that Sam, but it is getting me thinking. My husband Mark passed away a couple of years back, God rest his soul. But anyway, he too, played the guitar; I have it here just collecting dust in the closet, why when it could be put to good use."

I looked at her old, kind face. "No, I am not…I really can't play very good at all."

"Excuse me for a moment."

She left the room and returned with a guitar case in her hand, and plopped it down on the couch beside me. It was in a hard cover brown leather case. She opened it looking at me with her wide smile, she took it out. It was a beige color with a black guard and trim.

"The strap probably needs some adjusting…it is yours, Sam, try it on."

"Shouldn't you be giving this to one of your kids?"

"Why, they don't play music, I think it serves its purpose in your

121

possession, and I know Mark is looking down from heaven, very pleased right now, he is."

"Thank you Grace…" I said with tears in my eyes.

"You are very welcome."

She was so cool; she didn't have to keep me there half of the day like she had done, and the strange thing is, she was enjoying my company, I didn't feel like her patient anymore. She played the piano for me, and refreshed my memory on how to read the notes. From inside the guitar case there was a song book loaded with country hits, Johnny Cash, Marty Robbins, Charlie Pride, and a book of church hymns. I suppose I wasn't ready for those yet.

She took me to a music store; we had gotten there just before it had closed. The man at the counter smiled widely, probably from seeing mine when Grace asked him for the beginners hand book. I'm sure he was mistaken with his assumptions, that I was her grand child.

I never knew my father's parents, I suppose they were a lot like him, they just didn't care. My mother's parents died in a car crash together before I was born; more than likely, my mother had a real hard time with that too, they both could have been a good grandparent, at least that's what I want to believe.

I felt bad that she gave me a gift and even spent money on me, and I had nothing to give her in return. All I could say was thank you, and she was just happy with that, it hadn't seemed like it was a chore for her at all, or it was something she felt she had to do. That's when I realized some people give to make themselves feel better, kind-of-like killing two birds with one stone.

I carried my guitar out of her car a changed boy yet walked nervously into the house with it, Mae was in the kitchen with little Jeanie at her feet, receiving a gift, it would break Grace's heart if I had to return it, just because it was a rule of the house, not to take charity from those kind enough to give.

She stood there looking at me with a spatula in her hand.

"What is this you have Sam?"

She knew what it was, doesn't take no rocket scientist to figure that there was a guitar in this guitar case. I quickly found myself comparing her to my mother already. She better not be upset about this, she had just better not.

"It's a guitar…Grace, I mean Doctor Albey gave it to me…It's all right isn't it?"

Oh why did you ask that, I thought giving her the chance to ponder the thought of returning it, only to say thanks, but no thanks.

"Why on earth did she give you a guitar?"

"Well…I used to have one, and she just wanted to give it to me…I didn't ask for it, I swear." I said looking at her with fear in my eyes, don't take this away from me, you had better not, and maybe I should try to examine myself once more for that 666 etched on my body somewhere.

"All right then, I reckon there is no harm in that."

I let out a sigh of relief, and carried it up the stairs to the bedroom I shared. James and Josh were lying on the floor playing Chinese checkers, they both turned with wide eyes.

"You got a guitar where did…who gave it to you?" Josh demanded knocking them plastic marbles a skew from the tin game board.

I laid it out on my bed, whishing that my twin cousins were much younger, or older than I.

"Doctor Albey gave it to me and I'm not sharing, you have your own things."

"You got a guitar cause you're crazy, it's no fair, and this is our room…we have to share!" Josh protested.

"I'm not crazy."

"Our mom say's you are!"

"No she didn't…She didn't call you crazy Sam…She just said you needed help." James said, and then added. "Aren't you going to take it out?"

I had felt defeated already, taking it out for them to touch and pluck the strings. I found that James was gentler with it, when Josh had tired from it James just sat there watching and learning with me. This angered Josh, but what was I to do?

"Come on James, let's go watch Star trek, it's on in five minutes."

"Go ahead, there just re-runs anyway." James said as if to shoo him away.

I wouldn't have minded a bit if he had left me alone, for this family I was thrown into was too sudden for me. I would be content living with Grace, I'm sure she would have allowed me alone time, but James had questions, and I had the answers for him, I guess it wasn't so bad.

Sometime latter we were interrupted by Uncle Larry]s presence, standing in the doorway. He looked important, somewhat scary, and authorative dressed in his police uniform, at least to me.

"Hi Dad…Sam got a guitar from that Doctor Lady."

"So I gather…James why don't you go wash up for dinner."

"Okay," he replied only to scamper out of the bedroom.

"Sam..." He replied stepping up to me.

"Aunt Mae said I could keep it."

"And you can...the thing is we have a rule in this household called sharing..."

"I was...I am."

"Josh said otherwise...He may be jealous.'

"I let him mess with it for a while, it is mine, sir."

"I understand, just don't shut him out...Did you have a productive talk with Doctor Albey?"

"Yes sir." I reported placing my guitar back into its case.

"Come on...dinner is on."


I had hard feelings towards Josh that evening, I hoped they were temporary, I went to bed with a hint of anger, and at the same time I wondered if I was going to have the same bad dream, or a worse one. I took in the comfort that my inhaler was under my pillow. And I tried to think good thoughts as I drifted off to sleep. Grace was in my thoughts, we are going to be together next Sunday, after church again, I am going to show her what I learned, and she is going to be proud of me.

I woke in the morning feeling refreshed, so why did I feel robbed. Not waking in the middle of the night for some time to myself; a piece of the night was usually mine, once I got my breath back.

James and Josh were already dressing for the summer day ahead. I was looking forward to having some; alone time; with my guitar, but after breakfast, Mae announced that we were all going to the store to find me a skateboard.

"He's going to get another present!! What do we get?"

"Enough Josh…you have everything you need."

"No I don't…I want a guitar!" he bellowed.

"Fine, just fine, if by Christmas you still want one, put it on your list for Santa."

"There isn't a Santa…" Josh muttered, knowing that he would not get away that quote next year at this time, for it would brake little Jeanie's fairy tale world that was soon to come.

Balance wasn't something that could be taught, although James tried, and he made it look so easy, gliding down the sidewalks of Bristol Park on his skateboard, Josh too, whizzed by me. I was thankful for the knee and elbow pads, Mae had kicked in for me. I noticed she was watching me closely for an asthma attack while she sat on a swing with little Jeanie in her lap, but I wasn't moving very fast at all, only picking myself up from off the ground. I wasn't that fragile, come on Aunt Mae, give me a break. Luckily I didn't have any that first day in the park, just bruises.

I could be the average boy, by watching and observing James, even though he was younger than me I wanted to be like him, normal, average, quiet enough to get the right kind of attention, and respect. I found myself stepping one foot forward from keeping my distance.

I couldn't wait for Sunday to see Grace again, but I didn't want to appear too eager, I just smiled at her as we walked by only to take our place in the pew before church service had began. I didn't want to count on a visit with her, but it was her words last Sunday. Maybe she had more important things to do; I didn't want that from her, I wanted to be the one to tell her I had better things to do. I sure did not find anything more important than spending an afternoon with her.

Of course I had to sit through the service to get there. The preacher man didn't seem to be damming all these nice people to hell like he was doing last week. Today he was discussing faith, have faith and everything will be fine and dandy, buttoned up and beautiful. Did all these good citizens believe in fairy tales?

If so, why can't I create one of my own, I let my mind wonder. I'm growing up, what can I do, what can I be? A rock star, yeah, I would be the leader of a big ole band, just like Johnny-be-good. Would I sing, not necessary, I can't sing, I would sure have to be the best guitar player around. I get to name the band, I am the founder. The Sam Ross band, no, not catchy enough, what am I? Who am I? The answer was as plain as day, I am an orphan. That's a cool enough name for a rock band, Orphan.

I wore my title proudly as I followed James down the aisle, if Grace was going to bow out today, I wouldn't be hurt to much, I am a future rock star and I don't need her help in getting there. I walked up to her.

"You all set…I reckon you need to go fetch your guitar…you didn't forget?" she said with a worried smile.

"No ma'am…I will go get it." I happily replied, and then added spring into my step, and my lungs did not tighten.

At her home, she listened to me play, and was happy to see that what little practice I had gotten was paying off. They were the simple songs. On Top Of Old Smoky, Michael Row The Boat Ashore, and Amazing Grace. She said Amazing Grace was her favorite because it was her husband Mark's. Any time that she was down he would play and sing that song for her.

BRENDA LAMBERT

And then of course she wanted to know how my week had gone, I wondered if she was asking as a doctor or a friend, should I draw a line between them?

"And how about your nights Sam…Any more bad dreams?" she asked setting a bowel of chocolate ice cream in front of me.

"No…No bad dreams." I replied lifting my spoon, eager for the ice cream.

"Good…good, could it be the exercise that you are getting, I wonder."

I didn't have the heart to tell her that I didn't care for skateboarding and maybe I will get the hang of it whether I wanted to or not.

"Yeah it could be." I said spooning the ice cream into my mouth.

She sat on the opposite side of the table. "Did you learn anything from the message today Sam?"

Didn't she realize that I was too young to be expected to make heads or tails out of a church sermon? "No…not really."

"You didn't fall asleep, did you?"

"No…I didn't." I said simply, knowing that I didn't need god, and odds were I had a good fifty years ahead of me to decide my fate. She tested me anyway.

"What didn't you understand?"

"All that talk about moving mountains with faith…mountains don't move on demand, with out dynamite…and a hundred men getting paid to do it."

She chucked subtly, lightly offending me.

"What if the mountains were not made of rock and dirt, but were the obstacles, barriers, and troubles in your life that stood in your way?"

"It would make more sense." I said, not admitting for one moment

128

that the preacher man hadn't explained it, he may have.

"Have faith and you can move mountains…You will keep that in mind wont you Sam?"

"Sure Grace…I will."

Her nagging ceased, I was happy that it didn't last long, and we were able to get back to our music, all I wanted for my soul was for it to be happy and entertained for the moment, Did I think the moments would end, I did indeed for all moments end, I on my guitar and she on the piano, where did the time go?

Another Sunday spent with her, came and gone, and another, It was such a nice break from the day to summer days that I had spent at the park with the Casper's trying to get my balance on that no good for nothing Skate board. I didn't have to be a tagalong on Sunday afternoons, surely Josh was glad that I had given him time to reconnect with his twin brother.

It was my understanding that this Sunday in August, Grace wanted to take me to a picnic lunch at her daughters home, just outside of the city, I was not much looking forward to it, the tagalong that I had come to be was now true on this day.

On the way we had begun to exchange small talk, I was aware that she had seemed a bit nervous and preoccupied, it quickly became contagious.

"Oh Sam, it is so beautiful here out in the country…no smog…just the clear fresh air…"

Small talk that I could not find a reply for…I was just a boy, and it was just small talk, wasn't it?

"Sam...I'm seriously thinking about moving in with my daughter...Why with Mark gone...it just seems ideal...It's not going to happen for a few months yet, so we will have more Sundays together...and you will be starting in a new school...Sam you have come a long way, I think you will adjust to your new family just fine...yes, just fine." She reassured herself hiding what little guilt she had for her decision behind her smile.

"Okay." I said hiding my tears as I turned my head and looked out my window at the countryside.


At her daughters country home, Grace and I had learned that this was a "Surprise retirement party" I suppose I was a trinket, her last patient I gathered that I best be on my good behavior, and represent myself as of sound mind on her behalf.

Once her excitement eased, she introduced me to her daughter, and the family that she had, the same ole small talk.

"What grade are you going in?"

"It's a pleasure to meet you..."

My picture was even taken, and I can imagine it sitting in a photo album as, Doctor Grace Albey's last patient at her retirement party. They were kind, almost to kind, I am sure they had been filled in on me. I tried my best, still I felt like an outsider, especially seeing how happy Grace was, she truly enjoyed being here. It was my selfish plan that I would break away from her when I was good and ready, and Grace would bow out as gracefully as her name. Selfish plans fail.

Keeping my act, subsided once back into her car to head home. I didn't want to hear any more small talk, I didn't want to hear her talk at all, maybe, if she was to complement me on how good I conducted myself in front of her family, yes, I could accept that.

"Did you get enough to eat Sam?"

"Yes I did…thank you."

"Oh good because it's nearly six o' clock…I don't know what time your family eats, but as long as you had enough to eat, that's good enough for me…"


I didn't know it then, but "small talk." Is essential, in many ways, there was no reason for her to lift up my spirits at that time, no reason for her to bring them down, she cares, but soon, I'm on my own. At least she didn't ask me if I had a good time…


"My baby…my baby…Sammy…help me…my baby…" I heard my mother cry.

I got up gasping, couldn't see the fire, but it was there. I just knew it, for I couldn't breathe.

"Find her…find her…save her, save little Angie…" I told myself as I made my way though the dark, dark home…it didn't feel like our old trailer house, but she has got to be here somewhere…Where, where are you?

"Angie!!! Angie…" I gasped, listening for her cry, was it too late?

"Sam! Sam…" I heard a man call out. It wasn't my father. "Sam…"

Now I felt strong hands clutching my shoulders. "No…I got…" I gasped, who was stopping me from finding her?

"Wake up Sam…" I felt my inhaler at my mouth; I reached for it as it was pumped into me, raising my awareness.

Larry stood before me studying my face as I was catching my breath, the light was bright in the room, not where I bunked with my twin cousins, but in their room. Mae too, looked at me with a hint of fear; she was wearing a thin nightgown.

"I'm…sorry…I'm sorry…"

"It's all right…you had a bad dream." Larry replied handing me my inhaler turning his eyes to the hallway from where I came. "Boy's, get back into bed."

"I'm sorry…"

"Back to bed, Sam." Larry said calmly.

"Okay…"

I turned the light out and got back into my bed, covering up my head with the thin blanket.

"I told you James…He is crazy…"

"Shut up and go to sleep," James replied.

I should have been thankful for James and Uncle Larry, taking this charade I played out lightly, but it was something that they can hold against me, it was a strike, and how many strikes do I get before I am out? I heard my Aunt and Uncle talking in the other room, I couldn't make out what they where saying, and I wasn't sure if I would want to know. I lay there the rest of the night just humiliated at what I had done, and Grace, if she catches wind of this, I just wouldn't know what I would do.

I got up very early, knowing that Mae was getting Larry off to work; I could smell the coffee and the eggs. They were not entirely surprised to see me walking into the kitchen; I just hoped that I had interrupted their conversation in time, if they were talking about getting me some serious help, or worse.

"Good morning." Larry boasted, yet no where near ignoring what I had done three hours ago. "You didn't get back to sleep, did you?"

"No sir."

"Sit down Sam…would you care for some orange juice?" Mae asked setting a sippy cup down onto the highchair tray in front of little Jeanie.

I nodded, sitting myself down. "Aunt Mae…please don't tell Grace about last night…She's retiring and moving away, and, well she doesn't need to know…please."

Mae gazed at me setting my juice in front of me. "Well, my intensions were to do so. I knew she was retiring, but I didn't realize that she was moving away."

"You two have become quite close, I suppose this upsets you, hah Sam?"

"Yes sir, but I will get over it, and I'm sorry…"

Larry sighed tapping his fingers onto the wooden table. "All right then, it is against our better judgment, but if this happens again, we will have to arrange for you to see another doctor. You understand?"

"Yes sir."

Mae had given me a wonderful gift that day, she had let me stay home while she took her children to the park, knowing that they had a picnic lunch, and my sandwich was in the refrigerator, was music to my ears. I had quiet time to reflect on myself, time with me and my guitar. A small time in my life to remind me that independence will be mine one day, a long time from now, but one day.

Grace called me that following Sunday morning to tell me she wasn't feeling well and she would not be at church. She wished me luck in my new school, and said she would see me next Sunday.

I wished her well…

It was a big junior high school, glad not to have James and Josh anywhere near. I wasn't necessarily a new kid, in this ever changing city, but just an unknown face in the crowd. I kept quiet, kept to myself, listened to my teachers while I observed others, some more grown up than the others, some much more.

I wouldn't have imagined that it was a stressful day for the teachers until I had really thought about it. As I sat in the history class, Mister Dinn introduced himself by writing his name on the board with his back to us, a kid sitting next to me wadded up a piece of paper then took it out of his mouth and threw it at his back. The balding man with thick glasses quickly turned around peering at us all.

"Who did that?" he asked with a nervous demand.

He had failed already; I thought to myself, how did this kid next to me know that this teacher was a push-over? Word gets around, perhaps he had an older brother or a sister who had Mister Dinn in a previous school year, and because he began his very first day of school with his nervousness and uncertainties they will have to stick with him until the day he finally decides to retire.

"You…" the teacher pointed directly at me. "Who threw it?"

"I'm sorry…I don't know…really, I didn't see a thing." I replied lying through my teeth.

I wasn't the only one who didn't see a thing; no one did…not one…

Other than that Mister Dinn incident, I felt pretty good about my first day, I wouldn't cause Mister Dinn any trouble, but I cant be a victim of his failures ether, I hope he understood in his way, there was no hero inside of me, I was too small to bring him out of the hole he had dug for himself, just one kid. I was sure I could speak for half of his class.

Grace was right; I had my own life to live, time to move on, our last Sundays were slipping away with more and more, "small talk." On the very last Sunday I didn't bring my guitar, just my helping hands. I helped her take down curtains that her daughter had purchased for her a few years back and then we hung some old drab sheers in its place. She had told me that a former colleague of hers had purchased her home; they had already had their own plans for drapes.

As the minutes went on, it was getting closer and closer to good byes.

"Come...come, let's take a break," she said as if she were exhausted, she plopped herself down onto the couch. "I have something for you." She added reaching into a mesh bag she had on the floor.

She handed me a keychain, the base was thick see-through plastic coated, with a yellow dot in the center.

"Do you know what that is Sam?"

"Not, really...No."

"It's a mustard seed...turn it around, read the back inscription."

I did so, it read : Have faith as small as this mustard seed and nothing will be impossible to you.

"You will never lose your way if you keep that in mind Sam...always, can you do that for me?"

I nodded as my lips quivered. "Will I ever see you again?"

"I am sure we can arrange something...Sam you are going to be so busy, with school, and friends you will make many..."

I didn't believe her, yet found myself nodding. "I know..."

"Come on...give this ole lady a hug."

We hugged, it reminded me of our very first visit, not to long before, except this time, she too was crying.

"Okay...let me get my coat and I will bring you home." She said pulling herself away from me.

I wiped my eyes, with the back of my sleeve. "Grace...I'm going to walk home today...It's not far, and I'd rather..."

"Oh, I understand, completely...Sam, good luck to you."

I hugged her once more at the door and then turned away to suck up my tears, I didn't look back...


I sat in Mister Dinn's class, Jim, the trouble maker, who sat next to me was up to his old tricks. It was getting old, for me and most of the students; still, few thought he was bad and funny. He tossed a pen it and hit the chalkboard, just for a laugh. In the middle of an unexpected pop quiz.

Mister Dinn rose his head from whatever he was doing sitting at his desk.

"I have about had it from you, Tanner, come here and get your pink slip."

Bravo...about time I thought to myself.

"It wasn't me...I have my pen...ask anybody, it wasn't me."

"Yes it was!" I found myself blurting out.

I heard the class gasp, almost in unison, and perhaps I should have done the same for I surprised myself.

"Come get your pink slip!" Mister Dinn demanded.

Jim Tanner rose from his desk then gave my shoulder a shove, he didn't have to say anything, I got the hint. He took the pink slip from the teachers hand and walked out.

As we all left the classroom, I had gotten a few remarks from my classmates...

"Wouldn't want to be you..."

"Your dead kid."

I stood at my locker, fishing out my math book wondering how Jim Tanner was going to hurt me.

"Way to go." The older girl who had a locker one away from mine called out. She lifted her eyebrows and smiled in approval. I've noticed her before, but didn't know her, and how could she possibly know me, let alone what I had done earlier that day. "Thank you...thank you."

"I didn't do anything."

"Yes you did," she said keeping her smile. "I'm Gail Dinn...yeah he's my dad, I know, he's kind of dorky, but he's a good guy."

"How'd you know, did he tell you?"

"No...no, someone pointed you out in the cafeteria...do you always sit alone?"

"Ah, no...sometimes..."

"Well I have the same lunch hour as you, and if you got no one to sit with you can sit with me and my friends...I mean it I really do."

"Yeah okay, thanks...if I don't get killed first." I shrugged holding a smile.

"Odds are, he's got detention after school for a week. So you will be safe at least until next Wednesday."

The next day I stood at the cafeteria line asking myself if I had the guts to take her up on her offer, I didn't get the chance to test myself. Gail tapped me on the shoulder and playfully butted in line before me.

"You going to sit with us Sam?" She asked with a smile.

"Sure...lead the way." I said a bit nervously.

I followed her to a table where two of her other girlfriends were sitting there with their bag lunches. Gail introduced me to them, and to my surprise they were not the least bit angry with her for my presence, me a sixth grader sitting here with three eighth grade girls...Fonzie eat your heart out...

Small talk only lasted for a few short minutes, and then they jumped right into their girl talk, talking about Dan and Rudy, who was going to take who to the Christmas dance.

"Who are you taking to the Christmas dance Sam?" Gail asked.

"No one, I'm not going." I replied, nearly chuckling.

"Oh, there has to be some girl you are sweet on..."

"No..." I assured them, realizing I never felt sweet on any girl yet. It was time I started.


Back in Mister Dinn's history class, Jim Tanner tossed me a note. I opened it up and read his sloppy writing.

AFTER SCHOOL PARKING LOT BE THERE!!!

I wrote him back, and tossed the note his way. : START WITHOUT ME!!!

I guess I could have been a real pansy and taken the note directly to Dinn, but I didn't, I suppose I felt big and bad because I had girls who were my friends. I had not told the girls at lunch hour about my situation, and I hurried directly into the bus.

I should have been that pansy, for when I went to bed that night, fear was inside of me.

"My baby…my baby…Sammy help…Sammy…"

Find her this time…find her…find her. I said to myself as I searched the dark rooms wheezing and gasping. "My baby…My baby…" I kept hearing my mother call out.

"Angie…Angie!" I called, and thank god I heard her cry this time.

I found her…I found her…"Don't cry…Don't cry. Please Angie don't cry I'm going to get you out of here."

Through the darkness I found the door that led outside. We dropped down into a snow bank. She was screaming and I was gasping…

I was picked up with strong hands and pulled back into the house, where reality cut me like a knife. I clutched onto the arm of the couch waiting for my lungs to bust wide open I didn't care if they did right now…It wasn't Angie, that I took outside, it was Jeanie she was still screaming…Did I hurt her? I couldn't ask, I couldn't breathe.

One of the boys handed me my inhaler I held it tightly in my hand, but I did nothing with it. Jennie's cries were fading, everything was fading, and I didn't care. Larry pried it out of my hand, and took it upon himself to pump it into my lungs. I can't say that it had mattered one way or another to me at that moment that my breath was returning.

I looked up at Larry. "I'm sorry…I'm sorry…did, I hurt her?"

"Physically, no…but you could have…you have really done it this time Sam."

"I know, get rid of me…I don't care…"

I wanted to be tied to the bed for the remainder of the night, but I didn't ask. I knew Jeanie was safely tucked in beside her parents, The boys said nothing and if they had I would have probably let loose on them. No doubt, I wouldn't go back to sleep anyway, and no doubt, I wouldn't have school tomorrow, I will probably have a doctors appointment, and I may end up in a mental institution, I was glad of one thing, doctor Albey will not catch wind of this.

The lack of sleep didn't make the morning any brighter, in fact I was full of heartache and pain. I couldn't go down stairs for breakfast, nor was I coaxed to. To look at little Jeanie after what I had done, I just couldn't. I had imagined James and Josh going to their school reporting what I had done last night, at least their day would be eventful, it would justify their lack of sleep at their little sisters cost.

Larry tapped on the bedroom door and entered. "Are you ready to go?"

He said nothing to me on the way to the doctor's office, nor did I want him to. I couldn't be sure if he had taken the day off, and I rightly did not care.


Now I sat here before an overstuffed psychiatrist. He had read my previous mental health record, and I had told him about my dream that had caused havoc. He was concerned about demonism, I knew for he had asked me if I heard voices asking, or telling me to do things that I didn't want to do.

"No sir, only when I sleep, and it's just my mother." I answered pleading that I didn't have the devil inside of me.

In the waiting room, I tapped on Larry's shoulder, waking him, at least this time it was in a polite manner, and not taking his baby daughter out to the snow bank and throwing her to the wind.

"How did it go?" he asked with his wide eyes upon me, concerned for the well being of his little girl.

"He gave me this…" I said handing him a written prescription, he took it in his hands and studied it, reaching for his jacket at the same time. "He said I had, an overactive imagination and those will help."

"Does he want to see me?"

"No. he didn't say he did. They are supposed to help me from getting asthma attacks too."

"Well, good…if he says these will help, then we will give it a shot."

He stopped at the pharmacy on the way home. As I sat in the truck and waited, I wondered if Mae would be upset, seeing me walk into the door. Her husband was bringing me back into the house where I should not be welcome anymore, and how will I face little Jeanie…

She was sitting in her highchair, not to happy about eating her lunch, not to happy about seeing me either, from what I gathered anyhow. I went directly upstairs to my room without a word. Time flew by so quickly when I was by myself. I wish I had more, I just didn't have enough.

It had only lasted a minute, and then Larry walked in wearing his police uniform with a pill and a glass of water in his hand.

"There is no time like the present…Tomorrow you take one twice a day."

"For how long?" I asked swallowing my pill with a gulp of water.

"As long as it takes…The doctor will let us know…You haven't eaten all day, I suggest you come down for a sandwich."

"I can't…really I'm not hungry."

"All right then, I have to go to work for a couple of hours…I'll be home for supper, and you best be joining us."

"Yes sir"

As if I were a werewolf or a vampire, I waited until James and Josh were in bed before I took out an old boot lace that I had found, I tied one end to the spring of the bed, and the other around my wrist, only then did I allow myself to fall asleep. I wasn't the only one who was looking out for little Jeanie, she was in bed with her parents.

I began to feel the difference from within myself that very next morning. I felt calm and very much less worried of what The Casper family had thought of me; even little Jeanie, for if I had apologized to her now, she would probably sneer at me in a non understanding way. I apologized, that was all I could do.

And the Cylert pill I took again that morning was my little friend, I felt it easing me and my mind, telling me, that I'm all right, don't worry about this or that, I'll take care of you.

I went through the day with that in mind. My little pill was put to the test without warning. After Mister Dinn's History class, I felt the push from behind, and before I knew it I was up against a locker with Jim Tanner in my face.

"Trying to skip out on me…are you, you rat…?"

"Get your hands off me…!"

"Yeah or what…? You rat fink!"

This time it was a bigger and more confident teacher taking it upon himself to clasp onto Jim's arm.

"Come on Tanner; let me escort you to the principles office."

I was accused of nothing. Jim Tanner couldn't even accuse me of being afraid, because I surely did not show it, I looked pretty tough in my own way, and I had my friend; the pill to thank for it.

"Were you sick yesterday?" Gail asked as we walked over to our lunch table.

"Yeah, I was, still don't feel very well."

"Well, it's that time of year."

She simply replied without doubting me, she didn't pry, none of her friends did, they were just too nice. Sometimes I felt like I was in the twilight zone with them. Should I take it as a hint? Was I wearing out my welcome already?

"So...the Christmas dance is next week, you going Sam?" one of Gail's friends had asked.

"No, I...no."

"You know my little sister, don't you...? Katie Miller..."

"Oh, yeah I have her in my math class."

"I tell you a secret if you promise to keep it..."

"She wants you to ask her." Gail broke out in a chuckle.

"All I can say is that she won't say no if you do...so...you going to ask her?"

"I...I don't know...if I..."

"If you what...?"

"He doesn't know how to dance Gail..."

"No, it's not that...I don't think I will be able to get a ride over."

"Come on you can't live more than a mile away."

"I'm not going okay!" I said harshly then removed myself from the table.

I was not about to ask Mae or Larry if I can go to a dance after what I had done, and it was true, I didn't know how to dance. I didn't suppose, Gail and I were friends long enough for her to come over and comfort me, and she didn't. I sat there wondering if our short term friendship was over. I've lived on her complement too long.

Be careful what you ask for...You might just get it. I wanted to be left alone on my terms, not theirs.

I had thought about it in math class, Katie Miller sat one row over from me. I looked her way, she cracked a smile as did I. I was hoping I hadn't given her the wrong impression. I didn't ask her to the school dance.

Christmas came and went, I had gotten some new clothes and a song book, and oddly enough I was allowed alone time with me and my guitar, was it an understanding that was made behind my back? It didn't much matter to me just the same. I was in my own little world, day and night.

No more vivid dreams haunted me in the night. If I dreamed of my mother, it was subtle, her cries did not ring in my ear, yet her distant whimper disturbed me.

"Sammy, don't you care anymore about your poor mama...?"

"Go away...please, just go away..."

I heard the little one crying...no I thought, this was over my, pills were stopping these awful dreams. She was screaming, no it can't be me. Wake up! I told myself. And I did, thankful that I was in my bed,

I heard the screaming still. The bedroom light was just turned on. Larry stood in the doorway wearing his robe with his eyes upon me.

"It wasn't me…" I claimed with certainty, lifting my hand showing him that my wrist was wrapped and tied to the bed with the old boot lace.

He shook his head at me. "You tie yourself up every night…?"

"Yes sir."

"Your Cylert is taking care of your sleep walking." He said coming over to me, he took a hold of my wrist and began to untie me.

"What's wrong Dad?"

"Nothing, Jeanie just had a bad dream, go back to sleep James…"

"What are you doing?" Josh added.

Larry took the old bootlace into his hand. "Nothing…everyone back to sleep."

I had never kept my bootlace a complete secret, Mae must have seen it at least once or twice, when she stripped the bedding for cleaning. She must have had a clue of what I was using it for; she must have seen the chaffing around my wrist. I was hoping she did, I was hoping it was giving her peace of mind every night.

I felt less peaceful without it. It was my security, one of my friends. I will find another.

After little Jeanie's cries calmed, I heard Mae and Larry talking, again I could not make out their words, but I imagined, as far as my drugged mind would allow me, as to what they were saying.

After school the next day, I was sitting on my bed with my guitar, alone in the room, when Mae walked in with the clothes basket; she dropped an elastic type waist band on the bed beside me and then began to put clothes away.

"You didn't get it from me; it would be in your best interest to keep it in mind, I'm not telling you to use it, but if you choose to, well, there it is," she said continuing to put the clothes away.

I nodded, picking up the peace of mind; I stuffed it under my pillow. "Thank you."

"Like I said, you didn't get it from me; you must have fished it out of the garbage pail when I cleaned out my sewing basket."

"Yes ma'am."

"Well, it will be much easier on your skin than that dirty old bootlace…Don't you have homework to do?"

"No ma'am…"

The elastic band was not as easy to tie as was the bootlace; I had to use my teeth to assure that it was tied properly, much more comfortable on my wrist; this was a much gentler friend. I used it ever night for a week or better, and then one morning I woke up and it was gone. I knew Uncle Larry must have taken it away sometime in the night, he didn't say anything about it the next morning, and he didn't have to. It couldn't have been anyone else but him. He didn't understand, I needed it, I thought of a better idea. I found a long shoelace and instead of tying my hand to the bed, I tied my ankle onto the spring. I wore a sock to prevent chaffing. It was much easier on me; I should have done it that way from the start. I left it there for Mae to see for her peace of mind.

Summer was mine, I had spent it in the bedroom with my guitar while Mae enjoyed her family and her boys who would grow, and soon may feel the need to distant themselves from her, as I have the privilege to do. I jotted down some thoughts of mine on a notebook that I had rescued from being used for school purposes. I thought of ways I could make a song out of them. Time flew by; the twins always interrupted my time. I stuffed my notebook into my guitar case and slid it under by bed, time to get up and stretch my legs anyway.

I didn't ask; I assumed by now it was my chore to take out the garbage. Larry was mowing the lawn, I tossed the garbage into the can, and he motioned me over.

"Finish it up…!" he shouted over the roar of the lawnmower.

I took a hold of it with him walking away. Not angry, nor happy about mowing the lawn, I finished the chore and brought it back into the garage, the pollen in the air made me wheeze some, but I got over it without using my inhaler.

Inside, supper was cooking, I went upstairs to wash up, and briefly passing up the bedroom that I shared, I saw my guitar case on the floor and opened. I charged into the room. Both James and Josh were on the bed giggling at what they were reading in my notebook. The anger that I had felt inside was unbearable, and it demanded to be let out.

I took the twin who had my notebook in his hands and threw him to the floor, I dropped, sitting on his chest, and began pounding my fist into his face. With all my might I let my anger out. I didn't care if he was crying and pleading me to stop between blows.

"STOP!!!" Josh shouted out for his brother. He tugged on me, tying to pull me off, but my anger was much too fierce.

"DAD!!!" Josh screamed leaving the room.

The vigorous workout made me wheeze, only then, did I back away. James lay on the floor crying loudly covering his face with his hands.

Larry stormed into the bedroom with Mae following him; I suppose we were all gasping. My knuckles had blood on them, as I reached for my inhaler. James revealed his bloody face.

"This is enough…! I want him out! Do you hear me, I want you out!!" Mae screamed at me.

"Okay…" I wheezed.

Larry helped James off of the floor.

"I hate him! I hate him…Get rid of him Dad!" James cried.

"Come on, let's get you checked out."

Mae slammed the door behind her, leaving me alone in the room. My mind was setting; I wasn't going to be where I was not welcome one minute longer. I looked out the window as my breath returned, Larry was leaving with the twins, James held a rag to his face, and they drove away.

I crept down the stairs, if Mae was sitting in the living room, I was leaving anyway, but she wasn't. I grabbed my jacket and walked out the door, with the hope of never returning. I walked quickly, block after block, leaving the Casper home behind Me.:


Marshall raised his eyes from off Sam's words. He thought he should close this book. Sam would not be happy with him. Reading this is invading his privacy, what he had done to James was written proof…It was too late now, he will just have to get this book back into his apartment before he drops off his keys in the morning. He dropped his eyes back down to Sam's book…

I wasn't afraid, but would I be once my friend inside of me dissolves completely? Had I known ahead of time that I was going to totally lose it to the point of no return I would have snatched my pills from the cupboard before hand.

I should get off this street…go down a couple of more…go over a few more. I walked for more than two hours before I took a break. I needed to find the poor side of town; I felt that heading north was my best option. There has got to be a mission there, somewhere that I could curl up for the night and be fed breakfast in the morning, I could go from there. Maybe I can find people like me…somewhere I belong.

I wondered what the Casper's were thinking. Probably glad that I was finally out of their hair. Tomorrow I may make the missing persons list. Night was falling, I was tiring, but I had made it. I found a group of homeless people.

Sad, sad people, some talking to themselves over flaming trash barrels, what do they do in the rain, what do they do in the winter? I sat on the cemented ground near a dumpster as the sky darkened, still not afraid I watched and observed. A tall lanky woman walked by carrying a tote bag in her hand, her eyes caught mine; she walked backward peering at me.

"You need a blanket kid?"

"Yes ma'am."

"Ma'am…where did that come from kid?"

"I'm not saying."

"Do I look like a cop to you?"

I would have had to answer no on that one; she looked more like a prostitute, a slummy one at that, but I wasn't about to say so.

"No…unless you are undercover."

She laughed. "Yeah that's what this city needs, undercover cops to seek out the runaways…are you a runaway?"

"No…I'm just visiting."

She laughed again. "I'll get you a blanket, be back in ten…"

I sat there counting the homeless group, ten, no more than a dozen. Why were they here in Minnesota…why didn't they hop a fright train south, live on the Mississippi river like Huck Finn and Tom Sawyer? Some of them looked my way, I wondered if I was in someone's spot, if I were, I was sure to hear about it.

The lanky woman returned with a blanket, I had gotten a better look at her. Her face was caked with make up, and it appeared that she had a ruff day, as did I.

"Thank you ma'am…"

"Enough with the ma'am thing okay, what are you doing in a place like this…? Do you need bus money for the ride home tomorrow?"

"No…I'm…is the mission near by?"

"You are at that back door to the mission, but if you think you are going to get a free meal without a police ride home in the morning. Well you have another thing coming kid. In the morning you will see things differently…you will want to go home." She said as she reached into her pocket and pulled out a small handful of quarters. "The bus line is one block away, on Granville…If you decide not to take it, wait for me and we will talk about it tomorrow over lunch…okay?"

I nodded taking the quarters from her and slipped them into my pocket. "Thank you."

"Yeah sleep on it…and don't worry about these guys, they are harmless."

I watched her prance away, like I had imagined a prostitute would.

I covered myself in the blanket for the night was getting cool, this blanket was not dirty, ragged, or smelly, she must have lived near by I thought to myself as I cuddled with the gift, I even buried my head under it hoping no harm would come to me in the night.

The summer sun shinned through the woolly blanket treads, I squinted until my eyes adjusted. The homeless were reliving themselves over the storm drain in the alleyway with no pride or dignity. My heart ached for James and what I had done, no, I couldn't go back, but could I hop a fright train, how far would I get? My inhaler was not fresh, only if I was healthier.

I did what the others had done, reliving myself over the storm drain. They all lined up outside the back door of the mission for their breakfast, more had come, and I culled back down hiding behind the dumpster. I was hungry, but did not want to go in for that free ride home, the bus money was in my pocket, I didn't want to use that either. Instead I sat there waiting and wondering if that prostitute woman would return like she said she would if I was still, here. Yeah, her lunch is probably her breakfast. Bummed, I curled back up inside of the blanket. I dreamed of the chaos I had caused, "I hate him…I hate him…" I heard James cry.

"Kid…?"

I pulled the blanket away from my eyes to see that woman there. She didn't look quite the same, her face was without make up, and she was dressed more conservatively in denim. She could have passed for a regular woman.

"So you want something to eat?"

I folded up the blanket the best way I knew how on such a short notice and followed her past the homeless court to an apartment building near by. The place was run down; it was an ugly red with brown trim. We climbed up to the second level, the walls were thin I could hear the happenings inside almost every apartment as we passed them. Babies crying, children shouting, parents shouting, televisions blaring, the homeless were quieter.

Inside her apartment the scene was much more stable. Yes, it was run down, but tidy and glowed with a few candles.

"This apartment is dark. I'm not weird or anything like that, I just don't like bright lights…I'm not a short order cook either so you will have to settle for a couple of bologna sandwiches…one or two…?" She asked opening her refrigerator.

"Just one please."

"You don't have to be modest with me, I can see you are hungry, you're a growing boy…how old are you, twelve?"

"Thirteen…"

"Don't you think thirteen is a bit too young to be running away…? Are you just visiting…what are your plans?"

"I don't know, heading south?"

"Yeah…with what…? You have a wad of cash in your pocket other than that buck-fifty I gave you last night?"

"No ma'am." I replied quickly wondering if she had any intentions of robbing me if I had.

"You are not going to get very far before you call mommy and daddy, swallowing your pride kid."

"I don't have any parents…I'm an orphan."

"What happened to your parents?"

"My dad is in prison, and my mom overdosed."

"You in foster care?'

"Not any more..." I said as the woman set two sandwiches in front of me on a small coffee saucer plate.

She stood up against the counter stuffing her face with her own sandwich. "What'd you do...?"

"I got into a fight...beat a kid bloody...they were going to kick me out anyway...I did them a favor by leaving."

"So your politeness is just a put-on..."

"I guess so...Are you a prostitute?"

"No, I'm self employed...nobody, but nobody owns me or tells me what to do. My money is mine...What's your name?"

"I'm not saying, you can just call me kid...I'll get out of your hair in a minute anyway."

She laughed. "No I like you, I don't mind your company...you can stay a while, watch T V and decide what you're going to do...I'm going to go to work, if you leave, lock up...Don't steal from me kid."

"No ma'am..."

"Yeah I didn't think so; you don't look like the type..."


Full, from the two sandwiches I sat on her small tweed couch with the T V on. A bit dumbfounded I was over the situation I was in, the woman I really didn't know from Adam, had left for work. What did she want from me, could she possibly be that lonely to subject herself to harboring a runaway? It didn't make sense to me...I should go.

Why I didn't, I don't know. I spent hours watching the television wondering what was to become of me, if I stayed, if I left, if I took the bus back to the Casper's.

The woman had a phone, I didn't see any harm in calling, it was now after five, and Larry should be home by now, with any luck he will pick up the phone. I dialed.

"Hello?"

"Larry, I called—"

"Sam…! Where in the world are you!"

"I called to say that I'm sorry, tell that to James, and Mae."

"Tell me where you are, and I will come and get you…Sam!"

"No, I'm not coming back…I'm okay…I'm sorry."

"You are not okay…you need your meds. Tell me where you are at!!"

"I don't need them, I'm okay…bye."

"Sam!" I heard my Uncle Larry shout out before I hung up…

I felt bad about it, and wondered, he being a cop in all; if there was any way he could find me by the call I had just made, if there were, and he had went through the trouble I would be okay with that, cant say so much for this woman, a lessoned learned, don't harbor runaways.

A knock on the door bumped up my heart rate, I stepped over to the door.

"Who's there?"

"I should be asking that question…" A woman's voice called out. She knocked again.

It sounded like her, but I wasn't sure, I opened up the door.

"Where's Zee…?" She asked prancing inside.

"She is working…"

"You a new kid…? Oh, never mind…I'm going to hang out with you…" She said sitting herself down on the couch.

She pulled out a cigarette pack from her purse, and then pulled out a joint, from it.

"Smoke weed kid?" She asked before she lit it.

"No…go ahead…"

"Never heard of a goody-two-shoes runway before…" She said before she took a toke.

"I, can't smoke anything…I have asthma…What did you mean when you asked me if I was a new kid?"

"Oh…I don't know…I never seen you before, so you are a new kid to me, ya know…When is she coming back?"

"I don't know."

I watched her smoke the joint, now feeling some fear inside of me, why should I; I'm free to go anytime, she; Zee said so. Her mood was changing, to comfortably numb.

"What's your name?" I asked her.

"What's it to ya…?" She chuckled and then chewed on the remainder of the joint; I assumed she had then swallowed it. The smell got my head buzzing a bit, I didn't cough, and I didn't wheeze.

Zee walked inside, not at all surprised that I, and her friend were here.

"Can I see you for a minute Zee…?" Her friend had asked getting off the couch.

She and Zee walked into the back bedroom. The walls were thin, but not thin enough to hear what they were saying, and I wanted to know. I could leave now; I should, and forget I ever came in the first place. No, it was my wild imagination playing tricks on me, I had nowhere to go, and Zee was good to me.

I sat there until they returned; her friend said nothing, only left.

"Hey kid…I think it's time you shove off." Zee said pulling the pin out from the formed bun in her hair.

I nodded, not completely surprised. I said nothing, only grateful that I was able to leave. I left. My imagination was not as wild as I thought, something was up, I could have been of use to her, and her people that she claimed she didn't work for.

It was warmer than yesterday, I walked past the homeless court once again, and into the alley way, I still had that buck fifty, but I couldn't forget my pride and my words I had said to Larry.

A revved-up mustang pulled by and stopped in front of me, I took off running, but wasn't fast enough for the passenger who darted out and grabbed me. I was dragged into the car, immediately I began to gasp for breath.

"We got the right kid...he's got asthma all right!"

I reached for my inhaler and took a hit with a big bald headed man in my face, he clutched onto the collar of my jacket pinning me against the window.

"We are not going to hurt you kid." He said gritting his teeth at me. "We will let you and your Uncle, the Cop live if you keep quiet about your whereabouts today! You hear me?"

I nodded pumping my inhaler into my lungs once more.

"I mean it! It's a promise!"

"Okay..." I gasped.

He hit me.


I suppose it was hours latter when I woke with a pounding head, it was dark, lightly raining, and I didn't know where I was other than outside the city limits somewhere. I heard cars passing by, I saw the headlights, and the city lights in the distance.

As I made my way out of the bushes I vomited near the ditch, and dropped back down wheezing. The grass was wet, and I didn't care, I reached into my pocket, my inhaler was not there. I took in little air; I closed my eyes excepting death, I was okay with that…

"Sam…" I heard him say.

I opened my heavy eyes, felt like I had pennies on them. Larry was standing over me; he had his police uniform on.

"How do you feel?"

"I don't know."

"Your in a hospital…do you know why?"

"Yeah…I do"

"What's your last memory…do you know?"

"I was in the ditch."

"Who did this to you…?"

I shook my pounding head, I would never tell.

"Sam…was it the prostitute that you were staying with, when you called?"

"No…no!!! It wasn't…! It wasn't any of those people!" I gasped.

"All right, calm down…" He said placing his hand on my shoulder. "Sam, this is a serious matter, you could have been killed, and it's not far from being ruled an attempted murder…were you taken against your will?"

"I could have killed James…"

"I suppose it could have been remotely possible, you did bloody his nose and knocked out a tooth…he's got some bruises, and I'm not excusing what you did one bit, but your apology has been accepted…Now, tell me about this prostitute…did you know that she was, one?"

"No. Not at first…when I did, I left."

"And then what happened?"

"I don't know, a couple of guys…grabbed me, pulled me into their car."

"Can you describe the car?"

"No…I didn't get a good look at it."

"The color…large or small…? What about the men…can you describe them?"

"No…I was having an asthma attack."

"Before you had seen the car…? Sam? You saw the car; I know despite your flaws, you are bright and observant…Talk to me."

"I can't…" I cried, reaching for the oxygen tubes that led inside my nostrils.

"What are you doing, you have a touch of phenomena, let it be." He said pulling my hand away from my face.

"Why can't you talk to me?"

"I'm sorry…for what I did."

"Yeah, you totally lost it…it comes with holding anger inside…like a stick of dynamite ready to go off…Do you know that if you don't let out the truth about what happened to you, and who is to blame, it's going to happen again…? Why can't the bad guys get the raw end of the stick for a change?"

"They, said that they…would kill us, you and me, maybe even your family"

"That's not going to happen, Sam."

"How do you know?"

"Cause the bad guys lose, don't you think they deserve to?"

I nodded wishing I had him for a father all my life; I could have turned out a lot better. How lucky James and Josh were, and how I messed up my life, despite my efforts, I made the wrong decisions, and I wasn't sure if telling him the truth was one of them.

"Sam...?" He asked I imagined that he was pleading, not for my sake, but for his, he needed to solve this case for his own reasons.

"The guys in the car...a jacked up mustang, black...could have been a cobra...They knew who I was; they were looking for me...They knew who you were; they knew I had asthma...Did you report my disappearance?"

"Yes I did, yesterday morning, it was on the news."

"The prostitute...she, her friend, referred me as to the new kid...I don't know what that means, but it can't be good...When Zee figured me out, she told me to leave."

"Zee...the prostitute...when she figured you out?"

"Yeah...I'm sorry I messed up."

"Did the women, hurt you in any way?"

"No sir, Zee was very nice to me."

"Weaving her web on you...she was. What about the men, you said two men..."

"Yes...a big guy with a shaved head."

"Was he white, black...?"

"White...he had a tattoo on the side of his head...I didn't get a look at the other guy, honest I didn't."

"Can you describe the tattoo...? Was it a sword?"

"Yes it was."

Larry sighed deeply with a nod seemingly pleased, he lifted his eyebrows.

"Did I help you, sir?"

"Yes, very much…I'll see you latter."

He walked quickly out of the room.

I was glad to be of some help at my expense, I just hoped he would be safe. I deserved what had happened to me.


I saw a police line up on the television a half dozen times at least, but I didn't think it was this intimidating. Six of them in all, only one I was sure of, tattoo man.

Standing behind me, Larry put his hand on my shoulder.

"They can't see you Sam."

Yes, I've heard that too, it didn't make it any easier just the same; for there was one that probably knew I was standing on the other side of the two way mirror. I could only guess that Larry went out and arrested him. I didn't care for his expression even though his lips were closed I could tell he was still gritting his teeth, and I had imagined him saying…"Your dead asthma boy…"

"You recognize any of these men Sam?"

"Yes…number three…"

"Are you sure?"

I turned to him and the other two officers who stood as witnesses. They probably wondered if I was creditable after what I put my Uncle through.

"Yes sir."

I didn't mind waiting around for Larry at all, I could wait a week, and I didn't want to face the rest of the Casper family at all. It would be foolish to run again, Larry was right, I couldn't make it on my own. I have to live on the mercy of others, whether I was welcome or not. Uncle Larry trusted that I had learned my lesson, for he left me unattended in his office, I wasn't locked in, I know because I had checked. I suppose I could have snooped around at police files, but I was in no mood.

Larry walked in after some time taking off his weapon belt. The good, intelligent father never took his gun home; he locked it up in a drawer of one of those filing cabinets. I wondered if he had ever shot anyone before, I didn't feel it was my place to ask.

"You must be hungry for some real food after eating hospital food for three days. I've told Mae not to hold supper for us...I know a truck stop that makes one of the best burgers in town."

I wasn't hungry, but I didn't want to interfere with his plans by saying so. While we sat in a booth, I asked for one of their famous burgers, as did Larry. I could tell something was weighing heavily on his mind. I was beginning to feel like I was his pet dog that no one wanted except for him.

"Did you arrest him?"

"We are holding him, yes"

"Just holding him?"

"He's been booked...I can't discus much right now Sam, an investigation is in progress..." He sighed deeply. "Sam, we are also in the process of making other living arrangements for you...I have a couple in mind...their children are grown and out of the house...I'm looking out for your best interest as well. You will have the privacy that you need, and there will be no need in tying yourself up at night...You understand, don't you?"

"Yes sir"...I understood...people get rid of their dogs when they misbehave...

# *The Panes*

As Marshall continued reading Sam's story, he remains unaware of this one. His mother's.

Twirling the black phone cord around her finger, Gwen Banks wore an excited smile, sitting on her porch just outside her front door.

"You should have seen her face Nance—It was the most…! Just the most. Needless to say, Tom didn't have to give her the axe, she quit on the spot…on the spot, so the job is open if you want it…oh…Really? In that case, get me a job there…no just kidding; I will stick out the summer at the Dairy Dip,"

Gwen chuckled adjusting the strap on her sandal. "No…no, Tony is not even sixteen yet, and I wouldn't go for that anyway, not sure if he even would."

From across the green grassy field, the front door slammed, Jack Pane stomped out and then to his truck, the tires raised a lot of dust when he roared out onto the loop road.

"I have to let you go Nancy," Gwen remarked rising from off of the deck.

She came in; hanging up the phone then sprinted into the living room.

"He's back…! He just, just left the house."

Gwen's mother sat in her chair with knitting needles in her hands and an afghan on her lap only to shake her head in disappointment.

"Gwenie. We can't be running over there every time that lunatic comes and goes…" Her father remarked not taking his eyes from off of the wrestling match.

"Don't ask me either!" Tony bellowed from where he lay on the floor in front of the television.

"Come on honey…lets take Martha and David a piece of cake." Beth replied balling up her afghan and set it onto the floor.

"I want the both of you to high-tail-it back here the second he comes back."

"We hear you loud and clear." Beth replied entering the kitchen with Gwen.


"That's a good idea Gwen, why if it is the same shift you can give him a lift…He could be a nice boy if he didn't have that man as a father, now, he is probably ruined for life, cause they say the apple doesn't fall far from the tree…Yes, I hate to say it…or think of it for that matter, but he may end up just like his father…"

"What are you going to say to Martha…?"

"Well, Gwen, she has got to do this on her own, she has got to leave him. She can't expect him just to stay away."

"What about the restraining order?"

"Does no good if she drops or ignores it…" Beth replied as the two of them walked up to the door.

Behind the house, David sat on the grass leaning against the cracking white paint. He had a cigarette in one hand and a beer in the other.

Gwen came into his sight, His eyes widened.

"It's just me; I won't tell…I would hate to see you get in trouble." She said taking it upon herself to sit on the ground beside him. "When did he get out of jail?"

"Yesterday…" David said before he gulped the rest of his beer down.

"Your Mom forgives him…?"

David only nodded, and then took a drag from his cigarette.

"So far, so good, right?"

"It takes him a few days…maybe as much as a week before he starts pounding."

"Just your Mom now…or is he still beating you?"

"No…I got him good a while back…I don't think he will mess with me anymore."

"Good…he's afraid of you…that's a start, maybe he will leave your mother alone now too."

"I can't baby-sit her all of the time."

"I know…You are sixteen, right?"

"Yeah, why?" He asked butting out his cigarette.

"Well…do you want a job…? I can get you hired on at the Dairy Dip for the summer…and it's the same shift as me, so, I can give you rides…"

"Yeah...sure...But why me...? Don't you have any friends that want it...or does it really bite?"

"It's not bad, and you're my friend aren't you?"

"I don't know...I never paid it no mind."

"Well, you are going to have to start, because we will be working together." Gwen said standing up. "Be ready at nine thirty tomorrow morning."

"How do you know I have the job?"

"I just know...I told my boss, that I might have someone in mind...you weren't my first choice, but my first choice don't want it, so it yours."

"Alight, I will see you in the morning." David said with enthusiasm, lifting himself from off the ground.

"We brought you and your mother a piece of cake, so go eat it before your dad finds out."

"You kidding, I'll wait for him to get back and I will eat it in front of him."

"Not a good idea David."

"Yeah, probably not."

"Gwen...!" Beth called out.

Both Gwen and David came from out behind the house.

"Come on now, I want you to help me with the dishes."

Gwen nodded, knowing very well that she had already done the dishes.

"All right...Well I'll se you tomorrow David, nine thirty..."

"I'll be ready."

Together, they walked the short distance home,

"What were you two doing back there?"

"Talking, Mom, just talking…"

"I don't want you two getting sweet on each other…remember what I had said."

"The apple don't fall far from the tree…Mom we're just friends…David is like a year younger than me anyway."

"Your father is a year younger than me…just don't be getting sweet on him."

"He's not even my type Mother…" Gwen protested very much believing her words; she preferred the older, college type, like Carl Perry, who came to the Dairy Dip delivering his wide smile and sparkling white teeth.

He knew her by name, says he is going to law school, going to be a lawyer one day; he was just falling short of asking her out.


"What did Beth want?" David asked his mother as he plopped himself onto the couch.

"Same ole busy body she always is." Martha said putting the paper down onto her lap.

"She cares…so any jobs in the paper that you think you can handle?"

"One or two maybe."

"Are you going to do something about it this time?"

"It's not like I have transportation, we don't have a phone."

"I have a job…start tomorrow, I can save up for a car for you to use…and then, we can get out of here."

"It's not going to be that easy David…Jack won't leave me alone."

"We get out of here…! This place he calls his, you had better stick to a restraining order!!"

"Gwen, get you the job?"

"Yeah, it's for the summer, but it's a start…we will get out of here…we will…"


David lay in bed listening to his fathers loud truck pull into the driveway. His shouting always followed no mater what his mother had cooked for him; it was always too hot, or too cold, too spicy, or too salty. He heard his augment this time.

"What did you spend my money on when I was in the can…?"

"It's called child support; your son needs to eat, he needs clothes…"

"I NEED TO EAT!!! What do you call this slop!?"

"Jack." Martha cried.

"Don't you give me your excuses? Where did you hide my money?"

"I didn't hide any money."

"I'll have to find it myself!!" Jack shouted rising from his chair, he went to the cupboard and reached his hand inside, throwing the contents onto the floor, some dishes crashed breaking as they hit.

David grabbed a hold of his fathers arm and swung him around, slamming him up against the wall, Jack already wobbly on his feet held his stance.

"Give it a rest; there is no money for you! And if you lay another hand on my mother you are going to be sorry!"

Jack scuffled to his kitchen chair and dropped down; he picked up his fork knowing that he didn't lose entirely. He shoveled the food into

SAM'S SONG

his mouth with his eyes fixed on his son and his wife picking up the broken dishes and mess he had made, and because of it, He will let his son's words slide for now.


As always, David was worried about leaving his mother home alone with Jack. He spoke nothing about his new job to his father, nor did Martha, chances were, the day would be half gone before Jack realized he was gone anyhow, and that was a good thing.

He has never done it before, but this sunny morning he was sitting on the front step of the Banks home. Tippy their family dog timidly neared him with his head down low.

"Hey boy, what's the matter…?" David asked reaching out to pet the scruffy and thin terrier. This was the same dog that had barked for hours, nights on end. The same dog that Jack had threatened to shoot if he hadn't shut up, come to think of it, Tippy has been quiet lately.

"You're not so bad ole boy." David remarked gently scratching Tippy behind the ears.

The front door opened behind him, Gwen stepped out…

"You've been petting that dirty ole thing…? You're going to have to wash up good, the dog is sick…"

"What do you mean contagious sick?"

"No, just sick, my dad is going to take him out to the woods and shoot him once Tony leaves for camp."

"Why don't you guys just take him to the vet?"

"They can't help him, he's old and dying!" She huffed.

David stood, brushing off the dog's hair from him. He already was not sure of this job, and didn't take to kindly to Gwen talking to him like that, as if he were not going to wash up before he passed out ice-cream cones.

"I'm sorry; I guess I am so used to yelling at Tony…you all set?"

"Yeah…" He replied grateful for her apology, he now may be able to take orders from her, knowing that she wasn't as bossy as she appeared to be.


"Are you like, going to be training me in?" David asked while he rolled down the window inside of Gwen's car. Passing his house, he only briefly glanced.

"I guess so…You don't mind do you…? Really, there is nothing to it."

"No…I don't mind."

"Hey, do you have your license?" Gwen asked bringing down her visor.

"I have my permit…It really does no good with out a car."

"Well, you can save up for one…Can't you?" I mean I know how strict your dad is…"

"I don't call him my dad…"

"I know…I wouldn't either, the things he's done to you guys…I can't believe your mother lets him back every time."

"She's not normal."

"What do you mean, not normal?"

"Like yours…your dad is cool too." David remarked, not entirely sure that he was after hearing what he was going to do with Tippy.

"You think so…? I think he is a little…Well, he's not so bad…Do you think my mom is too pushy on your mom?"

"Not pushy enough…She don't listen to me…She needs someone to…I never know what I am going to find…one of these days he's just going to go too far and end up killing her…"

"Do you really think so…?"

"Yeah…"

"She needs to get a gun…do you guys have one? I mean isn't it legal to shoot someone in self-defense?"

"Of course it is…but your own spouse, I don't…maybe, if she would keep the restraining order in place…She could never shoot him…what if she missed? Or panicked? And she would have to be beaten up at the, time…You are talking about me…aren't you?"

"You couldn't do it…?" Gwen asked taking her eyes off the road to look at David in question, coming to a stop at the end of the loop road, to where the highway began.

"I rather not, but if it comes to it…I, I don't know…She's going to leave him, she says she is…And I'm hanging around forever…"

"Yeah, me neither…I am going to make something out of myself…"

"Going to college?"

"Me…? You kidding, my parents can't afford it…and making the B honor roll is not going to get me any scholarships either…I was thinking about moving to the city after the summer, and just checking it out, you know…My mom don't like it, but what can I do? There isn't any opportunity here…What about you…you're a senior this fall aren't you?"

"Yeah…I was thinking about getting into small engine repair, maybe being a mechanic."

"That's cool; there is money in that…You know the Dairy Dip is minimum wage?"

"I figured as much."

"Well it's going to be a warm day, we should be busy…"

David did wash his hands a good wash, Gwen was pleased, she handed him a smock. They jumped right into the routine. He was like most of the others she worked with, not entirely happy to be here, taking orders from people, and the young children who were dropping small change on the counter in front of him.

Gwen knew she was her boss's favorite, she seemed pleased to be here, even if it was a put-on, she wore a magazine smile for all of the customers who stepped up to her counter. Her heart fluttered when Carl Perry stood in front of her that afternoon, he too wore his dazzling smile, returning Gwen's.

"Can I help you?"

"What's good…everything?"

"Pretty much…"

"What about the steak and lobster?"

"Sorry, it's not on the menu." Gwen chuckled.

"How about you and me go somewhere that it is, Friday night…or do you have other plans?"

"I don't have any plans…"

Knowing that Gwen was holding up the line, flirting with a customer, David motioned the others to his side of the counter.

Gwen wrote her phone number down on a napkin, and with her smile she handed Carl Perry it, and an ice-cream cone. Her smile was genuine for the rest of the day.

"You did a good job today…" Gwen remarked on the drive home.

"I know, my boss told me."

"I know I'm not your boss Dave, but can't I complement you anyway?"

"Sure, if you want, but it's not like it is hard or anything."

"You don't like it, do you?"

"No, but it's a job for now, hey thanks…"

"You're welcome…" Gwen replied wondering if David was worried about his Mother right now, just the thought got her worrying about Martha's well being.

Her concerns were eased when she saw Martha sitting outside her door in her lawn chair, she had a glass in her hand, and no doubt it was probably laced with alcohol. Jack's truck was gone from the driveway, a short happy moment for Martha, Gwen guessed.

Gwen smiled and waved at her as David got out of her car, she waved back. "I'll see you in the morning Dave, same time."

"Okay." David replied shutting the door behind him.

Her Father was not home from work just yet, and it suited Gwen just fine, for somehow she would think her father would approve of her news, and she was just dieing to tell her mother about her date for Friday night.

Inside, her mother was at the kitchen table with a spiral note book opened in front of her, she was thumbing through a dictionary, reciting part of the alphabet keeping in tune with her best singing voice.

"L-M-N-O-P…"

Gwen chuckled. "Writing another letter to Aunt Vivian mom?"

"Yes and you never-mind, so what if I'm not the best speller around." Beth replied with a smirk on her face.

"What word are you looking for…?"

"You'd laugh…" She said still turning pages of the dictionary.

"No, I wouldn't…what is it?"

"Reap…as in we reap what we sew…"

"You're talking about Martha…right?"

"Of course I am…who else is reaping what they are sewing…? Is it Two E's, or—"

"It's R.E.A.P, mom…"

"Thank you…" She said writing it down, and then turning her eyes back up to her daughter. "What's on your mind?"

"I have a date, for Friday night…"

Gwen knew how to talk to her mother, letting the news out slowly, worked the best for the both of them.

"A college student, how old is this young man?" Beth asked setting the frying pan down onto the stove now giving her daughter her full attention she faced Gwen with concern.

"Mom, he's not that much older than me, I will be eighteen real soon anyway…I didn't ask him how old he was…Mom, he's going to law school."

"Oh…Law school…I suppose he is bright enough to date my daughter…Oh for heavens sake what are you going to wear…Tony!" Beth yelled.

Tony came jogging into the kitchen. "Yeah Mom?"

"Gwen and I are going shopping." She huffed taking the packaged chicken from out of the refrigerator. "I want you to fry this up, and put four potatoes into the oven."

"Are you serious Mom?" Gwen exclaimed in surprise.

"Yeah are you serious...I have to cook while you guys go shopping!"

"It's a special occasion, you mind your mother, and your day will come Tony." Beth replied ruffling her son's hair. "Tell your dad we will return, we are just going to Breton's here in Hudser.

Gwen was so pleased with this day, she did everything right, she loved her mother so much for understanding. With her, and her mother's excitement, how could her father be displeased about her upcoming date with the law student? She had to admit to herself she was falling in love with the dream of being well to do and worry free, even though she really knew little about Carl Perry, how could she be pondering marriage? It was just a dream, why can't she hold onto it, her mother was, what was the harm in that?

She loved the dress her mother helped her pick out; Beth smiled widely when Gwen walked out of her bedroom with it on.

"I need my camera..." She boasted.

Gwen posed for her, Beth giggled snapping the pictures.

Downstairs the doorbell rang.

"I think your date is here Gwenie!" Hank bellowed then went to answer the door.

He was pleased to see a handsome, clean-cut young man standing there, somewhat formally dressed in a dress shirt and a sweater vest. Hank raised a smile noticing the bouquet of flowers in his hand.

"You must be Mister Perry…Come in, please, Gwen should be ready in a moment."

"Thank you sir."

As the two men sat chatting about law school, reality was knocking on Tony's mind. He was too young to be considered a disappointment to his parents just yet. It wouldn't be acceptable if a rich, smart college girl with a promising career ahead of her came a calling on him. He felt very small here, sitting on the couch in front of the television with the sound turned all the way down. He got up and walked to the door.

"Tony…where's your manners son?"

"Oh, sorry, it was nice to meet you?" Tony replied with the doorknob in his hand.

"You too Tony…" Carl Perry answered with a smile.

It was nearly the longest day of the year, though it was evening the sun shinned behind the trees. A lawn mower was roaring across the way at the Pane home, it was David mowing the lawn. Tony shook his head looking at the fancy car that Gwen's date had parked in the drive.

"Rich daddy…I wish we were rich…" Keeping the conversation to himself; Tony added as he looked at David in the distance. "Yeah, you're not going to amount to anything either David Pane!" Tony picked up a rock from the driveway and tossed it into the field.

Gwen held a menu in her hand, as did Carl. She's never been in this restaurant before, she did not say so.

"Anything you want Gwen, money is no object. Did I tell you that you look beautiful tonight?"

"Yes, you did, thank you...It's a good change from that dull smock from the Dairy Dip."

"I agree...Your parents are pretty cool, old fashioned, but I like that."

"I don't mind their old ways either. So what are you doing with your summer?"

"My mother has her list of chores for me, besides it's a tradition, summers I spend here with her, and the winters I spend in Texas with my father, course when I'm finished with Law school I will get on at the firm with him...What about you...what are your plans?"

"That's funny...not funny, but I was just discussing my plans with a friend of mine the other day...I'm not sure, I was kind of thinking of going into the city and scoping out my options."

"You plan on staying close to home do you...?"

"I'm still undecided."

"What are your options...?"

"I think I will take the steak and lobster." Gwen said with a smile.

"I will too."

They both ordered, the waiter asked Carl for identification when he ordered a double shot of Scotch on the rocks. Gwen ordered a ginger ale.

"You don't mind do you?" He asked after the waiter had walked away.

"No, not at all."

"It's just that I get a little nervous on first dates."

Gwen was not that naive, she didn't believe that Carl was nervous at all, Lawyers are supposed to be good liars; Carl had a lot more practicing to do.

"So, how many more years of Law school do you have to go?"

"Oh…lots, I have five more years, but it's going good, I learned a lot from my father. I won't have any problem passing the bar when it comes to it."

"Is he a prosecutor or a defender…if you don't mind my asking?"

"Prosecutor…He's big, bad and mean, but that's where the money is…"

"Yeah, I guess so…"

"Did you know that Texas has the highest death row inmates in the country?"

"Yes. I think I've heard that recently."

Carl was pleased that Gwen wasn't as ditsy as she first appeared to him. His drink was placed in front of him. He took to it quickly, sipping it often so he could ask for a refill when the meal was delivered. A ringing came from a clip on his belt.

"Oh, it's my cellular phone, excuse me." He said pulling it from his pocket.

"Hello…Hey, Mike…what's up…? Yeah…Sounds like a blast." Carl chuckled, then he took a sip of his drink, he followed it by looking at his watch. "Give me a couple of hours…Yeah I'll see you there…Yeah. Catch you latter."

He hung up, and put the phone back.

"Sorry about that, Mike is an old friend of mine, from high school…He doesn't do much with his life but party, and odd jobs, it's a wonder why we get along and it's a good thing I only see him in the summer, but we have fun…and I'm enjoying your company too."

Gwen subtly smiled, she had some computation, somehow she believed that she might be going home after the dinner, instead of a drive or a movie, not that he had told her otherwise.

Dusk filled the summer sky; she may have some explaining to do for her early return. He opened the door for her and then pulled her close as she stepped out of his car.

"Do you work tomorrow?" He asked with his hands on her waist line.

"Yes, I do…"

"Well, maybe I'll see you, can I call you?"

She nodded saying yes, and they both turned their attention to the Pane home, and the shouting in the distance, two voices shouting.

"Get out off here…! Go…!" David demanded giving Jack a shove.

"This is my house…! You go!"

"What's up with them?" Carl asked.

"It happens all the time; it used to be worse, when David was younger…"

"We can do that!!!" David shouted barging into the house, where his mother was wiping her eyes with a course paper towel. "Come on Mother…lets go!" he demanded picking up his father's keys in his hands.

"We can't…where-…"

"You think you're taking my truck you got another thing coming!" Jack bellowed shoving himself into David.

"You want me to call the police?" Carl asked pulling his cell phone out from his belt line.

"I don't know, sometimes they calm down...it might stir more trouble if..."

Carl had dialed despite Gwen's doubts.


Jack lay on the front room floor holding his gut, he grimaced in pain. "Come on Mom!!"

"No David, don't stir up more trouble!"

"Fine...Stay here with him!!" He shouted with keys in hand he alone barged out of the house and stormed to his father's truck.


"Oh no..." Gwen cried, watching David peel out of the driveway.

"Was that David...?"

"Yes."

"Hey, Gwen...don't let this ruin your evening, the police will take care of this..."

"My evening is over isn't it...Go on, go party with your friends, and you best be getting out of here before the cops come...you've been drinking, and your driving, no fancy lawyer will get you out of a DWI." Gwen then walked away quickly to her front door.

"Gwen!" Carl shouted waiting for her to come to her senses, but she didn't, the door shut behind her. Carl Perry spat onto the ground and then got into his car.

Gwen came into her house crying, her whole family unaware of what happened until Beth saw her tears.

David had no idea where he was going, only that he felt more and more free with very mile he had put behind him, he couldn't go far, he had no money, and the gas tank was nearing empty as he entered the city of Minneapolis. What ever will become of his mother, well, she has it coming. He can find someplace to park in for tonight, sleep in the truck, and start fresh tomorrow.

Officer Larry Casper was making his morning rounds, alone in his squad car. This mornings meeting had provided him with a new list of stolen vehicles that may be in the area. Many went unnoticed, and those that were found, were found by accident, or natural causes, and this rusty old pick-up truck parked in a parking lot of a strip mall that wouldn't be open for hours yet certainly qualified.

He parked a distance away, and picked up his police radio. "Ten-forty-four, over."

David woke with the uncomfortable cramping in his leg. He lifted himself up off the front seat. A tapping on the driver's side window, he was disappointed to see a cop standing there.

Larry Casper had one hand on his gun belt as he backed away, David pulled the knob up that kept the door locked, and he opened the door.

"Hands on your head, where I can see them!" Larry shouted still keeping one hand on his gun belt.

"I'm not armed." David remarked placing his hands on the top of his head.

"Out of the vehicle, slowly."

181

David stepped out.

"Hands on the hood…now!"

He did so, and then spread his legs while the police officer frisked him.

"It's my ole mans heap, it's not like I stole it!"

"Stolen is stolen, he must be really proud of you, taking it without consent, don't suppose you have a driver license?"

"No sir."

"Don't count on getting one soon…Have you been drinking…any street drugs in the truck?"

"No sir, if there is, their not mine."

"You know how many times I've heard that?"

"I don't know…lots."

Larry cuffed him. "You are under arrest, anything you do or say can be held against you in a court of law…"

David sat in the back of the squad car while Larry searched the truck. Larry pulled out a check stub from Stillwater state prison from the glove box; it was issued to a Jack Pane. He was reminded of his ex brother in-law, who was still sitting there. This was how their son's turned out. He felt bad for the choice he had to make for Sam, but there was no other way, he supposed he should give him a call one day to see how he was doing.

Gwen was preparing for her work day, she hadn't had a good nights sleep last night, worrying about David, and then there was the frustration of last nights date that hadn't paned out well at all, so much for the dream.

There was a knock on the door; Beth was at the sink washing the breakfast dishes while Hank sat there with the weekend newspaper in front of him.

"It's Martha..." Beth said then let her inside. "Any word yet Martha?" She asked with curios eyes.

"Yes...He's been picked up...I need to ask you a favor, I have no one else to turn to..."


Hank was not happy at all, sitting behind the wheel of the Bank's family car, but there was no way he would allow his wife to transport Jack the ripper to the city to retrieve his truck and son, no matter if Martha had came along for the ride or not. He wanted no part in Jack even looking at his wife.

The tension was as thick and heavy as a fruit cake, yet it was silent, Hank didn't want to give Jack the satisfaction of small talk, and he didn't think it even existed in Jack's thick skull. Jack coughed and dragged on cigarettes annoying Hank, but he said nothing, for Martha was in the back seat doing the same.


Larry took it upon himself to follow the jailer to David Pane's cell, they had an understanding. The jailer opened David's cell at let Officer Casper inside. David stood from his cot and faced Larry.

"Your parents are here, seems your father is dropping the charges, does that make sense to you...?"

"No...not really."

"I didn't come in here blind, I read your father's rap sheet...I know of the years of abuse he has caused you and your mother...Did something happen last night in your home that you want to report?"

"What good would it do...? He's arrested for a day or two, six months tops, only to come back home steaming mad at us...My mother wont leave him...She's afraid to."

"And you want to leave...?"

"Course I do, I wanted to take her with me, but she won't."

"I can make a few phone calls and have you removed from your home if that's what you want...Of course my hands are tied in your mother's situation...the choice is yours."

"No. I can't leave her...but thank you anyway."

"Okay..." Larry replied then reached into his pocket for a small spiral notebook, he jotted down his phone number and handed it to David. "If you change your mind, give me a call...We can work something out."

"Thank you..." David said stuffing the phone number into his pocket.

"You're welcome and good luck to you." Larry said then nodded at the jailer.

"Thank you..." David repeated once more as officer Casper walked away.

Larry did not reply, he raised a smile just for himself.


Keeping himself content, Larry Casper left work early. He knocked on the door of the Anderson's. Earl answered the door, not completely recognizing him at first; for he was dressed in uniform. Larry lifted a smile.

"Hello, I'm Officer Larry Casper..."

"Right...right...come in please." Earl replied taking off his reading glasses. "Sally, we have company."

"Well. I can't stay long; I come to see Sam, if he's around...How's he doing?"

"He's no trouble, keeps to himself; sometimes we forget that he's here."

"Oh..."

"Earl, you make us sound like bad guardians...we know when he's here...he is doing very well, has himself a paper route, keeping his grades up..."

"Good...good, how about his asthma, how's that?"

"Well, he had a flare up in the spring, but with all the pollen in the air, it's no wonder, other than that he hasn't had a lot of problems...He's down in the basement if you would like to say hi."


Sam too, was content in his own world playing his electric guitar, he bothered no one in this home with his head phones on the music he made filled his ears.

Larry walked down the stairs to the finished basement; Sam was sitting on a couch with a guitar in his lap. Larry wished he could hear what he was playing for his own curiosity, no matter; it wasn't long before he was noticed.

Sam pulled off his headphones with wide eyes directed at his Uncle Larry now standing before him.

"What...?"

"You asked that as if you were guilty of something Sam...I just stopped by to say hi."

"I'm sorry Sir…Hi."

"You got yourself an electric guitar and all the fixings I see."

"Yes sir, with my paper route money."

"Do you still have the six string, Doctor Albey gave you?"

"No…I traded it in."

"Oh…I see that…For what you have here?"

"Yes…Did I do something wrong…Am I…getting transferred again?"

"No…no, Sam I just had you on my mind today, and I thought I'd come and say hello…I can't say that I wasn't disappointed that you refused to spend last Christmas with us…"·

"I'm sorry I didn't know that—"

"You didn't think that you were welcome…?"

"Well, Mae, and the kids."

"You are still a part of our family Sam."

"I like it here…we had a good Christmas…"

"I'm happy for you, I really am."

"Does James, forgive me, for what I did to him?"

"Yes, Sam I have told you that already…It's been a year since then, I teach them not to hold grudges."

"Then why is Mae…? She didn't want me back."

"Sam, we just wanted what was best for you…You said it yourself that you are happy here…Mae cares, I care. I'm sorry I've been a stranger lately but, I've been real busy, I just come to say a quick hello…"

"Sir, if it's all right, can I spend next Christmas with you?"

"Yes…I'd like that Sam…You take care okay…"

"You too, Uncle Larry…"

Sam sat there until his Uncle was up the stairs, and on the main level. Curious; he quietly crept up the stairs, and held his ear to the door.

"Does he spend a lot of time down there by himself?"

"Do you think we should be concerned about that?"

"Does he get out doors? Does he have any friends?"

"He has his paper route, and he is such a pleasure to have around."

Sally replied making Sam wonder if this was some kind of skit they had put on to boost up his self esteem.

"Okay, well his birthday is next month, July tenth…"

"Oh…no, we can't take your money, we will buy him a gift, be reassured…feel free to stop by, anytime…"

"Thank you, I'm sorry Sally is it?"

"Yes…Sally."

"I know, I should keep more in touch, do you have my number if you need to contact me for any reason?"

"Yes, we have it in our book Mister Casper…"

"I guess I'm concerned about him, he seems so withdrawn, if you two can encourage him to make some friends that would be great."

"Oh, I suppose we could be a little more assertive."

"Thank you very much…well I should be going."

Sam crept back down the stairs, and picked up his guitar.


Carl Perry had stayed away from the Dairy Dip all day until now; he stood outside leaning up against Gwen's car. It was Six o'clock. Gwen was not entirely surprised to see him; she didn't mind his presence either.

"Hi Gwen, how was your day…?" Carl asked without delivering his smile.

"It was long…" She answered standing before him.

"Want to go for a ride…?"

Gwen nodded. Carl took her hand.

"You know I didn't get a kiss last night…I thought I did the right thing in calling the police…I can't take you to a drinking party…Is that why you were mad?"

Gwen shook her head. "David is my friend and I just don't want to see him in trouble."

"He came back didn't he?"

"I guess so, today sometime."

"So, he gets a whipping from his ole man, he won't be doing that again." He didn't like the look on her face. "Come on Gwen; get over it…Do you want to play friends and neighbors with him, or do you want to play house with me…?"

Gwen pulled her hand away from his, he quickly took it back and somewhat forcefully he pulled her body close to his. He kissed her harshly and she didn't fight it. It felt good, someone taking control of her for a moment in this time of her life that she was so unsure of.

He wasn't so bad; she knew she shouldn't have given herself away like she had. She was almost certain that if she hadn't, she may have lost him. And knowing that he had the protection made it so much easier to give into his needs. He told her that he had loved her, and he even talked about her leaving for Texas with him come end of August. She had a decision to make, and she would secretly make it in the weeks to come. Yes it was fast, but right now she was contently pleased, to be loved for no reason other than being herself.

She pulled into her parent's driveway, noticing that the Pane home was dark and quiet. She hadn't realized how late it was, yet the summer night was warm, and stars twinkled in the night sky. Late or not, her home was lit. Her parent's were both in the living room.

Gwen dropped her subtle smile, ever so slightly, she had a feeling that it still showed through giving herself away.

"We were worried!" Beth announced.

"You could have called, let us know, if you had plans." Hank added.

"I'm sorry; I know...Carl and I went for a drive and then a movie."

"He's got one of those fancy cellular phones doesn't he?"

"Yes dad, I wasn't thinking...So, how did it go today, did Jack drop the charges?"

"Yes he did...David wanted to know if he still had a job."

"He's still got the job; I explained a little to my boss, we work in the morning..."

"If he's on our step he does...you are not going over there and knocking on that door in the morning...you hear me?"

"I hear you." Gwen replied.

"Your boyfriend...is he a gentleman?"

"Yes dad he is..."

"Off to bed, we're bushed; it's been a long day."


Gwen pushed everything out of her mind and slept until her alarm went off at seven a.m. She wondered if David may have an indication that he no longer had the job because she didn't get the message through to him. After she showered and dressed, she went outside and looked across the green grassy field, suppose she didn't knock on the door. That window has to be his bedroom window, the one with the red and black curtain that had a Harley motorcycle on it. She should check before her parents got up.

The window was partially open; the bottom of the curtain blew inward from the breeze. Gwen tapped lightly on the thin window it rattled some.

"David." She called just above a whisper.

David woke, not fully believing what he had just heard, he sat up in bed and then slipped on his jeans.

Gwen tapped once more. "David."

David pulled the curtain back to see Gwen standing outside of his window. Her face lost all expression, just seeing his. His eye was blackened, and his lip, caked with a bloody scab. She shook her head, and her heart sank.

He motioned with his head, as if to say he will meet her outside. She stood near the front door and he came outside.

"What happened…?" she nearly cried.

"I don't win them all. He hit me with a chair…Forget the job if I still had it…I can't go to work looking like this."

"It wasn't worth it, was it?"

"I don't know, maybe it was…I met this cop, he said he can get me out of here. All I have to do is say the word. I can't stay here Gwen" David said with tears flooding his eyes. "Even her, she's ticking me off…she told Jack that I had a job, and Jack wants me to pay rent. I'm not going to work to pay him."

"Rent…? You've got to be kidding; you're not even seventeen yet…"

"I'm thinking about giving this cop a call."

"Do what you have to do…"

"I can't…he will end up killing her…I don't know what to do…" He cried.

Gwen opened her arms, he did not take the hint until she stepped closer to him, and even then he had hesitated before he went into her embrace. He was not the only one with uncertainties. What was the right choice? She didn't know hers, let alone David's.

He held her tightly, Gwen didn't mind much, she asked for it. She wondered if anyone ever hugged him. When, he backed away, he was wiping his tears.

"David…do you have a gun in the house?"

"Huh…" he scoffed with a chuckle. "Yeah, a deer rifle, the ole man hasn't hunted in years,"

"How's your mom, did he hurt her last night too?"

"No, it was my turn; I didn't see that chair coming until it was too late."

"Well, I have to get ready for work, anytime you want to use the phone, just come over…I'll see you latter."


Beth was now pacing the floor with her own worries, she was a bit angry when Gwen came inside, and just the same she kept her voice down.

"What did your father tell you…?"

"Mother, I'm nearly an adult; I should be able to make my own decisions."

"Why were you hugging him?"

"I wasn't hugging Jack I was hugging David, just because he needed one Mother."

"We don't approve what he did, and neither should you…"

"I don't Mother…" She had told her what had happened last night as far as she knew, until Beth saw things in her perspective.

"Only two more weeks until camp, mom…" Tony happily remarked coming into the kitchen, he opened the refrigerator door and took out the juice carton.

"Oh, yes camp…" Beth huffed. "Gwen will you cook for your father while we're gone?"

"Sure, if he doesn't mind leftover's every other day."

"I'm sure he won't mind…I wish I could get away with that at camp Big Pine."

"How many cooks is there Mom?"

"Hopefully enough this time around…Why do you want to join in…? Oh, no heaven forbid, you have a boyfriend to tend to…"

"It's not just that mom, I have a job…You had fun there with the other ladies last year."

"Oh, I know, It's not so bad…If nothing else I will recruit Tony."

"No, mom…" Tony chuckled.

"I got to go." Gwen said then exited the home.


Hank was tinkering under the hood of his pickup when he sensed someone looking over his shoulder; he turned to see David standing behind him. Hank had been filled in on what had happened last night and under those sunglasses he knew David wore a black eye.

"Thank you for your help yesterday; this is for gas and your time."

David announced with a ten dollar bill in his hand.

"Oh, no…I can't say that it was my pleasure, but I won't take any money." Hank replied wanting to ignore the kid in hopes that he will go away; he wanted no trouble and no more part in their family squabbles.

"Well, then, I will just have to say thanks…What seems to be the problem?"

"What…Oh, nothing that I can't figure out, I have a short somewhere, in the wiring…It's my starter."

"Do you mind if I take a look at it?"


A distance away, weeding her garden, Beth was satisfied that her stubborn husband was getting some assistance in dealing with the problem. Hank was not mechanically inclined, yet he had insisted that he had some knowledge about everything under the hood.

Then there was David who spent hours under the hood of his rotten father's truck while he was in prison. He had taken it out more than a dozen of times since then, but they will never tell. There was no question that David may know a little more than Hank when it came to mechanics. It is too bad that Tony hadn't had interest in experimenting under the hood with his father; instead he was off with one off his friends for the day.

A bit worried, she was, the mad man hadn't done it before, but he may come a storming over at any time.

Hank and David worked on the truck half of the afternoon. Hank was happy with the results as was David; He refused to accept any money Hank had to offer.

"No sir, we're even…"

193

"Well then, tell your parents that I had accepted the gas money, and keep that money for yourself,"

"Oh, my ole man doesn't know about it anyway…but thank you."

"Thank you…Would you like to come in for some ice tea?"

Beth was sitting in the living room knitting her afghan when the two of them entered the house. The sick old terrier was lying on a blanket inside of the doorway. David knelt down to pet him; he took off his sun glasses.

"The starter is working like a fine tuned instrument Beth."

"That's wonderful, thank you David." Beth replied stepping into the kitchen seeing the attention that David was giving to Tippy. "I'm afraid the old boy there is on its last days."

"It was nothing." He said saddened for Tippy's fate. How could Hank just walk the old dog out into the woods and do the deed? David found himself wishing that the dog will die on his own before Hank had the chance.

"He's got a knack under the hood." Hank remarked pouring the iced tea, and then he nearly gasped seeing David's entire face.

"Can I use your bathroom to wash my hands?"

"Of course you may, it's up the stairs, first door on your left." He waited until the sound of David walking up the stairwell faded. "Why that no good for nothing son-of-a-…"

"Hank, remember your blood pressure…"

"What do we do Beth…wait for the lunatic to kill one of them? I'm going to have to make a phone call."

"Now, now, it will just stir up more trouble, Gwen say's that David has a phone number to call, and it's up to him to use it. We just need to stay out of it, or you and I might be regretting something that we shouldn't have reported."

"What if we regret saying nothing for something that we should have reported?"

"I don't know Hank…its nothing that they haven't heard before…"

Their discussion was short, and went nowhere, as it always had. And David felt somewhat exposed, it was an uncomfortable feeling not knowing if he had wore out his welcome, or was it his face and what it represented. He drank down the glass of ice tea and then politely excused himself.

Leaving the Bank's home, he learned that his father truck was gone; he probably went to Shaver's bar until he runs out of money or gets kicked out, which ever came first, and with any luck he would be to exhausted, to drunk to raise a fight, which was always a good thing. Then there always was that hope that Jack would never return under various reasons, all of them were acceptable to David, and his mother will just learn to deal with it.

All was acceptable for tonight, David had heard his father's return, and the vomiting he had done out side before he had entered, he then staggered into the bedroom, meaning tomorrow may not be so bad either.

Shortly after, another car was heard down this loop road, it had to be Gwen, she had been keeping long hours, and he was no dummy as to whom she was spending those hours with, the new boyfriend, the one with the fancy car. From his window, David watched her enter her nice family home. If she were in trouble, it would be settled the Brady Bunch way, no harm will come to her. Another day has passed for him and his mother, and so many more to go.

Strangely enough her parents were in bed, apparently not resting soundly. Hank came out to the hallway while Gwen was going into her bedroom.

"Another late movie…?"

"No, dad we were just talking…"

"What are your plans with him? You know he is only here for the summer."

"Yes, I know…goodnight."

Her father sighed, unsure if he should rebuttal for she will be an adult of eighteen in another month, and he did not want her to use it against him.

Gwen supposed she may have to have a talk with her parents soon about her plans to leave for Texas with Carl Perry, they probably wouldn't understand, yes it's a fast decision, but one that is required and she didn't think that she will be changing her mind in the weeks to come. They want her to be happy and finically stable in the future, this may be it, her parents need not worry about her, they should save their worrying for Tony's future. She will wait until her mother comes back from Camp. Her life will change, and if it does not work out she can swallow her pride and come back here.

Tomorrow was her day off; she had Carl's address where his mother lived, she was nervous about meeting her. Carl had portrayed her as high maintained; she owned and ran a hair salon here in town. Neither Gwen, nor her mother ever went to it for it was costly and ritzy. How is she going to explain that one to her?

She was a bit embarrassed driving her clunker of a car to this posh neighborhood, if the town of Hudser had one, this is where it was. And more humiliated parking it next to the two fancy cars in the driveway; she parked far enough away to avoid the clash that it might set off. She guessed that she can leave it behind when she leaves for Texas, perhaps Tony will have some use for it.

No one looking out for her, she somehow hoped that the door may open before she had the chance to knock, no such luck of having an overextended welcome. After knocking, she rang the door bell. After a long moment, the ritzy woman answered the door.

With a phone up to her ear, she wore a magazine smile. Her thick poofy hair was already set for the day, as was her make-up.

"Got to go baby…see you latter." She hung up the phone. "Come in, you must be Gwen, I'm sorry I have to take a rain check on our lunch…I had everything prepared too, it's a bummer I've been called in to the salon. You know I own the finest one in town, Pearl's…"

"Yes, I've heard, it's a fine place." Gwen replied lifting a smile as hard as it was.

"Oh…baby, I will have to give you a free consultation, then we can chat some, again I am so sorry, but I have to run."

"I see, ah is Carl here…?"

"Oh, yes he is…just give him a holler, he will get up…I suppose I can do that. Where are his manners, you are only ten minutes early…" She panted and then sprinted up the stair well.

It was one o'clock; they hadn't been out that late last night. She may need the rest of the summer to make her finial decision.

Pearl came back down the stairs. "He's getting up…out all hours of the night It's no wonder he wants to sleep all day…He doesn't take you to his drinking parties does he?"

"No…"

"Well thank god for that, I guess we should excuse his behavior, he does study hard, and he will be a fine lawyer one day…Well I must be going, hope to see you again soon, and again, I am sorry."

"No problem ma'am." Gwen replied before Pearl left.

She sat there and waited, and then waited some more, before she took it upon herself to leave. So much for spending a nervous summer afternoon with two people she so much wanted to impress despite her clunky car, her fifteen dollar K-mart summer outfit and her six dollar haircut. She will go home, perhaps call Nancy for a pep talk, much too early to talk to her mother about this. She pulled into her driveway grateful that she was alone, Mom must have gone grocery shopping, dad was at work and Tony's ten speed bike was gone.

Across the way things appeared to be quiet, although Jacks truck sat in the drive. Gwen sighed, and then gazed out to the edge of the property line. David was walking into the woods with a fishing pole and tackle box in his hands. She knew that the Fox River was near, somewhere out there.

Much too curious to let it go, she walked quickly to the edge of the woods where David had disappeared from. She was amazed of the path she had found, it was well groomed and so define. She thought about calling out to him, but chose not to. He might not want to be bothered, probably don't want no company either. She stayed behind and slowly followed the path. All these years, some boring summers went by with nothing to do, her and Tony could have made their own path out to the River, and all this time David had found a way to occupy himself.

After following the path for nearly a half of a mile, she could hear the rippling of the running River. She stopped just short of the clearing taking on the sight that she could see. David sat on a rock in front of the River setting his pole down.

"Hey Gwen do you want a can of coke?"

Gwen shook her head raising a smile coming out into the open where David reached into his tackle box. "How'd you know…?" She asked coming out into the open almost forgetting the upset she had just a short time earlier.

"I just did, I saw you…" He said handing her the soda.

"You only have two, were you saving one for later?" She asked almost in awe of the peaceful view that surrounded them.

"Course I was…I wasn't expecting company when I packed it."

"This is way cool…do you come here a lot?" Gwen asked sitting herself on the grass, she popped the coke. "This is way cool."

"Yeah, as much as I can…"

"You're not mad are you?"

"No…if I knew how much you would have liked it, I would have showed it to you a long time ago."

"I can't believe this; I guess I just didn't realize… What a place to get away to, did you clear the path?"

"Little by little, hey…Feel free to come here any time you want."

"Thank you…so do you catch any fish in this River?" She asked as she walked up to it. "It looks deep."

"It is, almost six feet in the center. I catch fish almost every time I come here and get a lot of pan fish, and when the time is right I catch a few Cats'."

"Catfish…?"

"Yeah, not your typical house cat...They mostly bite at night, I come here and start a campfire, a beer and a cigarette if there is any to lift, bug spray and I am set."

"Jack doesn't give you any trouble when you come down here?"

"You kidding, he likes eating the fish, and no, he never comes down here, I think it's too far for him to walk...you kept up pretty good..."

Gwen sat back down and watched him bait his hook. He kept the conversation going.

"Do you fish?"

"No, can't say that I ever had, my dad has taken Tony fishing on the St Croix a couple of times; he has a friend that has a big boat."

"Yeah this is small time compared to the St Croix."

"No not really, I mean if you can catch Cats here."

"Well if you want you can tell him about this place, we can hang out and fish, your dad is cool."

"I heard how you helped him out yesterday; with his starter...You know if you could give me a hand in changing my oil, I can give you a few bucks for it."

"Not a problem, I noticed it's sounding a little ruff, you might want to change your sparks and plugs too." David said as he cast his line out into the River.

"Sure, if you can tell me what kind to get..."


"Sorry I don't want to go back to the Dairy Dip, you know Jack will have his hand out, and I just can't give him the money I worked for."

"I totally get it Dave...Hey your bobber is sinking."

"I have a bite." He said with excitement tugging on the line, he

SAM'S SONG

reeled in and pulled out a large fish.

"It's a big one, what kind is it?" She giggled.

"It's a Cat..." David answered taking if off the hook. "Are you hungry...? There is enough for the both of us."

"You're not serious, you are going to clean it and cook it here?"

"Yeah, why not...there is a pan in that cooler over there."

"Over where...?" Gwen asked and the spotted between two trees some sort of lean-to, made with logs and tied with clothes line rope.

She held her smile taking the old cast iron frying pan from a cooler that was loaded with some necessities, a cooking spatula, a fork, a plate. Coming back with it she turned her eyes while David gutted the fish onto a flat rock nearby the bank of the River. "Looks like you had a lot of practice...we are going to need to start a fire, I will find some wood."

"Ah, Gwen, dry wood, not rotten, and we are going to need some twigs."

"Right..." She replied, nearly skipping out and back onto the path.

David left the unwanted Cat fish remains on the rock from where he had cleaned it, he tossed the fillet fish into the pan. He heard the scream; David took off running up the path. Gwen ran right into him, nearly knocking him over.

"There is a bear David...! A bear!"

"Was he chasing you?"

"I don't know...It's a bear...!" She cried putting herself behind him.

"It's all right Gwen he's not going to hurt you. Stay here, I will find some wood."

"No Dave, don't leave me here." She pleaded staying close to him while he picked up a few branches and twigs.

201

She followed him back to the River, trembling with fear. "How do you know he's not going to come charging at us?"

"He's just curious, he hangs out here Gwen, and I should have warned you." David remarked cracking sticks and then dropping them into the homemade fire pit. "I leave him fish guts, he waits out there until I am gone before he comes out and eats them...I know, I've watched him."

"That doesn't make me feel any better." Gwen answered nervously, keeping her eyes on the path ahead of her.

"Do you want to go back now...?"

"No...get the fire going...he won't come near the fire, right?"

"He won't, Gwen, he's a black bear, they rarely attack, this one has never bothered me, and I won't let it bother you either." He struck a match and knelt down to the fire pit, shortly a flame arose.

Though it was still warm out and the afternoon sun shined down onto them in this semi shaded place, Gwen did not mind one bit when David sat down beside her. She was warm as was he with some smoke from the fire in their eyes; he turned the fillets over with the fork.

"Can you do me a favor and don't tell your dad about the bear...I don't want him to come out and shoot it come Bear hunting season."

"He doesn't hunt Bear...don't worry I wont...I don't tell my parents everything you know."

"I barley tell mine anything...Your dad is cool an all but why is he going to put a bullet through your dog just because it's sick?"

"So he don't suffer...It's what people do when a dog is sick."

"I'm no dummy I know that, but people don't get shot because their sick, they have to suffer until they die."

"Well that's why there are hospitals and morphine, to make it easier on them. It's a God thing, you know, thou shall not kill…"

"It's short and to the point, does it just mean people?"

"Dave you don't have to listen to Tippy whine when she is in pain…It's not a good sound."

"Can't you guys find a potent pill to give her, instead of leading her off into the woods with a rifle in your hands as if she is going for a trusty walk?"

"You are really bumming me out when you put it that way…"

"I'm sorry…I just couldn't do that to a sick ole dog."

"My dad has some heart pills…"

"To slow it down or to speed it up?"

"I'm not really sure, he has abnormal rhythm." Gwen replied now taking her eyes off of the path entry and focusing on the fish frying in the pan.

"Give me a couple of those I'll mix them in with my ole man's fish tonight, and with any luck he will keel over."

"Are you serious?"

"No…I don't want to go to prison on the count of him."

"So, you are going to fish some more today…?"

"Yeah, we don't have anything for supper…If you want to go home after we eat I'll walk you home and then come back." David replied and then forked out a fillet onto the one and only plate.

He ate his fish out of the pan, picking it up with his fingers. She helped him wash the few dishes in the river.

"You ever swim here…?"

"Yeah, lots of times…It's my home away from home in the summer."

"That's funny, I never noticed…"

"You never needed to…" He answered placing the pan, plate and cooking utensils back into the old cooler. "You ready to go?"

"Yeah…"

David bunched up some sand putting the smoldering fire to rest. Gwen stayed close beside him as they started down the path.

"So what did you name him…?"

"The Bear, how'd you know I named him?"

"I just do…What is it…Smoky, Yogi…?"

"Wizard."

"Wizard, from the Wizard of Oz…?" Gwen chuckled.

"Maybe, yeah…"

"So what kind of…gift did he give you?"

"The wizard didn't have anything to give."

"Were you already brave with courage before you first ran into him…? Because I sure am afraid."

"No, he got me a little nervous; I threw all of my fish to him and took off running for home."

"Was he coming at you? I thought you said he stays away."

"It was a couple of years ago…He wasn't coming after me, he was just standing in place, in the brush grunting. He hasn't got my catch since, I leave him their guts."

"So he did give you courage, right?"

"Yeah, whatever Gwen…"

"That's a nice story…Thanks for sharing it with me."

"It's your turn…What are you looking for, some rich guy with a fancy car to sweep you off your feet?"

"That's not fair…"

"The truth hurt…" David cringed, his words just slipped out, but he meant it just the same.

"I'm not going to run off and marry him, and maybe I will, but for now I can date whoever I please."

"Yeah, well just make sure that he is pleasing you too."

"Where do you get your manners?"

"I don't know much about manners, I just know what's right and wrong. You will only be hurting yourself if you end up marring him because he's got money. Lawyers make a living out of lying, and you are not going be able to tell the difference between a lie and the truth."

"How can you say that about someone you don't even know…?"

"Because it's your day off, and you were supposed to have lunch with him today, and you weren't gone long enough for it."

"They told you…? My parents told you…? Which one was it, my dad?"

"What does it matter…? You want to talk about it?"

"No, I don't…! I can see myself the rest of the way." She huffed and then quickly walked ahead and away from him.

David sprinted into a jog beside her. "I can't go back just yet I have to give Wizard some time to eat…I'm not ready to test his courage yet, you know."

Gwen slowed into the walking pace that they had both began with. "No, I wouldn't want to either…"

Beth entered the kitchen as Gwen entered. "Where have you been? Carl has been calling; you were supposed to have lunch together today…"

"I am aware of that Mother…"

"Well, where were you? I was so worried that, that sick man was holding you captive or something, do you know I was just short of knocking on that door, and you know how your father feels about me going over there when that lunatic's truck is in the drive."

"I went for a walk, a long walk."

"What for, you were supposed to—"

"I know Mom!!!"

"Don't raise your voice to me like that Gwen!"

"I'm sorry…Carl's mother called off the lunch…Carl wasn't there, something must have came up I guess…I didn't think that I was supposed to wait around for him."

"Yes, he thought that there was some sort of misunderstanding…Why don't you give him a call. You mustn't lose a good man like him Gwen,"

She was hesitant and unsure who she was calling Carl for. Still the same she was happy that her mother had left the room.

"Hello…?"

"Carl it's me, Gwen…"

"What's up, why did you leave?"

"Because I was sitting in your mother's house by myself…"

"You weren't by yourself…I was coming down, I just needed a minute…And where were you? I called and got no answer, called again and your—"

"I went for a walk…I don't need to explain every thing to you, where were you last night…? Do you have to party with your friends every night?"

"My mother told you…? Hey Gwen, I'm on summer vacation, I

have friends I have to tend to…I really thought my mother was going to keep you company until I got down there…She left, why didn't you just come on up…?"

"I have morals, I really not that kind of girl, you were my first…"

"I appreciate that…I want to be your last too…Marry me."

"No…I can't make that decision yet…if you are serious…We've known each other for such a short time."

"Then you will come to Texas with me, to test the waters?"

"I have another month to decide Carl."

"You're right…it is much too soon to be talking about marriage, we will live together and take it from there."

"What do you see in me Carl…?"

"A beautiful girl that I care a lot about…Are we on for dinner tonight?"

"My mother is expecting me home for a change, maybe tomorrow night, if you'd like."

"Okay tomorrow night it is…"


Gwen helped her mother with the dinner dishes she was deeply saddened, almost in tears, but relieved that her father would not be leading Tippy out into the woods. Outside night was falling; Hank was on the edge of the property line digging a hole. Inside Tony sat against the wall near the doorway he held Tippy on his lap; he had tears in his eyes as he petted the deceased dog. Now he would not have to come home from Camp only to see a grave as a statement of his dog's death. It was about time he dealt with these issues, for the life of her, she didn't understand why her parents kept him somewhat sheltered from these issues.

"Take him outside honey…" Beth said with a cry in her voice.

Tony nodded and continued crying and then carried the dog outside. Gwen did not feel that she needed to be present; she went up to her room and cried, with her thoughts, she fell asleep and woke a few hours later. The house was dark, everyone had gone to bed.

She went down to get a drink of water; it was nearly eleven-thirty. She gazed out the window, Jack's truck was gone, and David's bedroom light was on from what she could tell. She went outside; it was a beautiful starry night. Not afraid that the Bear may be around, she walked across the yard and into another.

As she has done once before she tapped lightly on the partially opened window.

"David…?" She tapped again, "Dave…?"

After a moment he turned the curtain back to see Gwen standing there. "What's wrong?" He asked with wide eyes.

"Did I wake you up…?"

"No…no…" He lied. "What's up?"

"I just thought I'd let you know that Tippy died tonight, naturally."

"I'm sorry…you need help burying him…?"

"No, my dad and Tony buried him a while ago…I saw your light on and I thought you might want to know."

"I'm sorry…"

"Thank you, well I'll pick up the oil and spark plugs tomorrow…" She said handing him a twenty dollar bill. "Is it enough…?"

"Yes, more than enough…" He answered taking the money from her hand. "You have tomorrow off too…?"

"Yeah, I'll leave in the morning and let you mess with it in the afternoon, take your time, I wont be needing my car for the rest of the day."

The sound of Jack's truck was heard coming their way, the headlights neared.

"It's your dad...!" Gwen panicked ready to take off into a run for her house. David grabbed her arm.

"No! There is no time, he will see you." He gasped opening up his window fully; he then grabbed her and pulled her inside.

"I can't be in here! I can't."

"Shhh...you will wake up my mother...I'm sorry you have to get in the closet." He remarked franticly just above a whisper. He opened up his closet and shoved her inside. She plopped down onto some shoes looking up at David terrified. "Please be quiet, I wont let him hurt you?"

"Do you think he seen me?"

"No, I got you in-time..." He shut the door, leaving her in complete darkness.

Her heart pumped wildly in her chest. She quickly cleared the shoes out from under her until she was sitting on a solid floor. From the crack under the door the bedroom light had went out. The front door opened and then slammed shut leaving her wondering if she had been seen by the mad man. She should have broken free from David's grip and dealt with the conciseness, at least she would have been doing it in the safety of her own home.

He was cursing in the other room, perhaps it was the kitchen, banging things around.

"Martha...!" He shouted walking through the house, and into another room. "Fix me something to eat!!!"

Gwen wanted to leave now, why couldn't she go out the window from where she came? She heard things that were alien to her happy home. Perhaps Martha was slammed up against the wall and slapped. David got out of his bed and left the room.

The yelling and screaming, the ruckus and chaos that was occurring while she sat there helplessly, she dared to move in this tight spot that she was in, and felt it was safe enough to do so. She knocked over something and her heart raced again, was she heard, how could she be heard with all the commotion that was going on? Through the darkness she felt for the heavy object that had fallen against the closet door. It was the rifle, the deer rifle that had been brought up once or twice, she thanked god that it hadn't gone off and at the same time wondered if it was loaded.

How could David and his mother live like this, does this happen every night? Gwen reached up and pulled a sweatshirt jacket from its hanger. She covered her ears and buried her face into it wondering who was getting hurt. Was it David or Jack…? She heard Martha crying. She so wanted David to open the closet that she was in, retrieve this rifle out and put it to good use. She sure didn't have the nerve to do it, and now understood how easy it can sound, but the task so unbearably unthinkable.

Through the crack under the door, the bedroom light had turned on; Gwen's heart couldn't race anymore. The closet door from where she sat opened wide; she hid her face inside the sweatshirt, afraid to look.

"Gwen it's me…" He whispered kneeling down he reached for her hand.

Her heart ached helplessly for Martha and him, to afraid to speak or reveal herself. David took it upon himself to pull the sweatshirt away from her face; he held a bloodied tissue in his hand that he had used. He tugged on her hand and led her out of the closet.

"Is it safe?" She cried in a whisper, hearing Martha cry in the distance.

David nodded. "I got him good, he's out cold, he might come around in five minutes or not at all…I never know…"

"Oh god…" Gwen cried quietly laying her head on David's shoulder. She felt his hands on her back.

"I'm sorry Gwen, you better go…"

"Does this happen every night…?"

"No…Every night is different, some aren't so bad at all."

"You have to call that cop that you were talking about."

"I might…I don't know Gwen it's something I have to think about."

"Did you catch anymore fish today?"

"Yes, I did…It should have been enough to fill his face."

A harsh cough was heard by the both of them from the hallway.

"Hit him again." Gwen whispered raising her head from his shoulder.

"I can't push it when I want to give him to lesson…you have to go…"

Gwen left the same way she had come in, she ran quickly across the grassy field and then into her safe home.


She told no one of the incident last night. It was just another day in the life for David that she somewhat had felt a part of. She left for her appointment to please Carl and upset her parents if they ever found out that she was having pre-marital sex, and was requesting birth control. She could have been one of those few who saved themselves for marriage, then again she may not be a total failure if she ended up marring him. after all half of her friends have lost their virginity already.

She came home with her new pills tucked away securely in her purse and a bag of supplies from Auto Mart, a third bag; in the back seat. With the belief that David would be prompt, she laid the Auto Mart bag onto the hood of her car and went inside to get ready.

In her room she turned her stereo on loud wanting to shut everything else out, she has to try.

Tonight there will be no worrying about David for she has decisions to make concerning her own life. No worrying about him having to fish for his supper until Jack's disability check comes in the day after tomorrow. How primitive and in-humane it rings in her head. She had half-of mind to call the welfare department, her other half say's no.

It just didn't seem fair; the law doesn't mind that this no good beastly bad man is very capable of spending his last dime at the bar. It's that woman, that foolish woman not giving a blessed care for her and her son's well being.

Gwen put on the washable dress that her mother had bought for her, not really happy that she was repeating her wardrobe so soon, but it is the best she can do. With any luck, Carl will not announce to his mother that she has already worn it not more than a week ago. Perhaps Pearl had some other engagement that had suddenly come up and she would send her love and apologies her way, Gwen can only hope. In the back of her mind she wondered what Carl's father was like…Oh God forbid, and who divorced who?

Carl had thought it was a waste of time and energy, this kid under the hood of this old beater that Gwen proudly called her car. Tuning it up and such when there was no doubt that she was going to leave it behind, along with this hick town, well before fall hit the air. She ought to know that he would not allow this piece of junk to follow him traveling the miles that it will not handle.

Never-the-less he best be good in show. It was good for his image, even though no one was learning from him at this time, except himself. He kept his distance from the dirty car not wanting to smudge his finely dry cleaned clothing.

He cleared his throat, how rude can this punk be? Not paying any mind to a man of his stature any respect. This kid was going to get himself nowhere thinking that he was better than anyone else, especially himself.

Finally, David raised his head giving him a moment of his time.

"Hey…kid, thanks." He said holding out a twenty dollar bill in his hand.

David shook his head. "Gwen already paid me…and thanked me too…"

"Well…here is a little extra…do you think that you can give it a good washing while you are at it…?"

"What for…? This road…its dirt…it washes and dirties vehicles on its own."

"Humor me…"

David nodded and took the money without gratitude, not minding at all if he pleased him, yet wondered if Gwen had told him how needy he really was.

Gwen came out of the house nervous of the reaction Carl may throw at her for the repeated dress. David was in awe from the sight of her, the beautifully finely dressed young woman. Carl raised a smile as she neared him.

"You look niece Gwen…" David said beating Carl to the punch.

"Yes she does…" He added with an authoritative voice.

"Thank you both." She smiled.

"Ready…?"

"Yes…David there is a bag for you in the back seat…"

"Oh…okay…Well, have a good time."

She thanked him again, with a nervous smile, leaving him confused. He waited until Carl's car was out of sight before he went for the bag in the backseat. Somewhat displeased he was to see what was inside. A loaf of bread, a bottle of peanut butter, and a large can of stew. He will eat it no doubt; even his hateful father will welcome it into his stomach. It didn't matter where it came from, and if his son wants to go out and steal, beg or borrow for a meal, well, that was fine too.

He ought to try to get his job back and swallow his pride, pay the man who housed him and his mother. The last day will come around eventually, how and when is still a mystery. He can take up gambling and give his father all of his money, just enough for him to go out to the bar and get drunk. One day he will say the wrong thing, step on the wrong guy's shoes, and it might happen, he may not ever come home again. That was a gamble David was willing to make. David knew that there was a lot of guy's out there that despised the likes of his ole man. He wished they would do something about it; his money was on them…

Thank god Pearl walked into the restaurant with a man at her side.

"Well aren't you pretty as a picture Gwen and I do apologize once again about the other day…" She rambled as her friend sat her.

"That's all right ma'am…"

"Oh…no baby, call me Pearl…and this here is Gordy…"

"Hello…" She said continuing on with her nervousness.

Carl stood and shook hands with Gordy as if they had seen each other a few times before. The three of them chatted on, and on while Gwen listened in, the way she intended.

Not knowing much at all about business taxes, and foreclosures, that even hottsty tottsy Pearl had knowledge about sent her in an uncomfortable state. This was all necessary, a building block to a healthy relationship; meet the parents to find where you stand and you will know how to deal with them in the future. She thought she should speak up, just enough to agree with them, perhaps her nods and false smiles were sending out a lack of self esteem, for that matter her esteem may be draining right now. She couldn't let this happen to her. As she sat there, drinking ginger ale while the others sipped on an expensive bottle of wine she cheered herself up with a silent commitment, she will have to study up on such small business matters for her own self worth.

After an evening of quoting the Law to Gordy, He and Gwen used the basement entry of his mother's home to use the guest quarters. She will be a legal adult very soon, so this was not entirely wrong in her eyes, on the other hand her parents were old fashioned and would not see it this way. Only taking her pill for one day so far, Carl again used protection.

She laid there on the bed beside Carl wanting to ask him one of those legal questions. Truly believing that she already knew the answer, but felt the need to be certain about the self defense laws, would they be different from state to state. Then again, prosecution was his theme, not public defense.

"What's on your mind gorgeous?" Carl asked fluffing his pillow.

"Oh nothing…I should probably be getting home."

"I thought you were going to make a statement and stay here with me tonight."

"I don't know…you know…"

"No I don't Gwen…What's the deal…are you not going to Texas with me?"

"I didn't say that…you know how my parents are, I can't do this to my mother I have to go home."

"Am I wasting my time with you…? I can give you almost anything you want, and you want to turn me down because you think you are disrespecting your mother…! They aren't stupid Gwen…they know that we are having sex, and just because you want to go home after its done isn't going to make them any wiser."

"All right…I'll stay here with you."

"No…forget it you ruined the evening…get dressed I'll take you home." Carl bellowed in a huff grabbing his trousers from off the floor.


She sat in his car fighting off her tears; if her parents were still up she didn't want them to take notice.

"I need your answer Gwen."

"I told you I need some time to think on it."

"You know what it boils down to…whether you love me or not. Do you love me?"

"I think so." She said dabbing her eyes.

"No…you got to know so."

"Do you love me?"

"I told you I did…Now what is it…?" He asked turning onto the loop road.

"You said you loved me because I was pretty, and that's not enough for me."

"Yeah, well it's a guy thing…I can have almost any woman I want…there are other pretty girls out there but I picked you…Now do you love me?"

"Yes I love you."

"Then it is settled you are leaving for Texas with me…On the tenth of August…you have almost six weeks to tell your folks."


She lay awake the entire night, only dozed off for an hour before her alarm clock rang. She felt robbed not being able to make her own decision, those days should be over, she can over turn the decision he had made for her, and she may.

Careful not to make eye contact with her mother, she made it out as if to appear to appear be in a rush.

"I have to go Mom I'm running late."

"But you haven't eaten…" Beth replied only for a short glimpse of her daughter's tired eyes.

"I'll grab something latter," She huffed and was out the door.

It was clear to her that at least her mother had high hopes for her, and probably did suspect that she was now sexually active. It may not be a big surprise to her parents at all if they learned that she was leaving for Texas with him, Of course, they both had to suspect that by now, and no doubt it was what Tony wanted too.

The morning sun was bright and shined onto her rusted out car, even so, it was clean.

David washed it, why on earth for? She was pleased just the same. Once out onto the loop road the sun glared onto her windshield, she pulled the visor down, and an envelope had fallen onto her lap. She pulled over and parked on the side of the road to open the bulky envelope, inside was a plastic whistle hooked to a thin braided necklace rope. She then took out the letter and read.

Gwen thanks for the food, but you didn't need to do that, I can take care of myself. If that job is still open I would like to have another go at it. If it's already been filled or the boss doesn't want me back I understand. You are welcome down to the river anytime, for your protection and security wear this whistle around your neck and blow it if you see or hear the bear, he wont harm you, but I know this will help you with your confidence, just think of it as a gift from the Wizard...Talk to you latter and have a good day.

Gwen tucked the letter and whistle into her purse, she took out a tissue to wipe her eyes. After taking a few deep breaths she started back onto the road.

A plastic whistle wouldn't be enough to give her confidence in the real world, but out there at the river without fear, and with courage, one can make time stand still if they want it to, even if it's just for a moment. She had that sense of peace for a moment, out there, before she had seen the bear, before the fear set in...

Another day at this Ice cream shop, it's funny that Carl hadn't told her to quit this job and just take it easy for the rest of the summer. She should be glad that he hadn't, yet she would accept his suggestion on the spot. She could give her spot to David for his job had already been taken.

It was late in the afternoon when her friend Nancy approached her side of the counter.

"Hey Nance…What's up?"

Nancy looked at her with widened eyes and confusion, "You didn't hear…?"

"Hear what…no, what?"

"Carl is in jail…He was at a party, he and a couple of others got busted for contributing to miners last night."

"No, not my Carl…He dropped me off around midnight he said he was going to go home."

"Yes Gwen…Carl Perry…My sister, Tammy was there…You know he's not all what he's cracked up to be…Before the Cops came Tammy seen him flirting around with another girl, she was one of the miners."

"You're wrong, she's wrong, He went home."

"The bust happened at two-thirty this morning…I know this is a bad time but I thought you'd like to know."

"You said he is in jail…?"

"He's probably been bailed, but he was arrested."

Although, she had seen the truth on her friends face, Gwen spent the rest of her work day in disbelief. Instead of going home to use the phone, she used the Dairy Dip's back hallway payphone to call Carl.

He answered. "Hello?"

"It's me Gwen...I just heard something..."

"And what would that be?"

"You have been arrested...Is it true...?"

"I suppose it is...It was a misunderstanding, I wasn't aware that there were any miners in the house. The key word is that I didn't buy any of the alcohol, and it wasn't my home."

"Do you think you need to party every night...? You said you were going home."

"Yeah...Well I changed my mind. I am on vacation."

"Were you with anyone...I'm not talking about your guy friends."

"What are you implying Gwen...?"

"I heard that you were flirting with another girl."

"Yeah..." He chuckled. "Who told you that?"

"It doesn't matter who...were you?"

"Absolutely not...There were girls there...one was sitting by me for a while I guess, but I didn't fool around with any of them."

"I had to ask..."

"Sure, no problem...What do you want to do tonight?"

"I'm real tried...I'm just going to stay home."

"Okay, tomorrow night then...sound all right?"

"Sure..."

"Talk to you then." He said before the phone went dead.

She made it home for supper, at the dinner table she explained to her family that she was so tired; to tired to go out with Carl tonight They still asked her if everything was going okay between the two of them. Apparently they haven't heard the news, nor did she want them to.

"So Gwenie when is he leaving?" Her father asked setting his fork down onto his plate.

"The tenth of August."

"I see…where does that leave you…?"

"Are you going with him…? Can I have your car?" Tony asked with excitement.

Gwen disregarded her brother's question and looked to her mother. She was saddened by Gwen silence.

"He wants me to go with him…"

"Are you going to take your car…Can I have it…?"

Beth sighed. "That is no way to talk to your sister Tony…" She cried.

"What do you want…?" Her father asked.

"I'm thinking of going with him…"

"Then we are more than happy for you." Her mother cried. "Why it's not like we won't be seeing each other again, you can fly on an airplane and visit us often."

"I know its two days before my eightieth birthday, but…"

"Oh nothing doing, we won't let that stop you…We will throw you a party that you will never forget…"

"I wouldn't forget it anyway Mom."

"Are you thinking about further schooling?" Her father asked.

"Yes, I want to do something with my life, I'm not sure what yet."

"The sky is the limit; you can be whatever you want to be dear."

"I know Mom…I'm sorry to do this to you."

"Oh honey…we understand…you have to follow your heart."

Both Gwen and her mother rose from their chairs and embraced into a hug.

"Gwen…can I have your car.?"

Gwen laughed through her tears onto her mothers shoulder, Beth too chuckled.

"For all the crap I've given you Tony, it only seems fitting that you have that heap."

"Thanks, but I thought I had given you all the crap."

"We give and take…I'll come back next summer and teach you how to drive. Unless you want to Dad…?"

"No, no…He's all yours Gwenie…"

Tony smiled. "Well next year, I'll be here all summer long; this is my last year at camp…"

"Yes…our children are growing up, won't be long before we have an empty nest."

"Oh come-on Beth…Tony isn't going any where for a while."

"But they grow up so fast…" She cried.


Gwen went to bed early that night with the family conversation on her mind. It all seemed to be such a fairy tale. It can be maybe once in Texas and Carl's back into Law school, he will settle down again; after all it is his summer vacation. And if it doesn't work out she will be welcomed back home to start over.

Tammy could have exaggerated as to what she saw, or what she thought she saw last night…And maybe, just maybe, Nancy was giving her a line out of jealously; perhaps she didn't want her to go.

She went to work the next day passing David's house, recalling that she had forgotten to give David the message that his job had been filled. It would have been so much easer if there was a phone in his house. She will feel guilty all day if she didn't give him the message. She just had to put it in her mind that he understood her reasoning and press on with her day.

Why she worked all day and the man in her life slept and partied was beyond her. What was Texas going to be like? She needed to ask.

The two of them sat on the couch in front of the television of Carl's mother's home. She was in his arms.

"Well Gwen…You don't need to work…I just thought you needed to feel worthy."

"I'd like to take some classes or something in the fall."

"Yeah like what…?"

"I'm not sure…"

"I can get you a job Gwen…can you type?"

"Yeah, only about thirty words a minute."

"That's not bad…It's a start…I can get you on at the firm as a secretary, and someday you will be mine."

"You mean it…? Just like that?"

"Just like that."

"Whose job would I be taking…?"

"My father is head honcho; he can have one of his secretaries transferred. And you are in Gwen."

"It doesn't seem fair…You mean fired don't you?"

"It's no big deal…a good secretary can always find another job, he will pick one that is sloughing off."

"I would be the one sloughing, typing only thirty words a minute."

"Well he will just have to keep you out of the court room then, wont he?"

At least he came from a family that took care of their own, and Carl seemed to back his Father on that. She slept beside him that night, knowing that it was on the acceptable side of her parents, and knowing that her man was not out with his friends creating trouble but with her.

David was aware that Gwen hadn't come home last night, the reasoning was clear to him. Now he felt embarrassed about that stupid letter he had wrote to her, and the dumb ole whistle, as if he were going to win her over competing with a promising Lawyer to be. He didn't really want to know the answer as to why he has not heard back from her. Did she laugh at his letter…? Did she not want him back at the Dairy Dip?

He spent his entire day down at the river; there was now food in the house thanks to what few groceries Jack brought home yesterday with his disability check, and he will be at Shavers bar all day, so he didn't have to worry about his mother, more than likely she was happily drinking her spiked iced tea in the house or perhaps since it was a nice warm day she was sitting out side.

There was a difference between David and his mother. Her life as she saw it today was permanent, small moments of satisfaction breaking through her life of misery was enough for her. Telling herself and others that her life wasn't so bad, nothing she can't handle. Sure, Jack has his moments, but doesn't every man. The truth was, she was afraid of change, and she was just used to this life. One day David can be free from this one.

Martha's exercise consisted of the walked to her mailbox and back. Now she sat with an envelope in her possession. The envelope had no post mark on it, no address, it just read: David. It was probably from Gwen, next door thanking him for the work he had done on her car, or was it something more than that. She so wanted to open it up and read it, but with what values she did have she chose not to. Instead she waited on her sons return.

He did finally return with a small handful of fish, all cleaned out like a good boy would. Martha tossed the fish into the sink and ran cold water over them. "Oh…you have a letter of some sort…it's sitting there on the coffee table."

David walked over to the coffee table, picked it up and read…: David, I am quitting my job. I will talk to my boss today, he liked your work, so I'm sure he will be okay about you taking my place. I'm quitting regardless, just to spend more time with Carl and my family before I leave for Texas. My mother won't mind if you come over to call Tom at the Dairy Dip about it, talk to you latter…

"What is all about?" His mother asked,

"A job." He muttered, stuffing the letter into his pocket of his jeans.

"The same one, at the Ice cream parlor?"

"Yeah…"

"You know you are going to have to give half of your check's earnings to your dad."

"I know…I have to go use the phone."

David walked out of the house to make his way over to the Banks home, now, again uncertain if he really wanted the job. Early evening was setting in The Dairy Dip will be closing for the day soon. As he approached the drive of the Banks home, he heard Gwen's car coming his way. He now stood there while she pulled up.

The door of her car creaked loudly as she opened and closed it, and small piece of rust fell from it and dropped to the sandy ground.

"Hello David…"

"I was down at the River all day so I just got your letter…and I thought that maybe you didn't get mine, because I didn't hear back from you."

"Oh, no David I'm sorry, I should have, but your job had already been filled, and well I'm sorry."

"Don't worry about it I just want you to be happy."

"Well thank you, and your letter and the whistle it was so sweet."

"It was dumb."

"No it wasn't and I'd like to go down to the river to sit and chat one more time with you before I leave…We can have another picnic…I'll wear the whistle for the Wizard to keep my confidence…So did you want the job?"

"Yeah, I'll give it another go."

"Good, when do you want to start? I'll give you a ride…Hey why don't you set up an appointment to take your drivers test…You can use my car, as far as that goes you can use it until you save up enough for a beater of your own. I can't give it to you because Tony wants it next year."

"Why are you being so nice to me Gwen?"

"You're my friend David."

"Other than you dropping over a container of food when the ole man was gone and a hello here and there, we haven't been friends until now."

"I know…Both Tony and I have been told to keep away, for as long as we could remember, we grew up believing that your dad is a monster, and he is."

"I know that."

"Yeah…Well come in…were you going to use the phone?"

"Yes I was."

David followed her inside. He was greeted by both, Hank and Beth. He didn't mind so much that they were present when he made the call. With-in no time he was set to start in the morning. He carried an Apple pie home. Seems that Beth had made an extra, because she had an over abundance of apples. Gwen told him that she will bring him to work tomorrow.

"Its very kind of you, hon…giving him a ride to work and back, but what will he do when you have left?" Her mother said placing the dinner plates onto the table, in front of Hank.

"That car isn't going to last much longer, I was thinking that by this time next year, Carl and I will be able to spring for a nice used car for Tony."

"Come on Gwenie…you should not speak for Carl."

"I'm not Dad…I have a good job lined up as a secretary at the Firm."

"You've got to be kidding…"

"I know I can't type very fast right now, but I will get faster, and learn everything else as I go."

"Why that is wonderful news…Is someone resigning or retiring?"

"I guess so…"

"Oh I am so happy for you honey, isn't that wonderful Hank?"

"Yes, wonderful, did you plan on handing your car down to David then?"

"I am…he's going to take his drivers test this summer and he's going to need a car…I will keep my promise to Tony, I will Dad."

"In that case, I think it is a very kind gesture, I am proud of you."

"We both are honey…Tony is over at Pat's house tonight. So it's just the three of us."

"Just the two of you Mom…I'm going out with Carl tonight."

"Will you be coming home at all tonight?"

"It's no matter Gwenie…You are an adult now, just don't be a stranger."

"I wont, and don't worry I will be here next week to cook for you, I know its not going to be as good as Mom's home cooking."

"Oh, dear me it's coming up so fast." Beth huffed, laying her hand on her chest.

"One more time hey Beth, or will you do it next year too?"

"Decisions, decisions…I'll cross that bridge when I get to it."


Gwen had dropped David off at work; he was stunned by her news. He has a car come August. He promised Gwen he would make an appointment for his drivers test. With a car and a license he will be able to get away. David also said it was time to give his mother an ultimatum. A restraining order flied against Jack the next time he has an outburst, or he will call that Cop and be removed from the house. He can't be his mother's baby sitter forever. She hoped it wasn't just talk.

Worried of what kind of trouble Carl may have gotten him self into last night, Gwen went to his house, and low and behold his car was gone. Her heart ached and anger rose inside of her, for she knew him much to well to guess that he was already up and at-em by now, for any reason, after all he was on vacation. She sat there until after eleven o'clock.

There was nobody to turn to with her dilemma. Carl knew she was off today. Was he in jail…with another woman…or was he making a statement letting her know that this is what to expect of him in the future? Her second thoughts had told her that she made the wrong decision in the first place.

She kept it to her self and drove around town for a while. After stopping at the café to have a burger she went back to Carl's. Angry, she was when she knocked on the door. Carl answered. It looked as though he had just gotten out of the shower.

"Hey Gwen, come in." He remarked with a subtle smile.

Gwen stood her ground. "No, I don't think so…you want to tell me where you spent the night…?"

"Oh, I was at Pete's…He had a poker game there last night…I won eighty dollars…I was a little to drunk, so I spent the night…Come in." He said with no regrets.

She came in, letting some of her self esteem out. Perhaps she can find it again, but not right now. So why was he so angry when she left hours latter to go pick up David to take him home, it appeared to be jealousy, and she didn't like it.

She parked outside of the Dairy Dip to wait for David's shift to be over. To be really sure that he was cheating on her. She needed to catch him in the act. How was she to do that? Suppose she can talk to Nancy to have her or her sister spy on him. They had already suspected him of being untrue, and apparently they knew his hang outs more than she. Was it because she was a goody-two-shoe? Then again she can insist that she be with him night and day, now that she can. Did it really matter that she was under age?

Suddenly, her thoughts were interrupted. David opened the door got inside and then slammed it shut, as it needed to be in order for it to close.

"Hi…"

"Hi…how was your day?" She asked, seemingly still lost in her thoughts.

"Not bad, you know the job kind of bites…And how was yours?"

"Oh fine…" She replied pulling onto the highway, leaving David wonder if he was already a burden.

"You know Gwen; it's not that far, I can walk home if you want to stick around town."

"No, no…I was going to go home for a while anyway, been in town all day. Five miles is a long way to walk after you've been working all day."

"So what's wrong?"

"There is nothing wrong Dave." She replied with a cry in her voice.

David waited a while, with almost a mile behind them before he spoke again. "You could have fooled me?"

Gwen wiped a tear away from her cheek. "I don't know David I am having second thoughts. He parties every night, and not once has he invited me along. I think he may be fooling around with other women." She cried harder letting many tears out as she spoke.

"Women, as in plural?"

"I don't know."

"You want me to drive…? I need the practice."

"You drove to the City just fine, I can handle it."

"But can you see?"

"No, not very well…" She answered pulling over.

As they passed each other in the front of the car on the highway, David patted her shoulder, and then got behind the wheel.

"Did you come out and ask him if he's fooling around?"

"The other day I did, course he said no, otherwise I wouldn't of-…A sister of a friend said that she saw him flirting with another girl."

"It should be enough for you to call everything off."

"But he's on vacation…he may be a flirt but, I can't say that he actually cheated on me."

"Are you going out with him tonight?"

"I don't know I was a little mad at him I told him I'd give him a call. He was talking about Maybe we can just hang out at his place, at least I will know where he is. You know the couple of times that I have spent the night he behaves."

"So, when do you want to fit in our picnic…? Or do you just want to forget about it?"

"No…I'll let you know, there is a lot of time yet…and David; please keep this conversation between us."

"Who would I tell…your parents? I'm not that kind of person Gwen."

"I know…I'm sorry…"

Still secretly unsure of her final plans, Gwen helped her mother load her car with all the gear they would need for Camp Big Pine. Although the camp was only Fifteen miles away, just the same Hank had his head under the hood checking the oil. He kicked the tires and was satisfied.

"You take care of your daddy now hon," She sighed opening up her arms. Gwen fell into them.

"I will, you try to have fun now Mom."

"And I'm late for work." Hank added next in line to give his wife a hug goodbye for a week.

Gwen didn't mind giving her brother a hug. "See you little brother, have a good time."

"I will…this is my last year you know."

"Don't have to be, you can go back as a counselor."

"No not going to."

Gwen stood there waving off her mother and brother in one car, going to camp, and her father behind them in his truck off to work. Oh the glorious feeling that overcame her. Having the house to her self, it was like a piece of magic. What to do, what to do?

With David using her car she could not go any where, nor did she care to, she was just happy that he had gotten his license so quickly. She spent her day going through her things, deciding what to take with her to Texas and what to leave behind, for her space will be limited. She could have her mother mail a large box or two her way, but there were many things she could just do without. She separated and sorted in the quiet house with sadness. Boxes filled of memories and good byes. Her first camera, The Kodak Disc, not to long ago it was hot and flashy, Now, obsolete, good luck finding any film for it. A Girl Scout award, with the help from her parents, she sold the most cookies on her team, her mother framed it just the same, for that reason it truly was an award. What was she going to do when it came down to the long good byes with her family? Leaving them after all these years with a wing and a prayer that she will fall in love with the stranger she had meet not more than a month ago.

Through her opened window she heard Jack's loud truck barreling out of the drive next door. That sound always made her worry, more so than before since she has gotten to know David so well. She was sure that her mother would keep her informed once she's in Texas, about that foolish woman.

She enjoyed this time at home, cooking for her father. He came home to a fine dinner with his daughter. She cooked some fried chicken and rice. She sat and ate with him, knowing that this evening was like no other.

"Why aren't you out with Carl tonight...? Not that I'm complaining, this is wonderful, but I don't want to take you away from your love life."

"No Dad...I had some things to do anyway...and I just wanted to stay home with you."

"Well the night is still young...and I just plan on sitting in front of the television and being a couch potato. I could have always nuked something...regardless of what your mother may say, I can, fend for myself."

"I know Dad...He may call yet, but he was talking about going on a fishing trip with his friends today and they probably are not going to get back until late."

"Why didn't you go, because of us?"

"Part of it I guess, I'm not really into fishing, and he's…on vacation with his friends."

"Everything is going okay isn't it?"

"Oh yes…" She replied before the knock on the door.

"Oh what's wrong now?" Hank asked with a sigh.

Gwen went to go answer it. It was David.

"Hey, would you mind if I used your car again…?" I want to take my mother to the police station so she can file a restraining order."

"You mean it! Oh thank god…is she all right?"

"Yeah, I think so…she's got bruises, but I told her if she didn't file one that I was going to call that Cop and get myself out of here."

"Good for you…Of course you can use the car."

"Thanks…I'll talk to you later."

Hank waited until the door was shut and David stepped off the porch. "She better stick to her guns this time…What Cop was he talking about?"

"Oh, in the City when David was arrested for taking the truck…This Cop said he can have him removed from his home. All he had to do was say the word."

"You know…he's not a bad kid…I guess we have been set on keeping our distance, we all just didn't realize."

Gwen cleaned up the kitchen only a bit surprised that Carl hadn't called her my now. Hank was sitting in his chair undecided whether or not to read the paper or watch the news. Gwen's eyes winded as she spotted Jack coming to the door.

She sprinted into the living room. "Dad…Jack, he's here."

A loud knock on the door confirmed it. "Stay back." Hank replied quickly rising from his recliner. He stomped over to the door and opened it.

Jack stood tall and broad, his nostrils were flaring. "Where's my family!" He demanded.

Hank stood his ground. "I believe they went to the police station to file a restraining order against you…And if you come to my door again I will be doing the same."

"You tell that busy body daughter of yours not to lend her car out to my son."

"Don't you come up on my doorstep and threaten me!" Hank shouted.

"Did you hear me…? I'm his father, and I say he does not barrow vehicles…He stole mine and I'm paying for yours!!!"

"You don't pay for anything do you?" Hank sneered with his angry words; he felt his heart racing inside of him.

"Dad…? You want me to call the Cops?"

"Yes Gwen, why don't you do that…You can tell them where they can find him."

"Listen here! No one takes me out of my house!" Jack grunted.

"You tell that to the police…they're on the way." Hank shut the door leaving Jack standing there. With his daughter on the phone Hank sat at the table and reached for his prescription bottle inside the cubby storage near the wall. He spilled out one of his heart pills and popped it into his mouth.

He wondered how that man lives with himself; he certainly must be healthy enough to be angry all the time. And here he was taking a pill when his temper flared. Still on the phone with the police, Gwen poured out a glass of water from the tap and handed it to her father. Looking out the window, she stated that Jack was walking back to his truck and leaving.

Moments later she hung up the phone. "You okay Dad?"

"I'm fine…With any luck he is on his way over to the police station." He chuckled.

"Yeah…he's dumb enough." Gwen said sharing the laugh. "Why don't you go sit in your chair…would you like some ice tea?"

"Yeah…that might hit the spot." Hank got up the peered out the window of the front door. He locked it then sat back down in his recliner.

She handed him a glass of ice tea. "So this means he gets arrested again?"

"Hopefully…yes…she's been beaten again, right…? As long as she files a complaint."

"But a restraining order won't keep him away, and it's not like they have a phone…And won't it make him angrier?"

"Our hands are tied Gwenie…David is welcome to use our phone anytime."

"So if you or I see his truck over there, should we call the police?"

"I suppose so…if he steps foot over here you certainly call the police."

"We don't have a restraining order against him."

"No matter…if I'm not here you call the police."

The orders he gave his daughter were his concerns. Gwen was comfortable with them, and she would, miss his protective fatherly way. No matter how she tried to tame her own concerns for David and his mother, she found herself restless that night. So she went downstairs to get a drink of water, and to look out the window. All was calm, no sign of Jack, but she wondered how long the jail cell would last, usually not more than a day or two.

Gwen was cooking an omelet for her father, when he came down all ready for work, the first thing he had done was to peer out the window.

"It's still quiet." She said.

"David working today…?"

"I don't know, I mean he is scheduled to, but I wouldn't blame him if he didn't."

"What's Carl doing today…?"

"Oh, I don't know."

Hank sat at the table. "I'm sure he is back from his fishing trip…why don't you invite him over here for the day…He can have dinner with us."

"Yes, that's not a bad idea…maybe I will."


It seemed that David was set on moving forward. Instead of staying home, he came over to get Gwen's keys from her. She had no problem with it at all, for she was going to invite Carl over for the day, and would not need her car. She promised David that she would keep an eye on the house, and she will call the police if and when Jacks truck arrived. He thanked her.

Gwen waited until nearly Ten o'clock before she called Carl's cell phone.

"Hello…?" A female's voice answered.

"Pearl…?" Gwen asked in confusion. After no reply Gwen added. "May I speak with Carl please?"

The phone line went dead. Gwen hung it up and cried over it. Knowing she had the house to herself, she bawled loudly.

A while latter, she was cleaning the house, dusting and mopping. She thought perhaps she called the wrong number; maybe Cellular phone numbers can easily get mixed up. She couldn't deny the obvious, but still left room for doubt. Fighting off the need to call him back, the phone finally rang. She was quick to answer.

"Hello...?"

"Hey...how's it going?" Carl asked.

"It's going...Did you have fun on your fishing trip?"

"Oh...Yeah, it was great...it was a blast...you should have come with us"

"I really wasn't invited."

"You told me you had your day planned, with your family heading off to Camp."

"Yes...that was before you said that you were going out on that boat."

"Well I'm sorry if there was a misunderstanding...we can do it again next week, maybe just the two of us, I'm sure it wouldn't be any problem."

"Who all went...?"

"Well Mike and Pete, and their two ladies..."

"Doesn't anybody work...?"

"Their on a two week vacation...I told you so Gwen."

"You know I haven't met any of your friends...Why not? And why did I call your Cell phone a few hours ago and have a woman's voice answer...?" She huffed.

"What…? You didn't call my Cell…Gwen are you implying that I'm cheating on you?"

"Yes I am!" She answered sternly, wondering why he hadn't used the word; accused.

"Well I am re—ally sorry to hear that…It kind of putt's a damper on our relationship now doesn't it?"

"What am I supposed to think?"

"You are supposed to think that you were mistaken on which number you dialed in the first place…Gwen my phone did not ring…I would, like you to meet my friends before they all go back to work and get all grumpy…Why don't you come on over right now and we will see what's shaking?"

"I loaned my car out to David, so he could go to work. He wont be back until a little after five."

"Oh…I know it's a pile of trash, but it was a car…Tell that loser to get his own."

"He's not a loser Carl…David is my friend."

"Yeah…whatever, I will hang out here until you're hoodlum friend comes back…I'll see you latter." He hung up.

Well; so much for her father's idea, Carl didn't give her the chance to invite him over. What kind of explanation was she going to give to him; she had a few more hours to think on it.

With everything done in the house to her mothers standers, and more than enough food prepared for her father, she filled a container full of the tuna casserole she just made,

and walked over to the Pane home in defiance. She knocked on the door until Martha answered. Gwen didn't expect to see a clear face. And she didn't, but behind the painful eyes she lifted a smile. Was it the food or her presence? It didn't matter much to Gwen either way. Martha's house coat was ripped and tattered, in embarrassment she clutched onto it.

"I'm sorry I must look a mess...I wasn't expecting company."

"That's all right Mrs. Pane...I brought you and David some Tuna casserole."

"Oh thank you Gwen, you are such a nice person...Would you like to come in?"

"I suppose I could for just a minute."

The inside of the Pane home was not what she had expected to see. Sure, it was old and run down, but it was clean and tidy just the same. She supposed Martha didn't have a lot to take pride in except for her son and her home. After putting the casserole away Martha came back into the living room, she sat down, Gwen did the same.

"You must be excited to be going off into new territory..."

"Oh...I guess so..."

"David is going to miss you...He's not one for making friends...it's all my fault."

"It's not your fault Martha...you just have to take care of your self, and keep this restraining order in place."

"We go to the judge tomorrow."

"Oh good...Is David taking the day off?"

"It is his day off...He said that he would leave me if I don't do this, but..."

"You're afraid?"

Martha nodded, using her house coat to wipe her tears. "Dammed if I do and dammed if I don't."

"Well, our door is always open for you and David...and I will call the police if I see him, or his truck anywhere near here."

"Thank you…you are so nice…I never went to the judge before and kept my mind made up…Jack is going to be so mad…and I'm afraid he might hurt David again…because Jack is going to know that this was his idea."

"Something has to be done Martha…It's time to put your foot down."

"I know…"

"Martha, I took Home Economics in school, I can sew pretty good…Would you like me to mend your smock there?"

"Oh. You don't have to do that."

"I'd like to, I have free time, so if there is any other garments you have, that needs mending."

Gwen sat there on the couch nervously for what seemed to be eternity before Martha returned with a trash bag full of clothes. Gwen was taken by surprise.

"Oh it's too much isn't it…?" Martha asked after seeing the expression on her face.

"It's okay…but there isn't any of Jack's clothes in here is there?"

"No…I put my foot down right?"

Gwen smiled. "Yes." She said realizing that some or most of these clothes here in the bag may be the result of his beastly temper, why would he tare his own in his rampages?

Knowing that she had her work cut out for her, she set up her mother's sewing machine in the living room and began to sort the damages. One thing was clear; Martha was in need for some new clothes. She was about the same size as her mother, perhaps when she comes back from Camp she can ask her mother to weed out her closet, she had so many clothes that she never wore, and it was a shame that they just hung there for no reason, when they could be put to good use.

Though his supper was warm in the oven, she knew that her father was going to be upset with her. Gwen didn't mind, she was feeling mighty proud of herself for her decision.

"I told you not to go over there." Her father said with disappointment, placing his lunch pail onto the counter.

"You don't understand Dad…"

"No you don't…You're playing with fire…what if that lunatic had come home?"

"I would have high-tailed it home, and called the police…You have got to stop being so protective of me."

"I just want to send you off to a happy life with no scars on you…Where is Carl…did you invite him over?"

"No I didn't, he had some other plans for us tonight, we can make it another night, I should go get ready, David will be back soon with my car."

She was a bit angry, set in her own ways sitting on a lawn chair, waiting for David's return. He was late it wasn't like him.

Her father was eating his early supper at the table, when she came in to use the phone. He became concerned listing to his daughters words.

"Oh no…! You've got to be kidding…! Okay…Well good…All right, I'll have my dad bring me over to pick it up…Oh…that bad." She hung up the phone.

"What now?" Her father asked.

"Jack showed up at the Dairy Dip with a crow bar and smashed up my car."

"That Sun-of-a-be…! Now do you understand me Gwen?"

"He's been arrested…"

"That's comforting…for how long…That Sun-of a…" Hank continued to curse picking up his keys to his truck.

They were still on the Loop road when they spotted David walking home. Assuming they had heard the news, David stepped up to Hank's open window.

"I'm sorry…your car is totaled Gwen."

"What else did he bust up?" Hank asked hoping that he had went inside and caused a ruckus, so he can be put away for a long time.

"Just the car." David replied. "A wrecker already came and towed it away."

"Well then we're going to the police station to press charges…You need a ride home?"

"No thank you…I'll walk…I'm sorry, I should have called."

"It's okay David, I'll see you latter."

The damages wouldn't total a whole lot on her car that had no insurance, and it had little value, other than it used to be able to get from one place to another. And as for jail time she was told that he may be held up to forty eight hours, if he hadn't made bail. She believed that he wouldn't.

Her father dropped her off at Carl's mother's home. Carl was preparing for his evening with a drink in his hand. He sat there sipping it, while she told her story.

"Well I hope you learned your lesson…I don't want you interfering with the likes of that family any more." Gwen's silence gave him the hint of defiance towards his statement. "Tell me…how friendly are you two?"

"What do you mean…? I told you that we were friends, and that's all, nothing more."

"You two ever…?"

"No of course not…I also told you that you were my first." She answered somewhat sternly.

"Don't have a cow…I just want to know where you stand with your neighbor…It's nothing different than you accusing me of fooling around because you dialed the wrong number."

"Okay…are we even now…because I'm getting tired of fighting all the time, aren't you?"

"I don't want to fight…but I don't want you misunderstanding me neither."

"Yeah, well it goes both ways Carl…I've been nothing but true to you!"

"And I haven't speculated until now…and look what kind of; tizzy you're getting yourself into! What's the deal on that?"

"The deal is I am standing up for myself…Something you wouldn't understand…! You prosecutor!"

"I'm not prosecuting you!"

"Speculating…? Am I on trial…?" She now shouted. "You know what…You were, and you just lost…! I'm leaving…its over!" She then grabbed her purse and headed for the door.

Carl grabbed her by the arm and turned her around. "Get a grip on yourself Gwen…what comes around goes around…Have respect for me, and I'll do the same for you…Don't be a fool and walk out on me." He sighed releasing the hold he had on her as his voice calmed. "You're right…we're even…no more fighting…so what do you want to do tonight?"

"I'm open for suggestions…I'm sorry I just had a bad day."

"You want to meet my friends?"

"All right." She answered.


He took her to a backyard party. After meeting his friends she indulged in the same things that she had condemned Carl for. It put perspective on such tidiest law; after all she was nearly an adult. She preferred this over the restaurant ordeal with Pearl. Now in a much more comfortable mood, relating with others was much easier, with a bottle of confidence, she made her way into conversations with the small handful of girls at the party.

Carl was on the lawn playing horseshoes. Music was playing in the back ground and the mood was right, so right that she celebrated with another beer and another, until her mind told her that she had no worries, no problems at all. She remembered very little after that.

She woke in Carl's bed, with a pounding head and a bad taste in her mouth. She got up; at the same time Carl was stirring.

"You embarrassed me last night…you never had a drink before have you?"

"I'm not feeling very well."

"Yeah…no kidding…You acted like a school girl. You really made me look small."

Gwen rubbed her aching head, and headed for the bathroom. "Just shut up…" She said before she walked into the bathroom then closed the door behind her.

Carl waited for her to return to the bedroom. "What did you say to me?"

"I don't need your constant criticism…I know I had too much to drink."

"Don't you ever tell me to shut up again…you got that Gwen?" He demanded putting his face up to hers.

"Take me home, please…" She begged.

"I need your apology…So apologize…we could have had fun last night, but instead you were stumbling and staggering about like a sick cow."

"You talk to me this way, and you want me, to apologize to you?" She cried.

"Yes I do…I'm not the one who made a fool out of myself last night."

"I'm sorry you feel that way."

"And what is that supposed to mean?"

"You make a fool out of me!" She bellowed.

Carl slapped her across the face; his cold eyes looked upon her. "You have some learning to do!"

"As long as you're not my teacher…I'm out of here!" She cried, and then quickly walked out. She feared Carl may try to stop her, but he did not.

She left her purse behind; now there was no doubt that she will see him again. Nancy didn't live too far away, with any luck she will be home.

She sat in her friend Nancy's car, spilling out her troubles.

"I tried to tell you Gwen…He's no good, and if he was any kind of a man he would have taken you home."

"I'm sorry if I'm a bother…"

"You are no bother…I'm glad I can help…so it's over then, right?"

"It is…"

"Good…give me a call anytime you want to talk…I mean it Gwen." Nancy assured her as she pulled into the driveway.

Gwen opened the car door. "I will, I promise."

After a shower and some pain relievers, she felt better. Her mind was easing with the certainty of her decision, and no more will she question it. She had a lot of sewing to do. This will help heal her soul until her father comes home, maybe then she can tell him that it was over, all plans were off, she can cry some on his shoulder and be done with it.

A knock on the door interrupted the progress she was making having had four garments done already. She hoped that it wasn't Carl standing there with her purse in his hand. It was David. Gwen opened it widely letting him in saying nothing, yet she wondered why he was here.

"I just wanted to say sorry again about your car."

"Don't worry about it…I was giving it to you any way…How's your mom going to make that appointment with the judge now?"

"Oh my mother already left…she called an old friend…we were over here this morning to use the phone when your dad was still here."

"And how did you know that I was home…just now?"

"Well you know not many cars at all come down this way, except us, and the Wilson's...I couldn't help noticing that it wasn't your boy friends car that brought you home...is everything all right?"

"Yes it is...and thanks for asking."

"My mother told me what you were doing with her clothes...that was so cool of you to offer...You know she doesn't care what she looks like half of the time."

"It's no problem, I like sewing...so it works out fine." Gwen replied, doing her best to hold back her emotions.

"Are you sure everything is okay?"

"Yes...everything is fine David, thank you."

"All right...well I'm going down to the river to do some fishing...umm; you're welcome to come along, if you want."

"You know...I'd like that."

"Really...?" David asked raising a smile.

"Yes, give me a minute,"

"Okay...well I'll grab an extra plate to bring down...we'll eat some Cat fish."

"I'll grab some soda...and what makes you think that you are going to catch any?"

David said nothing keeping his smile; he just had to catch some.

Gwen packed the cooler, while David waited outside. Her father will just have to enjoy the tuna casserole again tonight.


She followed David down the path that led to the river. With a bag in his hand he turned himself around to look at her.

"Where's your whistle?"

"Oh it's in my purse…I sort of forgot it at Carl's"

"Did you get your things from your car yesterday?"

"Yes, what I needed…there wasn't much…"

They continued their conversation all the way down to the peaceful river, and then they collected wood together to prepare it for the catch. She sat beside him waiting for his bobber to sink with a jerk as the afternoon sun shined down.

"You are not going to get in trouble for this are you…? I mean if, what's his name…Carl finds out that you were down here…He just seems to be the jealous type, and he doesn't like me…Gwen…?"

"I…left him, this morning." She answered calmly and then looked away from the bobber, their eyes locked.

"Left him…I thought you said that everything was fine?"

"And it is…I'm so better off without him."

"Did he hurt you…was he fooling around?"

"I think so…it's over, and I am so okay with it…I don't want to hear you apologize about that car. It wasn't going to last very much longer anyway."

"Then I don't know what to say…except I'm glad that you're not leaving…I like you a lot you know…"

"Me too…" She said with a tear roiling down her cheek.

With his heart patting out of sorts in his chest, he reached for it; grateful that he had gotten away with wiping it dry from her soft face. He didn't know much about proper etiquettes, but he took it as an invitation to draw nearer. The look in her eyes reassured him that it was acceptable, and now her meting him half way was the deal maker.

As he tasted her lips, the pole slipped from his hand and slid into the river. He was aware of it, but wouldn't break away from her warm welcome that brought them down onto the grass.

# *Fear*

David will never forget the day at the river; he became a man with Gwen, the first and only real love of his life. All good things come to an end, as he saw it, too good to last. And he was told, Conner's remission wouldn't last, his abnormal bone marrow was certain to fail him. Tonight he stayed sober; no alcohol can give him comfort.

Conner went to bed a few hours ago, truly not feeling well. David was keeping a watchful eye. When his father stood over him to touch his warm brow, Conner opened his tired eyes.

"I don't feel so great Dad."

"I'll be right back...I'm going to warm up the truck."

# Sam's Song

Marshall was still lounged on his bed; turning the pages of Sam's book...He turned another.

: If tattoo head were chasing me, I had managed to dodge him another day. I was safe inside the Anderson home. I passed both Sally and Earl sitting in front of the TV, and headed for the basement entry; I didn't get away with it.

"Homework first." Sally noted.

"It's done...I finished it in study hall."

"You don't bring your studies home like you had last year." Earl remarked.

"Well...this year is different."

"Yes it is from what we seen of your first quarters report card. Your grades aren't so good...Sally and I would like you bring your studies home and spend a little less time in the basement with your guitar."

"Larry put you two up to this, didn't he?"

"He's your Uncle Larry...And he wants what's best for you."

"Why don't you worry about what's best for you guys...I won't tell...you like it when I'm out of your hair. You don't have to pretend you care…As long as you get that check in the mail for having me around, what's it to yaw's?" I felt better getting that off my chest. I continued with my first intensions and went down to the basement, and got away with it.

It was only a bit odd how they had let it go like that. I really did like the Anderson's, they were so easy going. I knew they could have had worse than me; they're many of them out there, and I didn't know what number I was, only that they had housed other foster kids before I came along. I'm sure they kept one thing in mind, how ever the kid's turned out; it wasn't their fault, they were already damaged goods. Why should I be an exception to their rule? It was Uncle Larry's pesky persistence that questioned their simple rules.

I didn't mind losing my paper route, because of my dropping grades. It was getting old, looking over my shoulder every time an engine revved behind me. The thought of Sword head and his friend searching for me, or running me down to finish me off was a constant echo in my mind.

I knew my life was taking a downward spiral; I wasn't totally in need of a reality check, just a little numb by it. My guitar was my only friend, we played well together, and it would never leave me. If Uncle Larry felt better about himself paying me an unexpected visit now and then, well so be it. I had no right to burst his bubble.

I was in the basement playing my guitar with my head phones on, when one of Uncle Larry's such visits occurred, he came down the stairs, and he wasn't alone. I could have accepted Earl or Sally, or any one I knew for that matter, but this stranger at his side; I didn't like it from the start. I took my head phones off in confusion as the two of them stood before me. I took in little satisfaction that Uncle Larry's side kick didn't appear to be a doctor of any sorts; he was dressed in jeans and a tee shirt. I had nothing against the fact that he was an African American, but he was just too young for house calls.

"Hello Sam…I would like you to meet Eddie."

"Hi." He said with a smile.

"Eddie is a member of the; Adopt a Brother Program…Have you ever heard it?"

"Yeah…"

"Good…He is going to hang out with you for a while…and you two can take it from there…Sam, I encourage you to give this a go, okay?"

I found myself saying nothing. If I wanted a friend I could find my own. Was I that miserable?"

"We're good Sir." Eddie said with a reassuring smile.

I didn't like him and his smile. Smiles mean nothing. The Joker smiles all the time and he's a bad guy. Bat Man knows first hand.

Uncle Larry smiled back at him. Ignoring my hidden hostility, he said. "Good deal, I'll see you again Sam." He walked up the stairs, leaving me here with this stranger.

His visits were always short, but this was the shortest of them all, it was as quick as the changing of the guards. I wondered if I would ever see him again.

"I don't need any friends…so you can leave now." I spoke as though my territory had just been invaded.

"Well you see, I'm with the Adopt a Brother Program…it kind of means I'm here whether you want me here or not…you know like a brother."

"So when do you leave?"

"When I want to…Don't worry I'm not going to move in or anything like that…Can I hear what you got…? I don't play an instrument, so show me how it's done."

"No…I rather not…you can leave, I'm not prejudice…but I don't want you here."

"Good…then I won't have to hurt you…just kidding…I would have at one time though, kicked your butt."

"What for…? I told you that I wasn't prejudice…"

"I would have found a reason…I was a bad kid, skipped school, did drugs, got into a lot of fights…caused my mother trouble…it wasn't too long ago…now I'm twenty years old and just finished getting my G. E. D."

"Yeah, well…I go to school, cant even smoke cigarettes because of my asthma…and my mother is dead…so we're not the same."

"You sort-of got me on that one."

"How much is he paying you?"

"Who…your Uncle…? I'm not getting paid a dime; I joined the program as a volunteer."

"For some kind of restitution, or community service?"

He looked at me for a long moment before he answered. "No, just because I wanted to."

"Your lying…you're not here on your own."

"I am too. I swear I am."

"Well…you're wasting your time, I don't want no brother, so don't believe everything that no-good Cop told you."

"He seems pretty cool to me."

"Yeah, well he's not!"

"Yeah…what's wrong with him?"

"Please, just go."

"It's because he ditched you, right...? He told me he did, you know, in his own words...If it makes you feel better, he said his wife put him up to it...Yeah, we talked for a little while. He said he was worried about you spending too much time here in this basement..."

"I like being alone, there's nothing wrong with it."

"Sure if you want to become a hermit, you're on your way."

"What makes you think I don't?"

"No one wants to be alone forever."

"I don't know about forever, but I want to be alone right now."

"All right...You don't like unexpected company...?"

"No I don't, it's worse than expected company."

"Well then...can I come back, maybe tomorrow, after school, I can help you with your homework if you want...What-do yah say?"

I said ok, not for my angry heart, but for my lost soul. Forever was a long time to be alone and I shouldn't desire it like I was. I could give this Eddie a little time, if it will make him feel better about himself, maybe it will do the same for me. Besides, I didn't want Uncle Larry to think that I was a quitter like he was.

In Biology class the next day, last weeks assignment was returned to me, and faced down on my desk by the teacher who walked up and down the isle. I picked it, turning it over. I wasn't surprised to see the grade, a; D. I knew better, I wasn't too confused with enzymes, and living cells, I just didn't care.

I came home from school with my back pack filled with text books. I went into the dinning room and spread my homework onto the table. Both Earl and Sally seemed to be pleased, they were probably getting tired of a policeman pestering them to be more assertive foster parents.

I didn't hold my breath and wait for Brother Eddie to show, it didn't matter one way or another to me if he came or not.

He came. I was a bit surprised, he must be getting paid. The Andersons welcomed him; Sally brought us some cookies and soda and then left the room. I didn't have the heart to tell him that I had the know-how in me to accomplish the average grade or above, so I didn't. He surprised me in his knowledge; he knew a lot about; genes and chromosomes. It was hard to ignore, it was one of his better subjects. He said he wanted to become a veterinarian.

"Have you ever dissected a frog?" He asked.

"No, not yet, I know it's coming though."

"You are not looking forward to it?"

"No."

"I skipped a lot of school but I didn't miss that day...It was the coolest thing." He said with a smile giving me the heebie-jeebies.

"Are you in college yet?"

"No I'm joining the Army for my schooling, so who knows where I will end up...I guess I will kind-of have to take it from there...What about you, what are your plans?"

"I don't have any."

"Well you have a couple more years yet to figure it out. Try not to do it the hard way, like me...Hey, can I show you something this weekend?"

"What are you going to show me?"

"There's this place, it's a youth center, and there is all kinds of cool stuff in there, it's not going to cost you any money...you want me to meet you here on Saturday, and we'll go check it out?"

"All right."

We took a bus. If I was alone, I would have been afraid, and then I realized that I had changed so much from that day I ran away from the Casper home. What was I thinking, I really messed up, leaving them and putting my trust in those strangers who would have left me for dead with no regrets, what was I thinking? I have to trust Eddie to help me out of the hole I dug for myself.

On the bus, He was telling me about the place, speaking as though it were some kind of Gym, or wreck room, equipped with a boxing ring. I suppose I didn't have to tell him that I wasn't athletic in any way, if Larry hadn't told him; he will figure it out on his own.

And now, inside the Youth Center, Eddie and I stood in front of the punching bag. He tossed me some gloves.

"Come on put-em on; let's work on getting some anger out." He remarked with a clap of his hands.

I so got it, he knew about my anger, he knew about everything. I hesitated for a moment and then put on the gloves. Eddie stood behind the bag and held it in place.

"How many times do I have to hit it?"

"As many as you want Sam…Just keep hitting it, it's not going to fight you back."

I seen it done on T V before, Eddie didn't need to dramatize like he did. "All the bad things that have happened to you…Hit it! For everybody who's let you down…Hit it!"

I started punching the bag.

"Come-on you can do better…Get mad!" He said that every time I drilled my fist into the bag. "Get mad…Get mad!"

I felt some eyes upon me as I continued punching the bag, it didn't matter much to me, what did surprise me was that I was breaking a sweat, and my lungs were fine. I hit the Sword man and his friend that I could never identify, I hit Zee, and her friend, my mother and father, and I hit Aunt Mae, but I couldn't find it in myself to hit the rest of the Casper family, including Uncle Larry.

Once finished, I felt lighter, as though I were carrying their ugliness with me the whole time. As little as I knew Eddie, he saw it in me.

"Way to go!" He remarked with a smile he put on his own gloves. I stood by and he showed me how it was done. He hit that bag like a pro, as he said he was a fighter, it was a good thing, the punching bag was invented, of course it's always been around, I'm sure it started out as a bag of grain, who am I kidding, it started out in a human form that's still around today.

I didn't need to thank him for the day at the center, I should have by rights, but I was learning that some things don't need to be confirmed with words of thanks, but just by words.

"So, when do you leave with the Army?"

"Come mid April…We can hang out until then…I can get you in the ring and show you stance."

"Ok…next Saturday?"

"You kidding…how about tomorrow?" He asked before I got off the bus.

"All right see you tomorrow."

I wasn't into boxing or fighting, but if it helped me release my anger I was all for that. I still questioned Eddie's persistence; there was no way someone could care like he was without getting paid for it. It mattered to me.

I went to bed that night missing my time with my guitar, from the basement, it was calling me, and I ignored it. Just Give me the beat boys and fill my soul until I drift away. I knew one thing was certain, I would never be the leader of a big ole band like Johnny-be-good, but I could dream about it, but I didn't have it in me, and couldn't imagine that I was military material with my bad lungs. What was to become of me?

No bad dreams plagued me, and with the new day I had hopes that I was crawling out of my hole, I still had my doubts, but I was going to enjoy this glimpse of reality while it lasted. It was funny how I never noticed Sally and Earl's love for each other, I caught them kissing in the kitchen that morning. I wondered if Uncle Larry and Aunt Mae ever done such a thing, not to my knowledge, I hoped that I hadn't interfered in any way if they had such a relationship, I felt bad for hitting Aunt Mae yesterday, but what she didn't know wouldn't hurt her.

"Sam, good morning, excited for the day?" Earl asked.

I wouldn't have gone that far, but I knew it was a step in the right direction. "I guess so."

"I bet it feels good to finally get some exercise, instead of being cooped up in the basement." Sally said with a smile, placing a plate of short stacked pancakes in front of me.

I never thought of it as being cooped up, I wouldn't have minded it one bit if Eddie were to call and cancel, but he didn't. We spent hours inside the center, I would have to say he was more excited than I was about boxing rotations, right jabs and left jabs. This isn't what future veterinarians do, but perhaps he was getting himself bulked up for the Army.

After spending a months worth of weekends and various week days with Eddie, I was beginning to feel comfortable with his company. The vigorous work outs at the center were still something I had to get used to.

We washed up in the men's room. "So, Sam do ya want to meet my mother…? She's making Sloppy Joes tonight."

"I don't know I should just probably go home."

"Ahh…just call the folks from my place and tell them you're eating over."

"I don't know…You live with your mother?"

"Yeah…not to far from here, we can walk it, and then I'll ride the bus home with you."

"I know the way I can take the bus home by myself."

"Then you'll come over supper?"

"I guess so."

I followed him out onto the street with an uncomfortable feeling; this was the same neighborhood I ran to, Even though it was nearly two years ago, at times it still felt like yesterday, and this was one of those times. With my hands in my jacket pocket, I held onto my inhaler tightly.

"I tend on getting my mother out of here, and into a decent neighborhood, it wont be long I will be getting a nice sized chunk of my enlistment bonus real soon…she cant wait."

I nodded, happy for him and his mother. "You got any other brothers or sisters?"

"Yes I do…They all didn't turn out so well…but me, I'm going to make my mama proud."

I nodded again trying to keep my mind off the surroundings. We were coming up on the apartment building that seemed to be too familiar to me. It was an ugly red building with brown trim; Eddie sprinted up the concrete stair. I stopped in my tracks feeling my chest tighten; he turned to look at me with wide eyes.

"Come-on...What's wrong Sam...?" He asked.

I took out my inhaler and gave it a pump, and then I shook my head. "I can't go in there."

"Why...what's wrong...? You going to be all right...? Sam...?"

"I'm just going to go home...okay..." I wheezed.

"No...not like this...I'll go with you."

On the bus, Eddie drilled me with questions while I held my inhaler in my hand.

"Is it the same building...? Where it happened to you?"

"Shut up...you know all about me, he told you everything...and you took me there because he told you to..."

"No Sam...it's not true...I live there, I have for years."

"Then you knew all along...why are you asking me if you knew?"

"Honest...I didn't know...Sam I didn't..."

He pleaded his case until I had gotten off the bus.

I said little to Sally and Earl, I told them I had eaten and that I wasn't hungry. They may have been content that I went into my bedroom instead of the basement. I knew I had paranoia, and no doubt Eddie now did too. I laid there on my bed for a long time just feeling numb and then the door bell rang. Knowing that Sally and Earl hadn't entertained guest on a regular basis, I suspected that it may be Uncle Larry; after all, his informant probably had called him.

I heard his knock on my closed bedroom door; it was a comfort to me. He then stepped in wearing his favorite jogging outfit that he wore to lounge around the house in on his days off. Once inside he grabbed the chair from my desk. He sat down and then let out a heavy sigh.

"You…um…You didn't have a good day I hear…Sam…no one is out-to-get-you…certainly not me, or Eddie for that matter…I didn't know his address, but maybe it was a god send, if you had some suppressed memories of that time, that you let out…Did you…?"

"You told him everything…you want me to have a friend, shouldn't I decide what I want to tell him?"

"You are welcome to do so when you find a friend…you know that Eddie is leaving soon…He enlisted in the Army."

"I know…"

"I'm sorry Sam…I just wanted him to understand you and your background…You Ahh…Did something trigger your memory of that time you lost…?"

"I didn't lose no time…"

"Sam there is a whole day that you are not telling me about."

"I called you that day, remember?"

"What about the day before you called me?"

"I hit James. At your house…I keep telling you…and I told that therapist the same thing."

"We know what you told us…" He sighed again. "I think you should have finished what you started and entered that building with Eddie…Would you mind giving it another try?"

"No…! I…So it's true…you guys set it up…! I told you!" I shouted jumping off my bed with no intentions of walking out, even though Larry may have saw it that way, he got up and walked to the door standing before it.

"You know better…I don't want to hear no more of your silly accusations…the case comes secondary to your well being, so there is a bad guy still left out there, they're a dime a dozen.

"You don't care about me...And nether does your family...!" He stood there in front of the door folding his arms across his chest, and then I retracted. "Your family doesn't...Aunt Mae hates me!"

"Have you given her a chance to care? You turned down every single invitation we gave you to change that...We were expecting you for Christmas...you back out every time Sam."

"I can't go someplace where I'm not welcome?"

"If you're invited, you're welcome...again, give them a chance...Sam what more do you want from me...? If you don't want to go into that building, then don't...but I would like you to try another therapist, can I set up an appointment for you?"

"I've done that, I mean, I don't...know what you are talking about, lost time...I think, you, had your days it mixed up...I was walking all that day, after I hit James..."

"Do you still tie yourself up at night...?"

"No...why would I do that?"

My Uncle took it upon himself to circle my bed. He lifted the mattress on all four corners. He found nothing, and I was pleased at that brief moment. I hoped he wouldn't lift up my pillow, but he did. He took a shoe lace into his hand and then held it out in front of me. "What do you call this then...? Do you still sleep walk?"

"Course not...that's what the shoelace is for."

"Can I set you up an appointment to see someone?" He asked as he stuffed the shoelace into his pocket.

"Can I see...Doctor Albey?"

"You know she's retired...?"

"Yes, course I do but can...I see her?"

"I'll see what I can do..."

After he had left I laid there, racking my brain one more time trying to solve the puzzle of the lost time I was supposed to have had. Every time I visited this scenario I came up empty. I believed someone was trying to mess with my head when I was probably the one and only culprit. Did I need to know? Was I being my best friend by surprising it? If I don't acknowledge it will it come back to haunt me, or somebody else? Because I had the tendency to do so, I wondered if I scarred Eddie away, he showed up when he wanted to. I guess I couldn't ask for promptness when it came to charitable reasons such as I was. That night I went to bed untied to the bed, it was time.

The next day I sat there at the dinning room table doing my homework, when I, of all people had a phone call.

"Hello?" I answered.

"Sam it's me, Uncle Larry...I'm sorry to be telling you this over the phone. But it has been a hectic day...Doctor Albey is sick...she has cancer...I did chat with her over the phone some, and she said that she wants to see you...She didn't sound so good, so I didn't tell her what happened to you, two years ago...I don't think she knows, so what I am saying is, she thinks it is a social visit, and I think we should keep it that way."

"Ok..." I said fighting back my tears.

"All right, well she's still living with her daughter out on the countryside, I have Thursday afternoon off, I can pick you up after school at the Anderson's there...Does that sound ok?"

"Yeah, that's fine."

"You all right...?"

"I'm ok…" I lied.

"I'll see you Thursday then."

"Ok." I answered as the phone hummed in my ear.


I saw Eddie the next day; he came over after school for a short social visit. I apologized to him; he played it by ear, and didn't pry. He said I should call him if I ever wanted to meet him at the Youth Center, he'd be hanging around for a few more weeks yet. I knew I had to remember the conversation I had with Uncle Larry; Eddie's purpose was not to be a friend, but just someone to lean on for the moment.


I remembered that day Grace took me down this long and winding road just a few short years ago, she said it was peaceful out here as if she were comforting herself and not me for a change. She must have already known she had cancer, I didn't see it as clearly as I should have, and I was too just wrapped up in myself to realize.

Even though the snow was melting, with the promise of spring to come, everything still looked dead to me. Uncle Larry was quiet; he had his eyes on the road ahead.

"Did she really say that she wanted to see me…?"

"Of course she did…I wouldn't lie to you Sam…She also thinks that you are still living with us, so we can keep it that way for her."

"I don't know what to say to her…and what if she asks me about the guitar she gave me…? I can't tell her that I traded it in."

"Well, you shouldn't have done that in the first place…Next time someone gives you a sentimental gift like that, I suggest you honor it and keep it in their remembrance…She is not going to ask if you still have it, she will just assume that you do."

"Sir…do you have my key chain…?"

"Key chain…? No, I don't have—you lost your key…didn't you say that you had it in your pocket that day you left our house?"

"I thought I did."

"Well no matter…I changed the locks just in case."

"Doctor Albey gave me that key chain too."

"I sorry Sam…If it was at the house, it would have turned up by now."

I didn't want the car ride to end; I just wanted him to keep on driving. I didn't want to see her, I didn't want to face her, I had disturbed and helpless written all over my face, and how dare I even wish that she would be too sick or tired to notice. Once in the driveway, Uncle Larry stopped the car and put into park, near the big house.

"Are you going to come in with me…?"

"Do you want me to?"

"Yes I do…please…I can't go in by myself sir…" I pleaded with a cry in my voice.

"All right, calm down, I'll be right next to you, but just try to suck it up, until the visit is over. Can you do that?"

I took a deep breath, and then let it out, then just nodded. We walked up to the door. My hand was inside of my jacket pocket gripping onto my inhaler. Uncle Larry rang the doorbell. A woman that I probably had seen before answered the door; she raised a subtle smile looking at the both of us.

"You must be Sam, and Officer Casper."

"Oh, just Larry ma'am, pleased to meet you." He said with a nod

"And you too…Well, I'm Jane, Grace's daughter…come on in, please…"

Uncle Larry patted my shoulder and then followed me inside. Jane stood before us clasping her hands together. She spoke just above a whisper. "Today is not one of her better days."

I found myself quickly speaking out." We can come back some other time."

"Oh, no, Sam she's been waiting for you."

I wanted to ask why, but didn't. We walked behind her and into a large bedroom where Doctor Albey lay. I felt Uncle Larry's hand on my back giving me a gentle push up to her bedside. I turned to look at him hoping that he wouldn't leave me there; he just nodded standing in place.

"Mom…!" Her daughter called out.

I didn't like the sight of her already, she looked so much older than she had two years ago, but when she opened her eyes I saw the yellow inside, She looked at me, and smiled anyway.

"Sam…you made it…it's so good to see you…look how you have grown…How have you been?" She asked in a weak, tried voice, and then she reached her hand out for mine.

I was uneasy, but took her hand. "I've been ok…been good."

"It's good to hear…your going to turn into a fine man one day…you keeping up with your studies?"

"Yes I am."

"And you have got such a fine family…you belong just where you are at…you see how things just tend to work out when the chips are down…?"

"Yes they do…"

"You stick with them, and they will never leave you Sam...ok?"

"Yes ma'am..."

"Come on now...I told you I have a name."

"Yes Grace..."

"I'm going to heaven soon...and I'll be looking down...watching out for you One can't have too many angels you know." She coughed, releasing her hand from mine, and then she regained her composure and smiled at me once more. "No more bad dreams Samuel?"

"No ma'am, none."

"That's wonderful...And your asthma...is it easing?"

"Yes it is."

"Good I'm glad...I bet you're a pro on that old six string...you didn't happen to bring it along with you, did you?"

"No ma'am, I didn't." I replied holding back my tears.

"Oh, what a shame...I would sure like to hear you play that guitar just once more, for the good times."

"You should have said something Mother..."

"I know...I should have...and it would be too much to ask...but you should hear him play...it makes my heart sing"

Yes, I told myself, it would be too much to ask, so please don't. I saw Grace's daughter lift her eyes to my Uncle Larry, only then did I turn to dart my eyes at him.

"We can come back tomorrow, same time." He said with a nod.

I shook my head, and then hoped that Grace hadn't seen it.

"You hear that Mother...Sam will play for you tomorrow."

"Oh how wonderful...I can't wait...Can you play Amazing Grace for me Sam?"

"It will be wonderful Mother won't it." Grace's daughter remarked with a smile.

I didn't smile back, and Grace closed her eyes with hers still on her face, I could speak for us all at that moment, we were in question, but Doctor Albey was breathing.

"She's been sleeping a lot lately," she whispered.

"We best be getting a move on then…remind her that we will be back tomorrow." Uncle Larry announced before he stepped out of the room.

Grace's daughter followed me out of the room; and as sad as it was, she thanked us both for coming. I got into Uncle Larry's car feeling numb; I wouldn't have minded an asthma attack setting in for some kind of distraction.

Uncle Larry turned the key to start the engine letting out one of his heavy sighs.

"What was the name of the music shop you went to?"

"Red's Music Box…but that was over a year ago, it can't be still there."

"It's worth a shot…if its not there we will pick out one similar to its liking…you know what it looked like don't you?" He asked pulling onto the road.

"Yes, but she will know that it's not the same one."

"What do you propose we do then…? Sam she's very sick, she won't be studying the guitar, she just wants to hear you play…I suggest you brush up on the song…Do you know it…?"

"I used to…"

"Used to, isn't that long ago for you… You're going to have to brush up on one or two church hymns in case she wants to hear more…Will you be singing?"

"I don't, I never have, and I couldn't…and don't you have to work tomorrow?"

"Some things are more important than working Sam…"


Back in the city my uncle and I searched the walls and cubby holes of Red's Music Box before he closed for the day. A man who I assumed was Red, because of his red hair and confident smile came up to us.

"May I help you with something?"

"Yes you may. We are looking for…Ahh…"

"Six string acoustic Fender, beige mahogany with a black trim and a spruce tip…it had a brown hard-shell case…I brought in here about a year and a half ago for a trade…do you still have it?" I asked.

"Well…what you see here is what we have, all the used equipment is priced to sell…I can't say that I remember that guitar in particular, but I'm sure it's gone."

"You have any records, some sort of log as of whom you may have sold it to?"

"No sir, I'm sorry, we do keep records, but after, ten, twelve months they get tossed."

"Tossed, you mean thrown out? Couldn't you just have found some where to store-em?"

"I suppose so, again I apologize."

We walked out of the music shop with one, somewhat similar to it, all the way down to the case. The trim was brown and not black and the mahogany was scrapped up, as though a house cat had had a field day on it, the strap was black, and it could have passed for her late husbands.

"Thank you sir, and my grades are coming back up, I can get another paper route so I can pay you for it."

Again, Uncle Larry sighed heavily behind the wheel. "I think its best you not have a paper route at all, and keep your grades up instead…Just think of it as an early birthday present, and a lesson learned ok?"

"Yes sir…thank you."

"You're welcome…I'll see you tomorrow, after school, you have some practicing to do right now." He said before I got out of his car.

"I have your supper warmed in the oven." Sally remarked reaching for her hot pads.

"Thanks, but, I already ate." I lied but truly I wasn't hungry.

Neither she nor Earl questioned the guitar case I had in my hand. I brought the imposter down to the basement, and shoved my electric guitar out of the way. I found the book of church hymns and searched though it. I found her song; Amazing Grace. I worked on it long and hard until Earl came down and told me that it was time for bed.

I laid awake most of the night worrying. If Grace finds out, what will I do? So many different scenarios came to my mind, some of them just horrifying, how could I think of such things? I had the feeling that I would never be sane. I can become that hermit Eddie spoke of. One day I will be an adult, and Uncle Larry will back off with his hands tied, after all he wouldn't be getting any younger. And I'd keep my madness away from the bad, bad world.

I did eat breakfast only because I had a nervous nagging hunger. Sally and Earl sat there with me.

"So, how did your visit go with your old friend?" Earl finally asked.

"It went ok, were going back latter today, after school so I can play her a song."

"You and your uncle found the guitar that she had given you a while back?" Sally asked with a tearful smile.

"Yes we did."

"How special that must have been…So what song are you going to sing for her?"

"I'm just going to play, Amazing Grace…"

"How wonderful." She said.

The phone rang. I swallowed my scrambled eggs harshly while Sally went to answer it.

"Hello…? Oh, hello Larry…Yes, he's right here."

I stepped over to the phone and took it into my trembling hand. "Hello."

"Sam…She passed away last night…I'm sorry…I will take you to her funeral…We'll go together…Are you all right?"

"Yeah…"

"Why don't you take the day off from school."

"Ok…"

"I'll talk to you real soon, hang in there."

"I will." I said hanging up the phone. "She died last night, and he said I didn't have to go to school today."

"By all means…I'm sorry Sam." One of them had said.

"It's ok…" I replied and then headed for the basement. They let me go.

Both of the guitars sat there teasing me. One, the imposter, the other two faced snob thinking that he was better than the one Doctor Albey gave me. I picked up imposter by its long neck raising it high then I slammed it into the snob as hard as I could. Knowing that they were not human I did it again, and again, and again.

Earl stopped me grabbing a hold of me. I dropped what was left of the six string. He shook me into place. "Look at what you have done!"

I stood there caching my breath, but it was far from being an asthma attack. "It wasn't the one she gave me! It wasn't!!!"

He shook his head at me. "So you destroy it! Both of them in the process!"

"Go ahead! Get rid of me, see if I care…! Just see if I care!" I shouted pulling myself away from his grip.

"We're not going to get rid of you!" He shouted as I jogged up the stairs, I ran into Sally.

"Sam…?"

"Let him be Sal—"

I did want to be alone, and for some reason, my bedroom seemed like a cage to me. With my jacket in hand, I walked into the living room and told them that I was going for a walk, they let me go. I'm sure they thought it would be good for me, for I haven't ventured out much, and it was about time I start again.

Once outside, I felt a hint of freedom, kind-of like I had that day I ran away from the Casper's. I had the guilt inside of me, I just couldn't do anything right, even when I had the nicest people around me, I was unfixable and untreatable, a dud. A car revved behind me, I wasn't afraid, I kept walking. After my legs began to cramp from the damp spring air and the long walk I finally took a bus; I didn't care where it was going. I couldn't say if I was running or just visiting the idea.

I got off the bus eventually. Near by there was a railroad trestle that ran over a channel of the Mississippi. It wasn't as close as it had appeared to be. I walked up the steep service road to it. Now it was clear to me that I was visiting the idea of ending my life. It was a shorter walk to the center of the trestle. I looked down to the cold partially frozen water below, directly below me about seventy-eighty feet were some big rocks. The drop would surely take my life away, it's what I wanted. I held onto the steel beam, I could just jump it now, and if I didn't die right away I can lay there injured, maybe the river would take me away and no one will ever have to know what ever become of me.

I stood there pondering in hesitation; I couldn't have been the only person who weighed out their options and their good-byes to themselves before they ended their life. There was no one around, but the busy people in their automobiles on the Interstate highway a quarter mile away going on with their busy day.

It wasn't much of a dare for me. I climbed onto the narrow beam and sat, the only thing left to do was to just let go, and drop. I came this far, I would have to tack on Coward to my list of defaults if I backed out on myself now.

"Hey…kid…did your god let you down…?

I turned my eyes to see that I wasn't alone. He was walking my way slowly. "Go away."

"What are you doing…? You can't be serious."

"I said go away…if you come any closer I'll drop right now." I said darting my eyes at him. He was somewhere between a man and a boy, he stopped in place about ten feet away from me.

"You can't do this…what if you change your mind half way down?"

"There won't be any time to think once I let go."

"Then give yourself some time right now to think about it…what about your parents?"

"I don't have any."

"Yeah, me neither…You must have somebody who cares."

"I'm a burden on someone." I answered.

"I know the feeling." He said taking a step closer to me and then he stopped at the edge of the beam, he looked down, and then back at me. "What can be so bad that can't be fixed?"

"Everything."

"Yeah, like what…?"

"I don't need to answer to you…so just go away. And don't come any closer."

"I'm not going to walk away…put yourself in my spot choir boy. Could you walk away?"

"Why…? Do you want to watch me?"

"Are you kidding…? My parents were killed right in front of my eyes, believe me it's not a pretty sight…my ole man had it coming. He beat my mother to a bloody pulp…My name is David Pane, maybe you have heard of me."


Marshall Quickly dropped Sam's book as he leaped up from his bed, and barged out of his room with his heart racing wanting to report to his mother. The house was dark. He turned on the kitchen light and looked at the clock; it was going on ten-thirty. It wasn't unusual for her to go to bed without saying good night, tonight was just one of those nights. He went to the refrigerator and grabbed a can of Coke.

In that short time, he decided that his news could wait, after all, how would he go about telling his mother that he believed David Pane was David Bear When he wasn't quite sure himself? The only thing he was sure of was that he was somewhat confused of Sam's words as he quoted David Pane's. His mother would probably be angry with him for taking Sam's property out of his house without permission, not to mention her sensitivity whenever David Pane's name was brought up.

Marshall went back into his room knowing that there wasn't much left to Sam's book, and maybe he will get some more answers, no matter, he was curious. He found where he had left off…

: "No, never heard of you."

"You never watched the news…? I was from Hudser…the kid who shot his father."

"I thought you said, your parents were killed in front of you?"

"I did…I was just seeing if you were paying attention choir boy."

"Why are you calling me choir boy?"

"Because you dropped your key chain…I wouldn't have seen you otherwise…I was down there when it fell onto the rock. I pulled it from the river then saw you up here."

I shook my head in utter disbelief when he dangled it from his finger. "I didn't…that's impossible…" I said still looking at the key chain from the short distance, I lost my balance.

In that split second I feared for my life. With one hand, I caught a hold of the steel beam that my foot had once rested on. I was losing my grip quite quickly when he hit the tracks face down. He grabbed my forearm; I saw the fear in his eyes when I lost my hold entirely. And then I saw the grimace on his face.

"I don't want to die!" I cried in a plea to him.

He said nothing as if he were saving every bit of strength he had to prevent that from happening leaving me to think I should do the same. He lifted me up just enough to allow me to grab back a hold of the beam to take some of my weight off of him. With his second hand he grabbed the back of my jacket, and from there, he pulled me back on the trestle.

We both sat there panting as a train horn wailed in the distance. Beside me, on the railroad tie was the key chain. I picked it up, it was mine, the one Doctor Albey gave me just a few short years ago.

"It's mine…but…I didn't drop it…I lost it almost two years ago."

"So you chickened-out two years ago…there's a train coming, unless you changed your mind about dieing…" He replied standing up. He started walking and I was quick to follow. I stuffed my key chain into my pocket.

I was overwhelmed, to say the least. I suppose I said too much, now this David guy thought that I was suicidal twice over. Have I been here before? It was a logical explanation, after all I had a day of missed time, and I couldn't account for that day at all. I was lead here today like I've been here before.

The train barreled across the trestle wailing its horn behind us, David had a car parked at the bottom of the service road in a small inlet near the river channel. It wasn't there when I walked up a while ago.

"You need a ride home kid?" He turned to shout at me over the sound of the trains' loud engine.

I nodded, and then caught up to him. I opened the passenger door, and on the seat were some mechanic magazines, he tossed them onto the back seat and then I got into his car.

"That was a rush…you need some help kid."

"You think I need help…you just told me that you killed your father."

"I'm not proud of it, it had to be done. I also said that my ole man killed my mother. I don't need any help…I'm ok now. I graduate in a few months, already have a job lined up as an assistant in an Auto repair shop…What about you?"

"I'm barely sixteen…don't compare me to you."

"You didn't go to school today."

"You didn't ether."

"It's almost four o'clock, I went to school."

"Well I have my reasons, and I don't need to answer to you."

"I saved your life…you see, if you would have had the time, you would have changed your mind."

"You're right, I'm sorry, and thank you…I owe you one."

"No you don't…I'm even. Are you done trying to kill yourself now?"

"Yeah…it won't happen again."

"So what was the reason? You said that you don't have any parents, are you living in a foster home?"

"Yeah."

"I know this Cop; he lives here in the city. He helped me out, even though we lived in two different states. He can find you some decent foster parents."

"The ones I have aren't bad." I replied as he went for his wallet.

"Then what is your problem?" He asked. My problem, I questioned. I didn't know. He handed me a slip of paper. "Here's his number if you change your mind. He's got four kids of his own, but he still calls me from time to time to see how I'm doing. He's pretty cool, he'll help you out…What your address?"

I told him my address and then I opened up the folded piece of paper with the phone number on it. There was a name included; Larry Casper. The number was his.

"What were you doing here?" I asked as he pulled onto the interstate highway.

"Me...? Just looking for a good fishing hole to take in...you're a long way from home. What'd yah walk all this way?"

"How many kids did you say this Cop has?"

"He's got four...Why?'

"Did you meet them?"

"No, I have no reason to meet them, kid, you're strange."

I supposed I was in his eyes, and I wasn't about to force my mind into more off the wall scenarios that just caused more trouble for me. I had to explain, I just had to.

"He's my uncle...He's got three kids, and me."

"No way...! Hey, that's pretty wild...Larry is your uncle?"

"I know I shouldn't have any problems, I lived with them once, but I caused trouble. I'm just a little messed up, but I'm getting better."

He chuckled. "You think so?"

"Yes I do...You won't tell him will you?"

"You're not going to pull any more of those stunts?"

"No, and thanks I really mean it, I owe you one."

"So why'd you do it?"

I questioned myself again. My attitude was changing by the second. I felt so ashamed and so glad to be alive at the same time. I was afraid of living, and every time somebody cared I somehow found the means to push them away with my own self pity. I've been taking a grim view of my day-to-day existence. It was time I lighten up.

Still I didn't have all of the answerers I was looking for, but I had what I needed, I've always had. What more could I ask for? Maybe I was on that railroad trestle before and maybe I wasn't. Maybe my keychain was there from a previous day and time, and maybe it wasn't. Either way I looked at it, it was a miracle, and that was good enough for me.

"Hey kid, you can just forget about what I told you, about—you know…I don't go around advertising…your uncle knows and stuff, and I'm not running, but I'd like to just—forget about it, you know."

"Yeah okay, it's a deal then. My name is Sam."

"Mine is David Bear, or it will be soon. I'm in the process of changing it. The legal way…Not to proud of your name either, are you?"

"No, not really, my dad is in prison."

"Mine would have been too. What did your ole man do?"

"Embezzlement and extortion."

"Are you afraid people are thinking you're no good because of him?"

"Not really…I messed myself up."

"You…the choir boy?" He chuckled.

I didn't care too much for that, but knowing that I had to lighten up, I passed it off, after all his life was probably far worse than mine. "I'm getting better."

"Yeah, me too."

"So you fish a lot?"

"I haven't for a while, but I want to take it back up this year."

"Well, if you'd like some company, I wouldn't mind coming along."

"Yeah, sure we can do that kid, I mean Sam."

He dropped me off with the promise that he would call me come fishing opener. Sally and Earl were both home. Earl was quick to speak in frustration,

"Where have you been all day? I was just about to call your uncle!"

"I'm sorry," I said calmly hoping that if he and Sally were at their; wits end with me and my behavior; they'd change their minds before they make any rash decisions.

"All right then…I want you to go down to that basement and clean up that mess you made."

"Yes sir."

Both guitars were just how I left them. They were destroyed as the result of my rage. It was for the best, if they were repairable I would have always been reminded of that angry boy I once had inside of me. I tossed the broken pieces into the dumpster, throwing away the old, and ready to begin to feel the new person inside of me, it was there, I just had to believe that it would last.

I would have had to accept the consequences if Uncle Larry had gotten wind of what I had done that day. Whether it would have been from the raging basement indecent, or god forbid, David went back off his word. Neither of the two possibilities happened, at least to my knowledge.

I was still a bit worried that I may be confronted after Doctor Albey's funeral. He picked me up after a half a day's school. I know that this was a day to respect her memory, but would Uncle Larry take me to a restaurant afterward and tell me that I was going to get transferred again because the Andersons just can't deal with me any more. I told myself that it was going to be ok, and I can handle it if it happened.

I shed tears at her funeral, not to prove to Uncle Larry that I was sane, but for me, because I was. He gave me his clean handkerchief and stood beside me all the way, and why not, I was one of his children.

So many good things were said about her, all of them touching. I was sure that nothing was exaggerated. I didn't know her all that long, but I wished I had. I supposed her knowledge was unlimited up there, but could she have been a guardian angel already? So soon after she had died? If so, she didn't have very much time to say hello to her beloved husband in heaven before; the big guy told her she had to come a calling to me. I bet she didn't think that I would have needed her that soon. She sure had her work cut out for her. If she knew about the key chain, she sure knew about the guitar, I wondered if that would somehow come back to me, but probably not. I hoped that she forgave me; I silently promised her that I would be good from now on. A woman stood in front of the church and sang Amazing Grace…She got her song.

We shook a few hands before we cleared the church. Uncle Larry spoke for the both of us with our introductions and our apologies, and then we walked out to his car. My emotions were still high, and if he was to say that we were going to a restaurant for a talk, well then, so-be-it. He started the car.

"You know it's Jeanie's birthday today…She's five, so we are having a little celebration…you know, just us, with the cake and ice cream, and the happy birthday song. Would you like to come over for supper and the fixings?"

I said nothing, yet I gave him my best, which was just a shrug.

"Then it's settled." It wasn't a clear statement, but I had the feeling that I understood him. And after he turned onto the street in the opposite direction of the Andersons, I understood him fully.

I thought of a reasonable argument I could bring up, but he's heard them all. It all boiled down to my self pity, I supposed it was a better time than any for a visit; I looked humble enough for a welcome after a couple hours of crying. "Do they know I'm coming?"

"I told Mae that I was going to invite you, only out of courtesy, you know women like to be informed of those things. You best keep that in mind for future references."

"Sir...? Do you work with other kids, like me?"

"What do you mean...?"

"Well did you know Eddie?" He said he was a bad kid and I was just wondering."

"I've been a volunteer at a rehabilitation center, a few hours here and there, going on ten years...I've known Eddie for a while now, but don't think of yourself as a bad kid Sam. Eddie was a bad kid, he got himself into the wrong crowd, but he turned himself around real fast. He fits the criteria for the; Adopt a Brother Program. Why do you ask, did you have a problem with him?"

"No...I was just wondering...I bet that kid who shot his father to death wouldn't fit the criteria...what was his name, David something?"

"David Pane...?"

"Yeah, that's it..."

"That was almost a year ago; in a town nearly thirty miles away...but yes, I know who he is...We can't be so quick to put a label on somebody Sam. What he did was justifiable, considering the circumstances at that time."

"So, he didn't get rehabilitated?"

"No, after an evaluation, he was dismissed all together."

283

I realized I was testing him and David, I couldn't help it, and my paranoia will go away soon enough. However Uncle Larry shouldn't have been so quick to label me as a good kid. If I was bold and brave enough to make friends, I may have gotten into the wrong crowd like Eddie had, and the only reason why I called him Sir, was because it was shorter than saying, Uncle Larry all the time.

I walked behind my uncle to his door. "Mae we have company!"

Mae come out from the kitchen with a dish towel in her hand. "Hello Sam."

"Hello ma'am."

"It's good to see you again, my, have you grown…The boys will be home from school soon…Just make yourself comfortable."

"Dad-dy…!" Little Jeannie called out racing up to him.

"And how's my birthday girl?" He asked picking her up into his arms.

"I'm good!" she said with a wide smile, and then she noticed me. "What's your name?"

"Well, this is your cousin Sam, don't you remember him Jeanie?"

She shook her head, "No…"

And for that reason I smiled. "Happy birthday."

"Thank you…" She replied shyly.

"You going to tell your cousin how old you are?" She looked at her father and then back to me spreading her hand out wide. "I'm a handful…five."

Jeanie was showing me her dolls when Josh and James came home. I saw the surprise on their faces. They said; hi and then went off to do their own things, I didn't mind that at all, but I assumed that Uncle Larry did. He left the living room, and soon after, Josh and James returned.

James showed me his walkman C D player he had gotten for Christmas.

"I got one too…" Josh had said with little enthusiasm.

It wasn't a warm welcome, nor did I expect one from them. Perhaps they suspected that I was going to move back in. I found myself thinking that maybe it wasn't so wrong of me; declining all of the invitations that Uncle Larry had given me. I might have stayed away just long enough to allow all the hurt that I had caused them to blow over. Time to forgive, and in little Jeanie's case; time to forget.

My mother was not a devil in disguise. I learned from her. I would have never been able to think positive if it weren't for her negativity. She didn't give up on me, she gave up on herself. She's given me patience.

I can't speak much for my father. I barely knew him. I don't know if I ever will seek him out. I doubt he will come looking for me after all this time.

I worry that my Uncle Larry is much to kind to be out there enforcing law, for he has excused me too many times with-out regret. He must not forget his needs. He reaches out too far and wide. I envy him; I want to be like him. I suppose he's got a back bone.

And Mae, may she find peace and forgiveness in her soul. Let God not judge her as she judges others. I wish for her to lighten-up as I have.

Josh and James are not as different as I once thought, at least to the role that they played in my life. They both make everything seem so easy. There're likely to strive and win without much effort. I was so jealous.

For Eddie and the temporary friends I had. I thank them for the moments. The temporary people in my life have much greater titles in their commitments to others. Like a lost puzzle piece, everyone is part of the big picture. We all fit, and together we make the world go around.

Doctor Grace Albey, my guardian angel. Thank you for giving me piece of mind. Thank you for pulling me out of the brinks of despair. Thank you for sending David my way.

Time heals all wounds, whether we believe it or not. Grief for a loved one, the hurt we cause them, and the hurt they cause us. We all make mistakes, and with forgiveness and time I will have sanity. And so ends my search for it…

Marshall shook his head and closed the book. He was a bit dumfounded, and at the same time felt that he violated his teacher's privacy by taking the book home in the first place. He could never tell, would his mother be able to keep a secret? Did she care to know what became of David Pane?

# *Sleeping Dogs*

At the Children's hospital, David had been sitting in the waiting room for hours now. He was fidgeting in his chair, didn't care to watch T V, he couldn't hold a magazine for more than a minute at a time. He just wanted to be with his son. Why can't the doctors realize that they needed each other at a time like this? Why is he being kept from his son?

It seemed forever before a doctor in a white coat came into the waiting room, and because David was very familiar to him, the doctor took off his glasses and sighed.

"I'm sorry…he's no longer in remission. His red count is very low…"

"Low as in…? Has it spread?"

"No, not that we see it…right now we can control his infection, but without a genetically matched donor."

"What…?" David asked fearing the doctor's next words.

"He needs the same H L A, at least a ninety percent match. Are you sure Conner's entire family has been tested?"

"You think I would have let that slip my mind?! Conner is an only child…His mother and I, are all he's got…Can't you check the registry?" He shouted in question.

"We've done that, and continue to do so, but like I said—" He nodded grimly.

"Are you telling me that you can't do anything for him?" He asked with a cry in his voice.

"We will control his infection, and take it from there...Conner is resting now, why don't you do the same. In the mean time we will continue to monitor him closely."

Advising him to get some rest was an imposable suggestion. But he did find little comfort in easing his own pain sitting in a chair next to his son's bedside, and then maybe he can close his eyes for a moment.

"Bear?" David heard Wendy's voice; she was crying standing over Conner.

David jumped up to hush her. "I told you, you didn't need to come until morning." He whispered. "There's nothing you can do for him right now, he needs his rest to get better."

"I'm his mother; I have a right to be here just as much as you do." She cried raising her voice just above that whisper.

"I'm not sleeping." Conner muttered, and then added. "I want you guy's to stop fighting, and Mom, don't cry, I'll be all right, the angel told me I will..."

"Oh God..." Wendy cried turning her head away.

"Don't say that Mom...The angel told me...she was here...I will get better."

"I know you will honey bear."

"It's nighttime, go home and go to bed...both of you please."

"You got it pal..." David replied.

They both kissed him good night, and then left the room. Once out into the hallway Wendy confronted him. "What did he mean; Angel...? He's going to give up and go to heaven because Sam fed him a bunch of—"

"You leave Sam out of this...Conner has a fever, His mind can be playing tricks on him, and if he believes he saw an Angel, then let him..."

"Hallucinating, David...? How high is his fever...?"

"It's not that high, a-hundred-and-two point-one, and he wasn't hallucinating, it was probably a dream...now go on and go home, come back in the morning."

She reluctantly did so. David did not; he went into the waiting room to sit for the night. When David woke a few hours latter he knew very well that he wasn't rested enough to even consider this a bad dream, and he was still here in this hospital. David learned that Conner was resting comfortably. He went down to the cafeteria. It would be morning soon...



Marshall was no expert on making coffee, his mother had always made it, and he rarely drank it. One scoop, two scoops? He wasn't sure. He gave it two and then turned on the coffee maker.

His mother entered the kitchen with her robe wrapped tightly around her. "Burr...its cold in here." She said before she turned up the thermostat. "You're up early...what are you doing making coffee...? I hope you didn't give it three scoops."

"No, I gave it two."

"Oh good...that's nice of you, and what are you doing up so early?

289

Look at you, you're ready for school."

"Well I have to make a stop at the hospital. Sam called me last night and he wanted to know if I'd drop off his keys before school."

"Is he going home today?"

"I don't know for sure, but he said Mia; his wife, is going to want to go into his apartment and, you know, get things unpacked and stuff."

"Oh, maybe then they will get back together…Well, I'm going to get dressed, it wouldn't hurt me none if I were to get an early start."

"Mom…I…"

"You what…Marshall?"

"I did something I shouldn't have done yesterday." Marshall confessed.

"What did you do?"

"I, ah, well…when I was at Sam's place; I found an Auto biography of his. You know his life story."

"I know what an Auto Biography is Marshall…What did you do, bring it here? Is that why you were so pre-occupied last night?"

Marshall sighed with a nod. "I'll bring it back before I return his keys. I wouldn't have even told you if I didn't find something out in his book."

"I don't want to hear it, your teacher's past has nothing to do with me or you…You get that back in the same place that you found it, do you hear me?"

"Mom…you know I've been asking you about David Pane, well…he's Sam's friend, David Bear, you know, the mechanic who helped us with the move yesterday. He changed his name…and I just thought you might want to know."

A warm rush of anxiety flooded through her body. "Put that back where you found it."

"Mom, you okay?"

"Yes I'm fine…Why all these questions about him?" She asked with her face turning pale. She took it upon herself to take a seat at the kitchen table.

Marshall set a glass of water in front of her. "Because every time I bring up his name you get so uncomfortable, and I want to know why."

"You have been told…you know what happened, he shot his father." She replied taking the glass of water to her lips. Her hand trembled, and Marshall took notice.

"I know, he even admitted it in Sam's book, but…he, Mom, were you there?"

"Was I where…?"

"Did you see it? I don't know, maybe before the police came…I just want to know why you are so shaken up."

"I saw it…off the record, yes I was there."

"Off the record…? So it's not in the police report?"

"No."

"What does that mean; you were there when it happened?"

"You're getting to technical on me…We don't need to discuss this any further…I'm going to get ready for work." She got up and walked away. Once in her bedroom, she shut her door behind her, and then leaned up against it sobbing. "Oh God…" She cried.


Marshall left the house with Sam's book in his hand. So she was there, inside of that house when David shot his father or was she not? It didn't make sense to him.

Sam had made his way to his wheel chair; it wasn't easy walking on crutches with broken ribs. He hoped it wouldn't take him out of his classroom too long. He was surprised to see Mia arrive so early. He returned her smile.

"You're early."

"I wanted to beat the morning traffic...How are you doing?"

"I'm doing good thank you."

"Any word on if you're getting released today?"

"No. I haven't heard a thing yet; it may take half the day before a doctor comes around. Marshall should be here any time with my keys...Again I appreciate this Mia, but don't feel that you need to do this."

"I want to, really I do." She remarked taking a chair beside him. She sighed. "Sam, I got a call from my brother Scott last night. He just came back from Florida. You know he's in the military?"

"Yes, of course."

"Well, Katie was packing up her things...The wedding is off because his duties as a military man took him away from home to much." She said with a cry in her voice. "She knew what she was getting herself into, the nerve of her."

"I'm sorry to hear that Mia."

"How selfish can she be...she knew he was a military man...She couldn't handle those short visits to Florida and back, what if he was called to Iraq?"

"We just need to be glad that he didn't get married to her."

"She kept the expensive ring that she just had, to have...and he

worked so hard for it…Scott is such a nice guy, and he's so broken up."
She cried.

"Katie will realize that one day…We all make mistakes…" Sam
sighed. "Mia I've been thinking that its time I get my head out of the
clouds and realize that not everything is a sign from God…I'm willing
to fill out that Adoption application with you, if it's not to late."

"Oh…" She cried tears flooded her eyes. "I was about to give in to
you…I want nothing more than to call this off."

"That's good news," he said reaching for her hand.

He slowly pulled her closer wanting her to fall into him, but they
both realized that it will cause pain. They kissed each other. The phone
rang, Mia pulled away from Sam's embrace.

"Hello…No you have the right room, this is Mia…Oh, David…yes
he's here." She handed the phone over to Sam.

"Yeah, David what's up?"

"I'm at the children's hospital with Conner. I brought him in last
night, he's got an infection, and he's running a fever…it's down some
from last night, but he's out of remission."

"Oh God." He grimaced, and then looked up to Mia. They shared a
solemn look.


Marshall tapped on the open door and walked in. Even though Sam
was on the phone, he was acknowledged by the both of them.

"Has it spread…?" Sam asked. "There's got to be something they
can do…"

Mia stepped up to Marshall, and he handed her the keys. "Thank
you." She said.

"No…Bear, tell him that I will be there as soon as I can…can I call him?…all right, have him call me…I'll be here for a while, and you hang in there."

Marshall already knew more than he should about his teacher and David for that matter. He wasn't sure of what was proper edacity in this situation. So he gave Mia a nod and walked to the door.

"Marshall." Sam called out stopping his student from leaving so soon.

"Yes Sir…?" He asked.

"Thank you for all of your help."

"I'm glad to help…is there anything else you need…a ride somewhere later? I couldn't help but over-hear."

"I'm here too Sam…is Conner out of remission?"

"Yes he is…and he wants to see me."

"I could pick you up after school, if you are getting released today."

"I'm not sure of that."

"Marshall you've done enough, I'll take him there."

"All right then…I'll talk to you later."

"Thanks again."


Gwen called her shop and spoke to her assistant manager. She was just too sick; she couldn't make it in today. It was the truth, her heart was breaking. Why now, she asked herself. Her son was no dummy; he can see the lies in her soul. Only if she were a stronger person she could have hidden the truth from him, at least until this blows over one more time. Just one more; Dad conversation, just one more time David Pane's name to be brought up, Why was her son so persistent?

It was time to tell him the truth…

Time to acknowledge her past…

She and David walked back up the path from the river.

"I need time to think about this…I'm not saying that I don't care for you David."

"Just tell me that you're not going to leave with him."

"I told you, it was over between me and Carl, but for us to have a life together."

"I'm not asking you to marry me right now…"

"David, we had sex, we shouldn't have because you are my friend."

"It doesn't make any sense…so it meant nothing because we are friends?"

"That's right; I don't want to hurt you, because if we go out together, we're going to end up breaking up. Now does it make sense?"

"So we're supposed to date heartless people, like you did with Carl…? Learn to love, learn to care and the hell with friendship! And if it doesn't work out, then no one was hurt."

"Someday you'll understand."

"Just because you say that, doesn't make it true! We're supposed to hurt, I hurt all the time!" David shouted trying to get his point across. He took a hold of Gwen's arm, stopping her in her tracks turning her around to face him. She feared him for a brief moment. "You know I didn't mind much getting knocked around by my ole man. To feel something, even if its pain is better than not feeling anything at all and I hope you never understand that."

Gwen nodded studying the seriousness on his face. "Can we take this slow…let me find a way to tell it to my parents, and officially break it off with Carl?"

"Yeah okay." David said with a nod and a smile.


Gwen was sitting behind her sewing machine when her father came home trying to piece together yet another house coat of Martha's. She wasn't happy with her work, Martha deserved better.

"Supper is on the stove Dad." She announced putting the garment down.

Her father washed his hand under the kitchen sink. "What are your plans for tonight? I hope you're not going to sit around with me again, because you feel you need to keep me company."

Gwen took the casserole from out of the oven. "I was wondering if I could use your truck."

"Oh, he doesn't want to come pick you up?"

"Um…we broke up the other night."

Hank shook his head, somewhat bewildered. "Gwenie…Why?"

"He's not a nice as he appears Dad…I have strong suspicions that he was fooling around on me. I'm sorry I know you and Mom wanted me to be financially secure…but I can't stay with him." She cried.

"It's ok Gwenie…" Her father spread his arms out and Gwen stepped inside of them. He hugged her tightly like he always had. "Weren't trying to pawn you off to the highest bidder, we just want you to be happy."

"Thank you for understanding…I bet you're hungry."

Hank patted her on the back releasing her from his embrace. "I'm ravished."

She was a bit uncomfortable explaining her suspicions to her father. A few short months ago she was an innocent young woman saving herself for marriage, and now she felt that she was a let-down.

"I left my purse at Carl's…I was wondering if I could use your truck tonight, I wont be long."

"That will be fine…if your mind is made-up about him; don't let him change it for you."

"No, won't…Dad…I ah. Well I want you to know that I made this decision on my own."

"That's good, that's what I want to hear."

"But, I ah…"

"Spit it out Gwenie."

"I have feelings for David."

Hank swallowed wrong. He coughed harshly and then took a drink of his milk.

"I didn't see that one coming…what brought this on?"

"Just getting to know him."

"Yes he is a nice boy."

"Well if you consider me a girl, then you can consider him a boy."

"I meant no disrespect, but his father is a mad man."

"I know you forbade Tony and I set foot near that house, but it was unfair to David."

"I'm sorry I was just looking out for your safety."

"I'm not blaming you Dad, I'm just saying…And mom tells me, the apple doesn't fall far from the tree…I'm, we're going to take it slow."

"So you've discussed this with him already?"

Gwen felt a bit shameful. "Yes…Dad, David had nothing to do with my decision."

"Don't kid yourself Gwenie, of course he did, one way or the other...You've got to be real careful, that lunatic will be back, restraining order or not, he'll be back."

"I know Dad..."

"David and his mother are welcome here anytime."

"Thank you."

Gwen was pleased with her fathers understanding; no doubt her mother will feel the same way. She and Tony will be back from Camp in a few days. Gwen was nervous about going out to retrieve her purse. With any luck Carl won't be home and she will just have to face Pearl one last time. Perhaps she will just stick her nose in the air and hand over her purse to her.

Gwen said good bye to her father, and thanked him for the use of his truck. "I'll be back soon..."

"Take your time...and Gwenie, stick to your guns."

Not a half mile down the loop road and she spotted David walking toward home like she knew she would, she stopped and turned around near a tote road that lead down to the river. David got in.

"Were you going some where?"

"I have to go get my purse David."

"Do you want me to come with you?"

"No, I got to do this on my own...Don't worry, I'm not going to let him sweet talk me into anything...I just got done telling my dad I broke it off with Carl...and I kind-of told him about us too."

"Kind-of...?"

"I told him we are going to take it slow...I know he's just worried about what Jack will do."

"He's not around; the restraining order is staying Gwen."

"Well, unless he's laying dead somewhere he'll be back, don't you think?"

"What do you want me to do...shoot him?"

"I don't know a whole lot about the law, but if there's a restrainer order against him, he'd be an intruder intending harm."

"Yeah, that sounds right...So I was thinking about going down to the river and doing some fishing...you want to come with?"

"What's the matter, don't you have any food in the house?"

"There's food...You don't want me to go?"

"What if he comes?"

"Just what I thought, you want me to sit around and baby-sit my mother."

Gwen stopped in the Pane driveway. "I'm just saying, I don't want to see you or Martha get hurt."

"Gwen, I gave her the rifle, I showed her how to use it, and she won't let him in." He said getting out of the truck.

"All right then, well when I get back I'm going to finish up on her mending...I'll be back in a little while."

David nodded, and then Gwen drove back to town.


It appeared that her wish wasn't going to come true. Carl's car was parked in the drive. She knocked on the door.

Carl answered, lifting a subtle smile. "Come in, please."

"No, I…just came for my purse."

"Please…I'll only take a minute of your time."

Gwen reluctantly agreed with his plea and entered. "Really I just…"

"Sit down for a minute."

"No Carl."

"I just want to be heard."

She found herself taking a seat on the couch. "What Carl?"

He sat next to her. "No one is here, it's just us…I called your house a little while ago and your dad said that you were on the way…Gwen I'm sorry. I'm a jerk." He said reaching for a lock of her hair; he combed it away from her face.

She backed away. "Carl…I'm not here to make up, its over between us. I just want my purse."

"And I just want you to hear me out, please." He said sincerely. "I've got problems…I've never had a steady girlfriend…all the good ones leave me, because of my ways. I'm willing to do anything for you. I'll get some help…Anger management, something, anything once we get back to Texas." He spoke humbly and Gwen was almost sorry that she had to refuse him.

"You get that help you need, and you'll be able to find a good woman, once you're in Texas."

"Didn't you hear me…? I promised I'd get help."

"And I'm happy for you, but you can't expect me to leave my family on a wing and a prayer that you will become a better person."

"So you think I'm—What do you want from me?"

"I want you to fetch my purse."

"I like that old fashioned talk…I know you don't care for my mother. I think she's a little big on herself too…I wasn't brought up like you Gwen. Give me another chance will you?"

If she hadn't grown to love David, Carl would have said enough to change her mind.

"Carl…"

"Can I take you out for dinner?"

"I ate already."

"So early?"

"My Dad is hungry when he gets home from work."

"Tomorrow night?"

"I don't think so."

Carl sighed with a shrug of his shoulders; he got up and went over to the corner of the room and he picked up Gwen's purse from a shelf inside the book case. He handed it to her. "I'll call you."

"There's no reason for that," She replied, heading for the door.

"I'll call you." He said again.

She turned the car stereo on loud, and let the music take her mind off her stupidity. How could she even entertain the idea of giving Carl another chance? She was going to give him another chance and she would have had it not been for the statements she gave to her father and David earlier. No matter, it was over; she didn't have to answer any of his calls.

She turned down the Loop road wishing all was well, another quiet night would be nice. The summer sun will be setting soon; she hoped that David had caught some fish by now, just in case he wasn't totally honest about having food in the house. In the morning she could take Martha her clothes, and she could take out one of those frozen loaves of banana bread from the freezer, she better take that out tonight, she thought.

Her calming thoughts ended abruptly.

"Oh God no!" She bellowed out loudly taking on the awful sight of Jack's truck parked in the drive. Could it be possible that he's already been taken away by the police? She asked herself barrowing into the Pane driveway. She turned the radio off coming to a sudden stop and heard screams coming from the house, and then she wailed on the horn continuously, at the same time shifting the truck into reverse. She raced the short distance home. Hank stormed out of the house. Gwen fell out of the truck and clumsily ran to meet her father.

"He's killing her Dad! He's killing her!!"

"I just called the police! Where's David?" He questioned clutching onto her arms with his grip and at the same time loud muffled screams came from the house.

"He's down at the river! Dad, he's killing her! You have to stop him!" She bellowed.

"All right…stay here!" He huffed and then took off in a slow sprint toward the house.

"David!" Gwen screamed uncertain of which way to run.

Even though she loved her father, she rarely listened to him. After standing there helpless for a moment, she started jogging across the long grass to the Pane home. She saw her father enter the house, and then she tripped over a rock hidden under the thick grass. She got up and continued jogging. An explosive bang of gun fire came from the house, it stopped her heart momentarily. She dropped down on the grass just short of the steps to the house.

"Gwen!" David shouted racing to her.

Gwen shook her head with wide eyes only watching David run to her and past her. He barged inside the house.

At that moment, she didn't want to know. It was a gun fire; it didn't mean her father was shot. She had to prepare herself if it were her father. What if he's hurt? She asked herself, getting herself to her feet. She felt like a lost girl, not wanting to go inside of the house. She was too terrified.

"Daddy…?" she cried at the opened door, it was quiet now; she didn't look in. "David?" How could she be so helpless? She questioned, she should do something, she was too afraid. She stood there helplessly, longer than she should have.

"Daddy…?" She cried once more.

"I'm here Gwenie…" Her father announced coming out of the house.

She fell into his arms and cried out loud. "I thought it was you…! I was so afraid."

Sirens wailed in the distance. "Hank, I can't let you do this." David said standing in the doorway holding the rifle in his hand, and then he set it down inside the doorway.

"David…your mom…?" Gwen cried.

He shook his head. "She's in ruff shape…You came in after me Hank…The rifle went off in my hands…Do you understand…?"

"Is he dead…?" She asked looking up at David.

"Yeah." He replied with a nod.

"And Martha?" She cried pulling herself away from her father.

"Stay outside, both of you." He said as the sirens grew closer.

Hank stopped his daughter from going inside, as David disappeared from her sight.

"Come on Gwenie…we are going to stick to his story…David was here…before us."

"Why…? He was a mad man…so you shot him!"

"It went off…he was beating her with it when I pulled it away."

Again, Gwen wanted to drop to the ground…The police pulled into the driveway. "Oh God…It was my fault!"

Hank lifted her up; hushing her and pulling her out of the way. "We need an ambulance!" He shouted while the police emptied from their squad cars, four officers in all.

"It's on the way…anybody hurt?" One of the officers stopped to ask.

"Yes…and one fatality." Hank reported.

"What?" The last officer outside asked, before he rushed inside.

"It was my fault." Gwen cried.

Hank clasped onto her arms pulling her up. "How could it possibly be your fault…? You hush now…It was an accident, what he did to Martha wasn't…Stand here and say nothing."


She did what her father had asked; she found no more words, numbness set in. David rushed beside his mother; the ambulance took them both away. She never saw, or heard from him again.


Marshall didn't go to school, and he found it a bit odd that his mother hadn't left for work yet. Could she be that upset still, or was she just running late? He had asked himself entering his house. His mother was sitting at the kitchen table clutching on to her coffee cup, wearing her sweat suit told him otherwise.

She lifted her tearful eyes to him as he neared. "How come you're not in school?"

"I'm not feeling well. What about you Mom?"

"It's not like you to miss school." She said and then wiped her nose with a tissue she had in her hand. He sat down on the opposite side of the table from her. His silence was no comfort to her.

Marshall felt in tune with Sam's Uncle Larry, as though he knew him. For that, he felt wiser, older. He waited for her to speak.

"I called in too...Did you put Sam's book back?"

"Yes, and then I dropped off his keys...He was on the phone when I got there, and from what I gathered, it sounded like David's son is real sick...Mom, what happened in that house, that night?"

Again, Gwen wiped her eyes dry. She spoke with a cry in her voice. "David's father murdered Martha."

"I know, but who killed Jack?"

"Why ask such a ridiculous question?"

"I'm sorry, what I meant to ask is, what's wrong?"

Gwen rested her head on her hand and shook her head. "Jack was an awful man...If you really want to analyze the situation that night. I killed both of them."

"What are you talking about Mom?"

Gwen lifted her head and continued crying. "David was my friend that summer. And I come to know Martha as well. I talked to David about self defense...I kept telling him he needed a gun, he needed to shoot that—Well he was strong enough to fight Jack off most of the time, but he couldn't be there all the time for her. I should have known Martha wouldn't use that big ole rifle on him...Jack used it to beat her to death."

"It's not your fault Mom."

"I put your Grandpa in danger too. He rushed inside before the police arrived. He grabbed a hold of the rifle and, it went off. And that was the end of Jack."

"Where was David…Mom?"

"I suppose he blames himself too. He was out fishing, he got there before the police arrived, and seconds after it happened…I told him not to go fishing."

"So he took the blame?"

"There was no blame in Jacks death, the only one murdered was Martha…You're grandmother doesn't know the truth, I guess I can't be sure, to my knowledge, she's not aware."

"Wow." He said with a sigh in his voice. "Well I won't say anything."

"So you've met David. Are you sure? This Bear guy—"

"Yeah, I know I shouldn't have read it, but yeah, he's the same one. I'm sure."

"And what, do you think of him?"

"It's hard to say, you know having a sick kid changes people. But from what I read in Sam's book he seemed like a nice person. But, I shouldn't talk about it."

"I thought that way too Marshall." She continued weeping. "It's such a small world. I was dating Carl that summer I befriended David."

Marshall looked at his mother oddly. "Yeah, that sounds about right."

"I was so unsure of him…Carl you know."

"Mom…?"

"David and I were intimate, we had sex Marshall." She cried.

"Are you saying, you're saying that…?"

"David is your biological father."

Infuriated, He jumped up from his chair knocking it over. "All this time...!

All this time, I was led to believe that Carl...Does he know?" He shouted in question. "Does he?"

"Yes...that's why there was no child support...I'm sorry, I meant to—"

"You've meant to!? Don't give me that! You're only telling me now because you found David, and you want to get him back..." He shouted pointing his finger at her in anger. "This has nothing to do with me!"

"Yes it does Marshall...I didn't want to lose you!"

"Well you ticked me off Mom...You ticked me off, all this time, I thought that my father didn't give a damn."

"I didn't want to hurt you."

"Well you did!" He shouted, and then he walked to the door.

"Where are you going?" She cried. She got no answer; he slammed the door behind him.


Sam was waiting for Conner's call, he lay there helplessly with his leg in a cast and his chest tightly wrapped he would be utterly lost for words if he did call. He searched his mind for words of comfort, but couldn't find any.

"Mister Ross?"

Sam turned and lifted his eyes to see Marshall standing there beside him. From the sound of his voice and the look on his face, Sam guessed he too, was upset. "Marshall what's wrong...? Why aren't you in school?"

Marshall too, stood there lost for words for a moment. "I took your book from your apartment yesterday."

"Which book?" He asked sternly.

"Your book, I'm sorry, I took it home and read it."

"Which one did you read?"

"Ah, you called it Sanity."

Sam now understood. He nodded. "Well, now that you know that I wasn't the poster child of mental health…I'm going to have to ask you, why'd you do it?"

"I have no excuses, it wasn't out of disrespect, and I guess I was just curious."

"And you read the entire memoir?"

"Yes I did…You can flunk me out for the rest of the school year, I don't care."

"This has nothing to do with the class room…Why are you so harsh? Why are you telling me this, for that matter?" He asked hiding a hint of anger inside of him.

"Because I, your friend Bear…I know who David Pane is…I mean my mother knew him."

"And your point is…? Your mother's opinions shouldn't affect your judgment of him or me as your teacher."

"It's not like that, my mother and David were neighbors and friends…she just told me that, he's my father."

He wasn't surprised to see the shock on his teachers face; he himself was still adjusting to the blow of his mother's words. "Sam, my mothers name is Gwen. Did he ever talk about her?"

"Are you sure Marshall…? I'm sorry I don't mean to imply any disrespect, but…"

"I'm sure. I mean she's sure. So he's never mentioned her?"

"Marshall David's son is very sick right now. He's got Myeloid Leukemia; He needs a Bone Marrow transplant. And if you're a sibling you can be the match he needs."

Chills ran up and down Marshall's spine. "For real…? Where is he, what do I do?"

"Your getting me out of here, we have to get a move-on." He announced with a smile hidden under his grimace, he sat himself up. "Can you grab me my clothes in the locker there."

"We're not going to wait for you to get released?"

"There's no time for technicalities."


Inside Conner's hospital room, David, wearing a surgical mask, dialed the phone number to Sam's room and then handed it to his son.

Sam was laboring, putting on his sweatshirt when the phone rang.

"Do you want me to get that?"

"It could be Conner."

"David's son?" Marshall asked in a long hesitation, long enough for Sam to pick up.

"Hello?"

"Sam?"

"Conner, how are you feeling?"

"Better than last night."

"Good, good…Well enough for breakfast?"

"Well, I had some juice. Are you coming to see me?"

"I sure am, I'm leaving here shortly. I'm bringing a friend, or he's bringing me."

"Oh, not Mia?"

"You'll see her latter."

Conner handed the phone back to his father; then laid his head down onto the pillow. His mother also wearing a surgical mask patted her son's shoulder.

"He says he's coming with a friend."

"A friend...?" David asked hanging up the phone. He didn't want to say it but would have preferred Mia who's been in the family, rather than that student, whom he guessed it would be.

"That's what he said." Conner replied, and then closed his eyes.

It should have been an exciting experience, dodging the medical staff and busting his teacher out of the hospital like he did. Under the right circumstances they could be having a good laugh about it right now, but under the right circumstances they would have never done it.

On the freeway Marshall was driving over the speed limit. The passenger seat was pushed all the way back allowing Sam the space he needed.

"You all right there?"

"Yes, this is just so overwhelming."

"I know."

"I'm not sorry that you read my book at all."

"It's like it was meant to be, you know like everything happens for a reason."

"God made me clumsy."

"And he made you a writer."

"You're not a nosy kid for any reason either, I'm sorry, let me rephrase that, curious. Your grandfather's death had a reason…if you think long and hard, you'll find it."

"Well he was almost sixty, and he did have a bad heart."

"I hate to think that we are all just a symptom of this life."

"But a piece of the puzzle."

"You've been paying attention."

"Sam…?"

"Go ahead ask me anything."

"What did David, what did he tell you about that night? You know, that night that…"

"I honestly don't know. I never asked, and he never spoke about it again. We just let sleeping dogs lie. I know that he is a good man, and a good father to Conner…He and Conner's mother never married. They dated on and off for a couple of years and then Conner was born. He never turned his back on his son…I'm sorry, I…"

"Don't be sorry, that's good news…I was so mad at my mother." He said sharply changing lanes. "She knew all this time! All this time I thought that my father didn't care."

"Look on the bright side, he does…He will."

"What about yours? Did you ever see him again?"

"I did."

"Well I'm still curious. How'd that turn out?"

"Not so good."

"Yeah, what happened?"

"I was in my last year of college, in a small apartment in River Falls, when he knocked on my door at about two in the morning. He was all

311

liquored up. he said he was my father and needed a place to stay for the night. I didn't ask for it, but he showed me his identification anyway...I tell you he must have found the closest bar to me, to show up like he had..."

"So what did you do?"

"I asked him to leave, he wouldn't, he started ragging on my mother so I called the police...if I would have let it go and let him spend the night. I don't know, I didn't want to get into that rut. It was just so much easier to drop him right then and there. I never saw him again after that night...Marshall, don't be so quick to judge your mother...David has been sort of, in hiding, he's changed his name. You can't be so sure that she has never tried to contact him...You're going to have to give her the benefit of the doubt, and you may have to call her soon. You are going to be a good match, and she's going to have to sign some papers for a procedure."

"I don't know a whole lot about this, but I'm only his half brother."

"All of this isn't for nothing."


In Sam's condition it was easier and faster to push him in a wheel chair. His crutches rested across his lap, took up plenty of space inside the elevator. David was standing there waiting, when it opened. He ignored the elevator going down and shrugged his shoulders.

"He's sleeping. I was just going down to get some coffee." He said distraughtly acknowledging the concentrated stare he was getting from; what's his name.

Marshall has seen his own refection in the mirror enough times to notice the resemblance.

"He needs his rest, so if your, student don't what to hang around, I'll make sure you get home latter. Or will Mia be coming?"

Sam nodded looking about, across the wide hallway to the small sitting area that consisted of four chairs and a couple of vending machines.

"I have something to say." Marshall blurted out.

David glared back at Marshall in question.

"Bear I think you should sit down." Sam added pointing to the sitting area.

Marshall wheeled him there. Puzzled, David reluctantly followed. "What's this all about?"

"Sit down." Sam announced.

David threw his hands up with a sigh and then took a seat. "What gives?" He asked coldly as if the matter were petty. Perhaps he broke a lamp yesterday during the move. How dare they put that above Conner right now.

Marshall waited for David to turn his eyes away from Sam and onto him before he spoke. "You knew my mother Gwen…She just told me this morning that you're my father."

David's face lost expression; he sat still, speechless and numb. His face grew pale.

"You all right there Bear?" Sam asked. "Just take some deep breaths."

His voice was shaky. "Gwen Banks…?"

"Yes, she just told me today."

"Why now…How'd you—?"

"He got a hold of one of my books I wrote, and you were in it."

"And I told my mom, that you were David Pane, and then she told me."

David shook his head dumfounded, he studied Marshall's face.

"You know Bear, he's not here asking for college tuition. Should we skip the coffee and head on down to the lab?"

"I'm sorry, what's your name?"

"It's Marshall…"

"Right, yeah, lets get a move on." Bear said standing up.

Inside the small waiting room, three of them sat impatiently while Wendy paced the floor.

"I can't handle this waiting!" She remarked annoying David.

"Sit down like the rest of us." He stated sitting on the edge of his chair with his elbows on his knees.

"Our son's life is at stake, and you want me to sit down? Why don't you sit there and try to remember if you have any other children, just in case this one doesn't work out!"

"That was un-called for!" Sam blurted out.

"Well I'm sorry if I offended your, Christian ears! But we could have used this information a long time ago. What if it's too late?"

"It's not!" David shouted.

"Oh, that's comforting, now you're an expert!"

"Stop fighting!" Marshall demanded.

Almost immediately David was reminded that he sounded a lot like Conner. "Do your parents fight?"

"My parents…? My mother and he divorced a long time ago. I thought he was my father but, I was wrong."

"Did he know?" David continued with his questioning.

"She say's he did. I guess I believe it now because he never paid child support, nothing."

"Did you call her yet?" Sam interrupted.

"No I was going to wait for-…I'll call now."

He was about to step out in the hallway to use his cell phone when a doctor holding a clip board walked in.

He tisked looking at David and then to Marshall. "A long lost son huh…The resemblance is un-canny…We have a perfect match."

"Is that possible?" Wendy cried in question.

"It is…Lets not argue the results. This is good news."

"It's just a lot to take in." David replied swallowing a lump in his throat.

"I'm sure it is, I have no idea how this came to place, but in my profession I've come to realize that miracles do exist…No doubt Conner will have a long road to a complete recovery, but it's possible with this transplant."

"A long road?" Marshall questioned.

"Yes there is a chance of infection and rejection, even if it's a perfect match."

Now Marshall understood the lack of excitement in the room.

"And if all goes well, he will be sick for a least a couple of weeks after the procedure…its well worth it, the odds are with him." The doctor added.

"When do we do this?"

"As soon as possible, Conner isn't going to get any better without new marrow." The doctor stated.

"You lied to me Bear!" Wendy shrieked.

Everyone else, including the doctor ignored her comment. The doctor turned his eyes directly at Marshall.

"We can get you admitted and start prepping. I understand that you are a miner."

"Yes. I'm going to call my mother. Will she need to sign for this?"

The doctor nodded, "Yes we will need her consent."

"And if she doesn't?" Wendy asked coldly.

Marshall stood and faced Wendy in anger. "You don't know my mother, so don't pretend you do. She's not like you!" He shouted at her and then left the room pulling his cell phone from out of his pocket.

He was out of character in there and he knew it. He had his reasons.

Walking down the hallway, he dialed home. He became disappointed, four un-answered rings. The answering machine played in his ear. "Mom, if you're there, please pick up. This is an emergency…Mom, call me back. I'm at—" He stopped his words seeing his mother walking down the hallway toward him, he met her half way. She had a tissue in her hand. She had been crying, and she still was.

"How'd you find me Mom?"

"I'm so sorry Marshall…Are you a match?"

"A perfect match, Mom, how'd you know?"

"Oh thank God!"

"How'd you know?"

"You said he owned a garage here and he went by the name Bear. I looked him up and I was told…I thought I might find you here. I'm so sorry."

"Why didn't you tell me?"

"David was a nice boy, but I thought Carl would have been a better father for you."

"Because of Jack?"

She nodded dabbing her bloodshot eyes with her tissue. "Your grandmother had a saying; the apple doesn't fall far from the tree. I was young, and if you knew Jack you would have understood."

Marshall shook his head. "I'm sorry, it doesn't make everything better right now."

"It's all right. David's son is what's important right now. What do we need to do?" she asked looking long over her son's shoulder at the small gathering empting out into the hallway.

Marshall took notice, "That's David, Conner's mother and Sam." He said.

David saw them in the distance. He wheeled Sam in the opposite direction.

"You're taking the long way." Sam noted.

"I know."


Conner was becoming aware that he no longer was alone in his room. He heard quiet voices around him as he recognized his mother and fathers. He listened without opening his eyes.

"Yeah, I called…Her mother said she left for Texas with him."

"So she was two-timing you."

"No, she had broken it off with him."

"Yeah, right she did."

"She did. And we only done it once, there's nothing left to say."

"You don't need to explain it to me. It doesn't take a rocket scientist to figure out why she left with the other guy, doing what you did, I'd leave you too."

"He didn't do anything wrong."

"You stay out of this Sam."

"No, you stay out of it Wendy…It's not wise to argue in front of your son, and you're constantly cutting his father down."

"Are you calling me a bad mother Sam? At least I acknowledge my sons father, un-like, what's her name."

Conner opened his eyes and looked at his mother. "Who are you talking about?" He muttered.

Wendy came close to his bedside wearing the required surgical mask. "Good news honey bear, you're getting new bone marrow today…we found you a perfect match."

"For real?"

"For real." Wendy reassured with a smile.

"Good, I want to get better so you and dad don't have to see each other so much. And when I get older we can fix it so you don't have to see each other at all…Sam wasn't calling you a bad mother, just stop fighting, please."

"Okay honey bear." She cried.

"What were you guys talking about…Dad…? Sam…Who's what's her name?"

David stepped up on the opposite side of Conner's bed. "Hey pal, we all just found out that you have a brother."

"You Dad, you have another son?"

"Yeah."

"How'd you find him, how'd you know?"

"Well Sam sort of found him, it's a long story."

"Where is he, can I see him?"

"Well right now he's getting some of his bone marrow extracted."

"For me…?"

"Of course, for you."

In a separate wing of the hospital, Gwen sat in the corner of another waiting room. There were others scattered about, some watching the T V, some reading the magazines available. She did neither. She still held a tissue in one hand, and a Styrofoam cup in the other, she sipped her coffee.

She didn't pay much mind to the man on crutches nearing her until he spoke.

"Excuse me, Gwen?" He panted, somewhat out of breath.

She immediately assumed that he was Sam Ross. "Yes…"

He sighed in relief and took it upon himself to sit in the empty chair beside her. It took him a moment to do so. "I'm Sam Ross, Marshall's teacher."

"Yes, of course…How's Conner?"

"He's doing well, he's excited…How are you doing? If you don't mind me asking."

She dabbed her eyes. "Mister Ross, I know I owe David an apology, Conner too, everyone for that matter. And my son, I don't know if he will ever forgive me."

"I'm not here to remind you of what you already know. You're a good mother; Marshall is living proof of that. I just want you to know that he thinks the world of you. And he forgives you already."

"What makes you think that?"

"He defended you today…It wasn't against anything Bear, I'm sorry, it wasn't against anything David had said about you. It was

Conner's mother. She's a little, ah, out-spoken, to say the least."

"So I wouldn't have her forgiveness?"

"It starts with your son's. The rest of them will follow, granted she will probably be the last."

"I take it; you're not upset with Marshall for taking your book home like he did."

"No ma'am, not at all. I got over that quite quickly." He answered with a smile, and his eyes fixed on Mia walking his way. "But I have a feeling someone may be upset with me."

Even after she guessed that this was his, soon to be, ex wife. Gwen didn't fully understand. Why…? Was her heart filled smile deceiving? She even spread it around to her. She sure didn't look upset. Her question was answered when she found out that her son had busted his teacher out of the hospital without proper dismissal.


Marshall was already antsy, a bit sore and tender, but ready to leave just the same. He was informed that he had to stay the night for precautionary reasons. Like Gwen assumed, her son's words were limited.

"I can't say it anymore Marshall…"

"Then don't, Mom its okay…I want to go see Conner, will you take me there?"

"Oh, no…it's not my place, besides he's getting your marrow right now. It's a family thing."

"I'm his family…"

"I cant, not right now. Maybe Sam and his wife are still here, they can take you, and maybe David will come and get you."

"I can walk Mom; I just wanted you to come."

"I can't. I know I have a lot of explaining to do. I'll go home and start with a phone call to your grandmother."

"How long are you going to keep this up Mom?"

"Marshall you saw him; he walked the other way when he saw me."

"You should have followed him and told him that you were sorry."

"Not tonight, I just can't do this tonight. I will see you tomorrow. Have a nice visit if you do see, your brother."

Gwen left the hospital, grateful that she had eluded David. And why wouldn't she, after all he was doing the same on her behalf. She was honoring his wishes. She could do this forever.


Marshall was disappointed. The recording over the P A just announced that visiting hours were over, and he didn't do anything about it. He re-grouped his thoughts, tomorrow was another day. He found a Scfi movie that had just started. He could watch this and then call it a night.

Someone had lightly tapped on his half opened door and stepped in. He didn't know what to make of David's expression. He turned off the TV, giving him his full attention.

"How's it going?"

"Fine here…how's Conner?"

"Oh you know, time will tell. He wants to see you. I told him that you'd probably come up tomorrow."

"For sure, I want to see him too…Did Sam and Mia leave?"

"Oh yeah…" He replied with a chuckle in his voice. "She was so set on getting him back to the hospital for the release papers…so you guys busted out of there huh?"

"Yeah, it was kind-of fun, would have been, you know."

"Yeah I hear ya."

"Are they back together?"

"I guess so…All that work, time and money, for nothing. Divorce papers, lawyers, the selling of the house."

"Can I ask why did they want a divorce in the first place?"

"Oh, Mia wanted a baby. Sam can't do it, he's sterile. She wanted to adopt…He told her no. He was too afraid to do it. You know, a woman who's giving up a baby has the right to change her mind, and Sam, he can't handle that. You know he's not as tough as he appears. His asthma just scratches the surface."

"My mother isn't tough either." Marshall dared to say.

"Your mother made a mistake."

"We all do…I know what really happened that night, she told me…I mean no disrespect, but the truth wasn't so bad. Why'd you take the blame for an accident?"

"Your mother told you what really happened?" David asked.

"Yeah…she said the gun went off. And it wasn't you it was, my grandfather trying to pull the rifle away from, your father…Isn't that how it went?"

"I don't know…It doesn't really matter. I should have been there."

"That's why you took the rap?"

"I didn't think I would have gotten a rap for it. It was less likely for me than it would have been for your grandfather, just in case it wasn't an accident…How's your mother been?"

"She's been all right. She's a good mother, even though she's kept this from me. I guess she had her reasons. She didn't know that you were going to turn out so good. She's sorry now, she really is…You changed your name. Maybe she tried to find you, I don't know, but maybe she did…"


Conner knew not to expect immediate results from his new bone marrow quite yet, but he told himself and everybody else that he was. He told his new found brother the same thing, he was felling better already. Marshall saw the strength in his brother's smile as h stood beside him.

"He's a good guy…he likes fishing. I haven't been able to go for a while, but come spring, he says were going to get a boat. Do you like fishing?"

"You know I haven't really done a lot of fishing, but I'd like to."

"Good then we can go together. It will be fun."

"Yes it sounds like it will be."

"What else do you like to do…? What do you want to be?"

"Well, I want to be a writer."

"Oh like Sam…He tells good stories."

"I know." Marshall said with a smile."

"What kind of stories does he tell you?"

"Good ones."

"Yeah, that's Sam."

"So what do you want to be when you grow up?" Marshall dared to ask.

"I want to be a mechanic like my dad…I'm going to get better."

"I know you are."

Gwen believed she knew what she was in for today. Marshall already had called her wanting her to meet him in Conner's room. She was nervous when she stepped into the elevator. Alone inside, she took a deep breath. The elevator stopped at parking level number four. She moved to the far left side, and lifted her eyes to see David step inside. And to him, there was no mistake about, she was Gwen.

"Hello David…I'm on my way to visit Conner."

"Oh…" David only replied, but it was all he could give at the moment, until he followed his heart. "He likes company…You're just as pretty as you ever been…I'm sorry I dodged you yesterday."

"Oh don't be." She said shaking her head. "I'm sorry for all of this."

"It's all right…Marshall says Jack is to blame, does that sound fair to you?"

"Yes it does."

"I had a long visit with him last night. He told me about your dad, I was sorry to hear that he had passed away."

"He lived a long time with that bad heart, and we're grateful for that."

"Your mother, how's she copping?"

"I called her last night and told her that you were Marshall's father, and you're Conner…I told her everything…She was so happy." She cried as the elevator opened once more at their floor.

David led her out gently touching her back. They walked side-by-side To Conner's room.

"If I ever thought that you were going to look me up, I would have never changed my name."

"I could have tried harder."

"I understand."

"Bear…The bear from the river?" Gwen asked with a cry in her voice.

"Yes…He gave me my courage."

"I still have that whistle you gave me."

David smiled. "Is that right?"

"The wizard, right that was his name."

David nodded. "Yeah…Wizard, you remember."

"I can't forget…You meant so much to me…and again I'm so sorry for leaving like I did. I was so unsure of myself…But enough about me. How's Conner felling?"

"He's going to be okay…Ask him and he will tell you so."

"He sounds like a strong little guy."

"You got that right," David replied when the two of them slowed their walking pace down as they neared Conner's room. He was only a bit surprised to see his eldest son there along side of Conner. "It Seems our boys have something up their sleeves…It has a nice ring to it doesn't it?"

"Yes it does." Gwen replied.

Both Conner and Marshall smiled…

# *Christmas*

Riding down the Loop road in his father's truck, Conner was bundled up warmly. The snow was softly falling.

"So this is where you used to live when you were a kid...around here?"

"Yeah..." His father replied nervously, he didn't want to see that house, oh God he didn't want to see it. He prepared himself just the same, and he would have to point it out to his son. Agony was coming just around the bend. He shook his head in disbelief. There was an empty lot where it used to stand.

"It was there." He said pointing to the empty space in total relief now that it was gone.

Conner was a bit disappointed; he wanted to see the house. "Oh, you mean they tore it down?"

"I guess so." David replied with a smile. He pulled into The Banks driveway.

"So this is where Mom Gwen grew up?"

"Mom Gwen?"

"I asked her if I could call her that...that's what step kids do."

"She's not your step mother."

"Well, aren't you guys going to get married? Isn't that why you bought her that ring?"

"What do you know about a ring?"

"Well I was snooping…I won't say anything. Are you going to give it to her today, for Christmas…? Are you Dad?"

"It was supposed to be a surprise."

"Don't worry she'll be surprised." He assured as his father parked the truck next to Gwen's car. Conner barrowed out the door and ran up to the door step.

David sighed with a smile. It was so good to see him run again.


This was the first year Sam and Mia made Christmas visiting a two day event. Once off their early Christmas morning flight back from Mia's parent's home in Arizona. They rushed off for the long drive to Iowa border. It's been a long time since he's seen his Uncle Larry, or any of the Casper family for that matter. They moved away ten years ago. He was told that his aunt Mae just couldn't handle the city living any longer, and she had a fear for Larry's safety as a police officer. So he had to take a transfer to a smaller town where crime was low. Sam hasn't seen his uncle Larry since his wedding. And there was no reason to expect the rest of the family to be there. It wasn't unusual to be invited over every Christmas. The invitation always came with the early card in the mail. This year was an exception. A couple of phone calls from his Uncle to see how he was doing after his spill down the stairs. Since then Larry has learned of the near divorce and David's son bone marrow transplant from a child he didn't know he had.

As the miles tacked on the snow was coming down heavier. Mia had the map in front of her. "Okay we just passed the town of Fairview."

"Did you get a fair view?"

"No. I blinked and I missed it." Mia chuckled. "Highway S should be up here on the left a spell."

"How long is a spell?" Sam asked. He squinted his eyes looking for such a sign in the snowy weather.

"A mile it seems."

Sam found it. and took the left. He was told they lived about five miles down this highway. This road was even worse.

"Sam there's a car in the ditch up there."

"Yeah. I see it."

He drove slow and stopped behind it. It was clearly in the ditch and wouldn't be easily removed without a wrecker. In a rush he jumped out of the car and raced to the other. The driver of the car rolled down the window. She was a young woman.

"Miss. are you all right?"

"Yes..." She shivered. "Do you have a cell phone?"

"No. I'm sorry I don't...Let us give you a lift somewhere."

"Okay." She replied getting out of the car.

She reached for Sam's hand as he led her to his car. She got into the back seat. Mia turned around in concern.

"You're not hurt are you hon?"

"No I'm fine...thank you."

After popping the trunk Sam grabbed a blanket, and then handed it to her as he got back into the car.

"Are you Sam?" The young woman asked.

Sam turned to look at her curious. "Jeanie?"

"Yes it's me...I heard you were coming. Well this works."

"It sure does…Are you sure you're all right?"

"Yes…and what about you? I heard you broke you're leg and, some ribs."

"Oh, I'm on the mend. I've never been better." He replied with a smile.

Jeanie walked them to the house. Inside the house the aroma of turkey and all the fixings surrounded them.

Jeanie showed her face stepping into the living room. "Surprise!" She boasted in laughter, with her arms flung out wide.

Larry jumped up from the couch, happy to see all three of them. "Mae, look who's here…Jeanie made it…! And, Sam and Mia are here!"

Sam and Mia stood there while Jeanie's father gave her a big hug. He acknowledged Sam with the same smile reaching out his hand. Sam shook it.

"It's good to see you two. I'm glad you could make it."

"And we're glad to be here."

Mae, James and Josh came out of the kitchen. Mae ran up to hug her daughter with a wide smile.

"My lord…I didn't think any of you were going to make it with this unexpected snow storm."

"I know…my car is in the ditch a few miles up the road. I don't know what I would have done if Sam hadn't came to rescue me."